ISBN 13# 9780982798607

Printed in the United States of America.

KENNEDY'S KIDS

A Novel

By Richard Landerman

Sortis Publishing

This book is dedicated to the Yuba City
High School Class of 1960.

KENNEDY'S KIDS is a work of fiction. Some of the names, places, institutions, business establishments, and situations have been changed to fit the author's concept of the story; some are totally fictional and are solely the result of the author's imagination.

PROLOGUE

Late October, 1959: One of the most important events that would ultimately shape the course of history for the remainder of the Twentieth Century and beyond was taking place in the privacy of a family compound in the small village of Hyannisport on Cape Cod, Massachusetts, a private residency owned by one of the wealthiest and best-known families in America.

On a Saturday morning in October, a select group of men were gathered in the spacious, plainly-appointed living room of the younger brother's home. Inside the room a large fire crackled in the spacious fireplace. Outside the day was frosty but sunny. Outside the house one could see Narraganset Bay nearby, could hear the sound of waves hissing upon the fine sandy beaches. Gulls screeched in the crisp salt air as they glided above the surf searching for scraps of food. Across the vast lawn away from the beach, at the edge of the private compound, one could see a line of dark green pine trees and beyond, the fiery oranges and reds of New England hardwoods turning in the cold autumn air.

In the gathering room, the sun streamed in; piles of sweet rolls and tea biscuits on large trays had been prepared and placed strategically around the room conveniently in reach of the guests. Silver urns of hot tea and coffee with china cups, small pots of sugar and cream, silver spoons and linen napkins were set conveniently on mahogany serving trays.

Other than the two hosts – brothers - the others had been hand-picked for their particular political skills, contacts, money-raising abilities, or simply because they were family members or long-time loyal friends and supporters of the family. Their names would soon be known around the world: Ted Sorenson, Kenny O'Donnell, Lawrence F. O'Brien, Stephen Smith (brother-in-law of the candidate), pollster Louis Harris, Pierre Salinger, Edward Kennedy (youngest brother of the candidate), and Joseph P. Kennedy, Sr.

The older brother, John F. Kennedy, junior senator from the state of Massachusetts, stood with his back to the fireplace, facing the gathering. He was casually dressed in a smartly hand-tailored Scottish tweed jacket, complimenting slacks, and loafers. As the meeting progressed he would lay aside his jacket and unbutton the top of his fine wool long-sleeved polo shirt. The senator was young and in his first term in the United States Senate, movie-star handsome with his now-famous swept back shock of thick reddish-brown hair, his gray-blue eyes, his ready smile and perfect white teeth. He was also a family man: married with an equally handsome wife, Jackie, and a cute young daughter, Caroline. He was also rich. Very rich.

His younger brother Robert, whose house this was, called the meeting to order. Robert (or "Bobby" as he was known to only a few insiders who were allowed to address him in the familiar) stated that the purpose of the meeting was not to make any major decisions; that had all been done months and even years before today, in numerous strategy meetings in Washington, D.C., New York City, Miami, and Boston leading up to today. No, it wasn't the "what" they were gathered to discuss; it was the "how do we do it?"

Today's meeting was to lay out the general campaign for the presidency of the United States of America, the most powerful job in the world, and how that prize could and would be captured. Confidence bordering on hubris - full of ambition and pride in their collective intellects and skills – palpably filled the room and hung in the air. There was no doubt in the minds of these young political warriors that the ultimate political prize in America was theirs. The only detail to be hammered out was assignments for the execution of the battles that lay ahead in order to claim the prize thirteen months ahead.

After Bobby's brief introduction, John began in a relaxed but cerebral monologue defining the challenges that lay ahead and how they would capture the presidency.

First, he said, was the obvious problem of religion: he was Catholic, and no Catholic had ever been elected president of the United States.

Next was his age: he was forty-three, and his youth would definitely be made a campaign issue by not only the Republicans but also by his many rivals within his own party.

Finally, he was a U.S. senator and no senator had ever been elected to the presidency. Someone in the room pointed out that three of the four other possible Democratic challengers were also senators: Hubert Humphrey from Minnesota; Lyndon B. Johnson, the Senate Majority Leader, from Texas; and Stuart Symington from Missouri. John silently nodded and respectfully acknowledged this comment.

John Kennedy stated that the nomination would have to be secured by winning approximately ten or eleven out of sixteen state primary elections. Several primaries they would logically avoid because of the favorite son factors and not wanting to alienate those candidates who might prove crucial to help them in the general election.

He said that this strategy required that they win big enough in the primaries to not only capture delegates to the national convention in Los Angeles, but also to send a strong statement to the Big City political bosses from New England, New York, and Chicago who could derail the candidacy if the convention became deadlocked in the early round of voting and no clear winner emerged. The nominee would most likely be anointed by those bosses after a back room deal was made. This meant that whoever got anointed by that process would be burdened with favors to the same bosses who put them in office, and he didn't want any part of that process. Someone quipped that in any event they would still need the help of the Big City bosses later down the road. John shot back, "But we don't have to be bought by them. If I sell my soul to anyone, it will be to my own father and his millions!"

From memory John Kennedy then ran down a list of the primary election states they would enter, starting with the obvious: New Hampshire because he was a New Englander, virtually the favorite son, and the odds favored his taking that state. Among the others they discussed there would also be Iowa's caucuses, plus Indiana, Maryland, Nebraska, West Virginia, finally finishing up with Oregon in June, just before the convention.

John discussed each state from memory: elected officials and political bosses by name, local organizers, donors, numbers of registered voters, and so on. His memory was legendary and amazing in detail. Everyone there that day already knew the story of how John, as a young congressman, had once driven down the main street of his district and from memory could point out which store fronts had put up his campaign posters and which ones had not.

Strategy would wait for the afternoon session. They took a lunch break and in groups of twos and threes headed across the broad expanse of manicured lawns in the crisp autumn air to the home of the senior Kennedy and patriarch of this famous clan, Joseph P. Kennedy, Sr., for stacks of turkey and ham sandwiches, tureens of chicken noodle soup, New England clam chowder, deep-dish apple and pumpkin pies, coffee and milk – always milk.

* * * * *

Bobby took charge and conducted the afternoon session. Cardboard file boxes had been brought in, which were full of files on each state, with sub-files for specific issues, complete with well-researched position papers. There were thick files on problem areas, files for supporters and others for donors. They also had complete files on their most likely opponents: Senate Majority Leader, Lyndon B. Johnson of Texas, Senator Hubert H. Humphrey ("The Happy Warrior") from Minnesota, Senator Stuart Symington from Missouri, and the venerable and widely-respected Adlai Stevenson.

The most concern and attention would be focused on the delegates. Delegates were valuable; delegates had to be cultivated, nurtured, pampered, watched over, contacted often and listened to. Delegates were golden – they were the capital, the stacks of poker chips on which a campaign was won or lost.

Stacks of multi-colored 3x5 file cards had been accumulating for many months; these special cards contained precious, detailed information on the expected delegates to the national convention in July. They would be regularly updated as needed, and would be used by the Kennedy people regularly, especially during the convention.

iv

Bobby, as everyone in the room acknowledged, would be Jack's national campaign chairman. He had earned it and was ready for the job. He was widely considered as the toughest of the three living Kennedy brothers. The one person *not* present in the room, but whose ghost hovered over the proceedings, was Joseph P. Kennedy, Jr., the oldest of the Kennedy sons. He had been the rightful heir to fulfill their father's political ambitions. A Navy Lieutenant, Joe had been killed in combat during the War.

Robert had the qualifications needed to be the campaign manager: feisty, smart, hard-working, loyal to his brother Jack to a fault. Most of all, he was tough. Bobby, many recalled, had served as counsel to a major Congressional investigating committee and had stood up to one unsavory union leader, Jimmy Hoffa, the Teamster's Union boss, grilling him relentlessly about possible Mafia ties during several days of hearings. This earned the instant dislike and mistrust of the Kennedys by the unions.

Bobby methodically worked through the afternoon, handing out assignments, discussing chain-of-command and communications charts; and passing out the boxes of files that would be the central intelligence for the campaign. He acknowledged several men, valued for their experience in raising campaign finances, and discussed strategies.

The Kennedys knew from Jack's failed run at the vice-presidential nomination in 1956 that nothing beat hard work, organization, and intelligence. But most of all, they had come to value communications, based on a painful look back at the 1956 experience, when vital communications had broken down at a crucial moment.

Bobby had been attached to the 1956 Stevenson campaign, had ridden in the buses and airplanes, always in the background as an observer: nobody ever had a specific job for him to do. So he kept quiet, asked a lot of intelligent questions, and filled notebooks and files with his observations on how the Kennedys would run a national campaign, should the time ever come. And the time had now come: Jack was as ready as he would ever be; Bobby was ready; these men were ready and eager.

Jack wrapped up the meetings with a brief pep talk and ended by paraphrasing a quote from Shakespeare: "Now, it's time to let slip the Dogs of War!" Jack grinned as the room erupted in cheers and applause; Bobby was grim and determined.

When the gathering finally broke up late that October afternoon, these men all had their marching orders and would fan out across the country for the next several months laying the groundwork for the road leading up to the nominating convention in July to be held in Los Angeles, and for the grueling general election campaign beyond that. A lot of work had already been done, but there was still much to be accomplished.

As evening fell over Hyannisport, Massachusetts, and the sun sank in the west, private cars took these newly-drafted field commanders to the waiting airplanes where they would then be flown to Washington, D.C., New York City, Chicago, and points west. As John Kennedy watched them leave, Bobby standing by his side, the Senator knew he had confidently embarked on one of the greatest quests that can cha,lenge men: the race for the presidency of the greatest nation on earth.

Totally unaware of the drama unfolding a continent away, in an obscure small town in Northern California, lived a small family whose lives would forever be touched by the events shaping up in faraway New England.

Alex Rodgers lay in bed, thinking back about the events of his day. Overhead, he could hear the cries of migrating Canada geese calling to each other – *Honkers*, as they were known in these parts – searching through the low-lying valley fog for a place to hunker down for the night. The air outside was damp, chilly, foggy; autumn was almost gone and the long, damp winter would soon descend.

CHAPTER ONE

January 2, 1960, Boston, Massachusetts: *John F. Kennedy, U.S. Senator from Massachusetts, announces to the press in front of historic Faneuil Hall that he is now a candidate for the office of President of the United States and will seek to win his party's nomination. Kennedy, in his first term as junior senator from his state is a Democrat, a Catholic, is forty-two years old, married and has one child, a daughter, Caroline.*

Allison told me about her best friend Angie cheating on a quiz in Mr. O'Farrell's junior civics class. She was upset that Angie could be so reckless. "She kept leaning against me or yawning and stretching like she was sleepy or bored or something," Allie said. "But I knew all the time what she was doing."

"Did you talk to her about it?" I asked.

"No. She's a jerk. I could've gotten into big trouble if he'd caught us."

"Us? You mean you let her copy your answers?" I asked.

"No, not exactly," she said. I looked hard at her. "Well, what am I supposed to do? She's my best friend."

Mr. O'Farrell. Tommy. Crazy as a pet coon. I remember sitting in his honors civics class last year when I was a junior. Tommy O'Farrell is a good guy, but crazy, I tell you. Not in the dangerously-scary sense, where he needs to be locked up. No, he's just a little… off.

He got decorated for gallantry in the War. He almost lost one leg to gangrene in a German field hospital. Then he spent eighteen months in a German POW camp somewhere (he won't say) until the end of the War when they were liberated by the Red Army.

Before the War Tommy, played halfback for Notre Dame. By his own account he was pretty darn good. He hates the Trojans; just mention University of Southern California and he sees blood. The war injury ruined his football career so he switched to political science and history and decided to become a teacher.

But like I said, he's crazy. And we've discovered how to make him get weird - we egg him into it. All we have to do is mention one of his three pet subjects: Notre Dame football, Nazi prison camps, and JFK – John Kennedy, Democratic senator from Massachusetts.

In addition to being Catholic, O'Farrell is also a rabid Democrat from Boston; he has predicted for two years now that John Kennedy will be our next president. Like, I'm too young to vote anyway, so who cares?

If you want to see the crazy part of Tommy O'Farrell come out, just raise your hand and ask him to show you his moves from when he played football. Or ask him about one of the other two subjects.

Notre Dame football. He gets this sly expression, sort of looks around to make sure Mr. Sumsion, the principal, isn't lurking outside the window or out in the hall. Then he opens up his closet and takes out an old pigskin football. He passed it around the class once so we could all see the autographs of his Notre Dame team-mates and coaches.

He gives us this long narrative, about the history of Notre Dame football, the student involvement in the South Bend riots in the early days of the Ku Klux Klan; the glory days of Knute Rockne. Sort of sets the scene for what follows.

Tommy crouches in a three-point down stance and he has Mike Burke, the center on our varsity team, hike him the old pigskin when he yells "hike!"

Mike hikes the ball, Tommy takes the snap and charges around the class room juking, faking, and straight-arming the shadowy Trojan defense. All the time he's giving us a running, verbal play-by-play. It kills us every time. It also kills about twenty minutes of class time so we don't have to listen to that much of his dry lectures.

The POW thing is even better. It can easily burn up an entire class period.

Every time it's the same routine, too. Tommy goes to his special closet, but this time he hunches in front of it so we can't see inside or what he's up to, even though he's done this routine dozens of times. He reaches in with both hands and pulls out a tattered red and black Swastika flag. Twirling around, he unfurls the flag, all in one deft move. He finishes his little drama with "ta ta!"

And here's where the scary part comes in. He drapes the flag over one arm, like a waiter with a towel, and digs into the closet again. He comes out with a metal German helmet on his head. He puts his index finger across his upper lip, under his nose, like a moustache. He stretches out his other arm, really stiff, and starts marching – actually, goose-stepping – around the room. The effect is kind of sad because of his limp from his wounded leg.

All the time he's singing at the top of his lungs: "Deutschland, Deutschland, uber alles!" Like I said, crazy as a pet coon.

But lately, Allie tells me, Tommy doesn't want to do the Nazi act any more. She says he knows what we're up to.

"Meaning...?"

"I think he knows we're trying to trick him into getting off the subject."

"Uh, yeah," I say. "So what are you going to do about Angie?" I ask, steering her back to the original subject.

Allie shrugs her shoulders and scrunches up her nose. She wanders off and I go back to practicing piano. We have a gig coming up.

I'm lucky to have a small room in our house where I can practice my piano. We live in a tract home, one of the first developments built in our town after the War. The subdivision is named Estates de Espana. That's a fairly pretentious title for three-bedroom tract homes with two baths. The streets are named *Sevilla, Madrid, Pilar, Barcelona, Pamplona,* and so on, if you get my meaning.

We live on Toledo Street. Our house is supposed to look like a country cottage in France. Now that's mixing your metaphors. It's got a white plaster exterior, blue trim and blue faux shutters, with a faux red brick chimney on one end. We have never built a fire in it because, on the inside, there's no fireplace. But on the outside, the street view shows tangles of ivy clinging to it that we planted when we moved in.

The rest of the homes on our block – four on our side, and five on the other – all went for the Southwestern ranch house look: single-story, beige stucco, with red tile roofs. Boring. Ours is the only two-story home on the block. All three of our bedrooms – Allie's, mine, and our parents' – and one bath, are upstairs.

At one end of the block is the Reorganized LDS church. The minister (I think you call him a minister) is our neighbor. I don't know the difference between this brand and any other Mormons, except this minister says it's okay for him to drink coffee.

At the other end of the block is the Park Avenue Elementary school where Allie and I attended through sixth grade. I still have a scar under my chin from when I was hanging upside down on the monkey bars on a cold day and lost my grip and fel, head first. I was out for two hours and it required twenty stitches to sew me up. That's the only time I've ever been in a hospital since Allie and I had rheumatic fever when we were little kids.

Mom chose the house design because she has French ancestry. She once said she came from Louisiana where there's supposed to be a lot of French people. She speaks French – teaches and tutors to private students. She also teaches classes in French cooking and once a year takes a private group on tour to France as their guide. Every year it's a different region in France noted for their unique cuisine. Then they end up in Paris for several days and eat themselves sick.

All I know for sure is she helps me with my own French homework (I'm in my fourth year) and I always get A's. She was a great help when we got into all that *passé composée* stuff. Mr. Pomeroy, my French teacher, says I speak it almost as well as a native. Mom's name is actually Julia; her maiden name was Peters before she married Bud just after the War and they built this house on the G.I. Bill.

She's smallish – *petite* - has curly brown hair, and the most incredibly beautiful brown eyes I've ever seen. The girl I marry has got to have brown eyes. Must have! Mom's eyes actually remind me of Sadie, my Uncle Arnold's English setter. .

Our house was the only one on our block that withstood the famous flood of December, 1955, when the levee broke and the Feather River engulfed us. We live in one of the lowest spots in the area, so we got water clear up to just below the second floor. Our bedrooms upstairs never got damaged. But the entire downstairs was submerged for several days.

The foundations stood, an engineer said, because of the extra weight of the top floor. The other nine homes on our block all had to have substantial foundation work done before they were safe for people to move back in. We had to shovel out tons of mud, rip up wall-to-wall carpet, and throw away the furniture, pictures, books, appliances, and food that were all ruined. Our little spinet piano was destroyed, too.

I remember three days after the flood waters had gone down enough we could go back into the house. What a stink! I also remember how the books in the room we called the library, where the piano now is located, must have floated at first before they became too waterlogged, because there were clean outlines of books all over the ceiling in contrast to the brown stain that was left by the muddy waters.

We got a new piano to replace the old one. It was a pretty little Baldwin baby grand with a rich brown walnut finish. Many of the oak floor boards had buckled and needed replacing; we decided to forget wall-to-wall carpeting and refinished the hardwood floors. Mom covered the floors with an assortment of Oriental rugs she buys from some Jordanian dealer she knows in Nice, France; she brings another new one back from every trip.

Some of my friends didn't get out quickly enough. They drowned in the flood.

CHAPTER TWO

February 28, 1960, Squaw Valley, California. *In a stunning upset, the American hockey team crushed Czechoslovakia 9-4 to take the gold medal in the Winter Olympic Games. The U.S. Americans squeaked into the final round after first defeating Canada 2-1, then besting the vaunted Russian team 3-2.*

Thursday nights at Shakey's Pizza Parlor in Marysville can be slow. It's only a few blocks from Yuba College and you'd think the preppies would want a break from studying. Man, I'd be burned out by Thursday night, looking for a break, hanging out with my friends, checking out the girls, eating pizza, drinking beer on a boot-legged driver's license, grooving on cool West Coast jazz.

Played by us. We're the Cool Standards Jazz Trio. Myself on piano – I'm the leader. It's my group. I organized it two years ago when we were still sophomores. My buddy Hugo Sargenti ("Sarge") plays trumpet and my other buddy, Freddie Gomes, plays bass.

We play mostly standard jazz repertoire stuff, tunes from the 30s and 40s. But lately we've been trying to move out doing our own improvisations. We're not so great on the improv yet, but in time, we'll get there. That's why I'm practicing more, so I can make it sound like it's easy, nothing to it.

I subscribe to *Downbeat* Magazine, and I belong to the Columbia

Record Club. Actually, the record club contract's under my Dad's name since I'm under age. I try to buy at least two LPs a month from my part-time income and the money I make from doing gigs like this one at Shakey's.

I'm racking up a pretty good collection: Dave Brubeck, Cal Tjader, Ahmad Jamal (my favorite – I love his easy, lyrical style), Oscar Peterson, Bill Evans – a new guy on the scene who I really like. I have some Coltrane, Charlie "Bird" Parker, Thelonius Monk, Duke Ellington, and Count Basie. I like J.J. Johnson on trombone. He's made some really good albums lately with another 'bone player named Kai Winding. Who would've thought that a trombone duet would sound so good? But it's all in the way the tunes are arranged. And there's this great trumpet player named Miles Davis. There's also a white trumpet player, a new kid from Bakersfield I've been listening to – Chet Baker.

But my favorite arrangements, believe it or not, are Frank Sinatra doing some Nelson Riddle arrangements of the old jazz standards as well as some new tunes. Riddle, like Stan Kenton, is not afraid to use strings, flutes, oboes, and French horns in his arrangements without making it sound gooey.

I play all my discs on the stereo and play along on the piano, trying to copy their riffs and fills – especially when they go improv, which is usually by the second chorus. I'm thinking I'll pick up a class or two in music theory and improvisation this summer at Yuba College if they offer any.

Allie – Allison – is my twin sister, but I'm a year ahead of her in school. That's because of the rheumatic fever we both had when we were five years old. So she lost a year of school – actually kindergarten. She almost died.

People can't believe we're really twins, other than the year apart in school thing. I have dark hair with dark complexion and brown eyes. Allie has blond hair, fair skin and blue eyes. As my Jewish buddy Kenneth Adelman is fond of saying - Go figure. Mr. Belka, who teaches biology, sure has fun using Allie and me as examples when he teaches genetics. We're really a lot different in other ways, too – apart from the obvious: boy-girl.

Allie likes to be involved in everything: school assemblies, school plays, pep rallies, student government. She has loads of friends and is popular with everyone. And not just at school. Everyone in town knows her as "Bud's girl." Wonder what she's up to now?

Allie had two paper routes from when she was eleven until just recently – six years in all. She delivered *The San Francisco Chronicle* in the morning and *The Appeal- Democrat,* our local daily, in the evenings. She plays on the girl's softball team at school. Also basketball, volleyball, and swim teams. She's the jock Bud wishes I were.

It's a miracle, considering the rheumatic fever when she was a kid; the doctors told my parents she'd never be able to play any sports. It's like she's determined to prove the doctors wrong. She also thrives on the competition. She's never complained about being a year behind me in school. She compensates in other ways.

Me? I'm athletic enough, in my own way. I'm on the varsity tennis team; that's plenty of sports and competition for me. I like to keep my time free to write stories and play with my combo. I've had a few articles in the school newspaper and I published some poetry and two short stories in the school's literary journal.

Miss Jensdatter, my English teacher, says I have promise. She reads the things I write and is kind enough to take time and make notes and suggestions in the margins. In red ink. But this is different from the red ink you see on homework or tests. I only think it means anything if the person criticizing does it in red ink.

I have a world history teacher this year, Mrs. Fillmore (old prune!). She uses different colored pens to grade papers – "depending on my mood," she says. One week it's purple. Next it's orange. Then yellow. Then green. But never red. She's called the "Rainbow Woman." Behind her back, of course.

I like Miss Jensdatter. Speaking of behind the back, she's known as "Hawk Face." That's because she has eyes that bug out of her red face, a thin hooked nose, and thin lips, with thin, dark hair (she says she's "Black Norwegian"). She's tall and flat-chested with wide hips. She won't win any beauty contests. She can't help her looks – nobody can. But she does look like a hawk.

Except when she smiles. I can tell if I've done okay on a paper or exam because if I have, she always smiles when she passes it back – all marked up with red ink notes and comments in the margins. If it's an A paper she'll write "Good job!" next to the grade at the top, or something encouraging like that.

I'm starting to think I could like being an English teacher. I've pretty well decided I don't want to major in music. I like playing piano; I like it a lot. But I'd rather study literature and writing and someday become a writer. I've always liked to read and write. I don't see myself making a living at music – a really tough life.

But Jensdatter says the life of a writer is even tougher, " a lonely life, full of disappointment." She says if I'm serious about writing, I should get a teaching position first – the bread and butter and rent income – then write part time, on the side.

I could do that. But I wouldn't teach high school or junior high. I see how many of my friends really are jerks about getting an education. They don't want to be there and they only are because the law says they have to.

Honors English is different. At least in Jensdatter's class. We're here in this class because we want to be. I could probably teach honors English in high school. Or maybe I'd teach in a private school, like those characters do in novels like *Catcher in the Rye,* or *A Separate Peace.* I'd definitely teach college, if the chance came along.

My dad owns a barber shop – Bud's – on Main Street. Everyone goes there to get their hair cut and their shoes shined by Murphy, the Negro boot black. Bud never got a degree, even though he went to college for a couple of years after the War. Mom never got a degree either. But they both are exceptionally sharp - Mom with her French; Bud knows a lot about politics, geography, and economics and business. He also speaks French and is really fluent. Says he picked it up during the War.

I will be the first one in our family to finish college. And then Allie right after me. But she's so smart she'll probably lap me down the stretch and graduate before I do. I tend to procrastinate a lot, especially homework.

I don't think I have a shot at a choice scholarship from a top school like Stanford or Cal Berkeley. I'll probably get one to either Chico State or Sac State – in writing, hopefully, or music, if I have to fall back on that major – and that's okay, as long as it pays the tuition, books and room. Lately I have been thinking about Southern Oregon because they have a good program for English majors. Smaller classes, less pressure, and a lot less money, which we don't have a lot of in our family. Jensdatter thinks I have a good chance and she's written some letters of recommendation for me. That helps.

Allie won't have any problem getting a scholarship. If she doesn't get one for student leadership, she will in sports. It's only a question of where she'll choose from all the offers.

We pass the hat three times a night at Shakey's and whatever we get we split three ways after I take ten percent off the top to help pay for sheet music and gas. Tonight we'll be lucky to make three bucks each. I hate Thursdays here because it's slow. I think of Thursdays at Shakey's as a practice session where we get paid a little on the side.

Sarge is screwing off on trumpet tonight – trying to be Maynard Ferguson, trying to hit high notes that aren't written in the score. He thinks he's a lady's man. Whenever a cute little co-ed from Yuba College shows up he has to put himself in the limelight. He ought to forget it. If he wants to pick up chicks as a musician, he should switch to sax. The sax player always gets the girl.

I really like my bass player, Freddie Gomes. I like his sister, Carla, too. Freddie was born in Sao Paulo, Brazil. Maybe music comes naturally to Brazilians. Maybe it's the African blood in them; I don't know, but he keeps the steadiest beat I ever heard. He likes to play an upright, acoustic bass - the old "slap" kind that real jazz artists prefer. I know a lot of bass players are going to the newer, electric guitar kinds. But Freddie sticks with the traditional kind.

Freddie keeps a steady beat better than any drummer I've ever had. Drummers, I've concluded, are flakes. We've been through four drummers in only two years since I formed the band. They all want to play rock and roll, and that beat isn't anything at all like what jazz is all about.

Question: How can you tell if a drummer knocks at your door?

Answer: The knocking speeds up!

Question: What do you call a drummer who's broken up with his girl friend?

Answer: Homeless!

Drummers: Screw them all. I can do without a drummer. I'll take a solid bass guy like Freddie any day.

I'll take his sister, Carla, any day, too. She's the same age as Allie, and I've started dating Carla recently. Maybe "dating" is stretching the truth a bit. So far it's just been, "Hey, let's go and get a coke together" stuff - nothing serious – yet. Maybe if the band ever breaks up I might go farther, ask her to go steady. But as long as Freddie's playing with me and he's still one of my best friends, no messing around.

If she were Sarge's sister? Maybe. If he had a sister that I was interested in. He has an older sister, Becky, and she's a piece of work. Sarge even says she is.

CHAPTER THREE

March 8, 1960: *Senator John F. Kennedy, as expected, wins the Democratic New Hampshire primary by a margin of nine to one. Because New Hampshire borders Massachusetts, Kennedy was always considered a "favorite son" in New Hampshire. The win came as no surprise to the political pundits and professionals.*

April 5, 1960: *In a surprise upset, Senator Kennedy wins 56% of vote in Wisconsin primary, shocking "favorite" Senator Hubert H. Humphrey of neighboring Minnesota.*

Early April in the Sacramento Valley can be either stinking cold or tending toward steaming hot. This year it chose to be cold. The peach farmers were worried that if the temperature dropped too much in the night the young fruit that had just barely set on after blossoming would be hit by frost and they could lose their entire crop. They gave us a pass from school for a couple of days so any high school kids that wanted to could be available to help set out smudge pots if needed.

I volunteered to help my friend Freddie Gomes's old man, Pedro Gabriel. He doesn't like me very much. Just a few weeks ago I remember he scared the living daylights out of me when I showed up to take Carla out for a coke and do some studying at the city library for a midterm. Mr. Gomes came to the door wearing some old tan, torn and oil-stained Dickies with suspenders, no belt, plus a wife beater shirt – nothing more, no slippers even.

He was sharpening a straight-edged razor with a leather strop.   He opened the door and just stood there looking at me, like I was being accused of some felony with his daughter, stropping that razor on the leather: whish-pop, whish-pop, whish-pop! Like that.

He hollered something to Carla in Portuguese that I didn't understand and she came to the door. She said something back to him in Portuguese and he sort of grunted at her. Then he says to me, "Okay young fella, you get Carla back here by nine, understood?" And he just kept sharpening that damn razor. Whish-pop. Whish-pop. Whish-pop! The razor looked meaner to me than Mr. Gomes. And his face was clean and shiny, like he'd already shaved. In fact he still had shaving cream in his ear.

It was already seven and Carla lives a half hour outside town on their farm, and by the time we got in town it was seven thirty so we had a quick coke at the A&W and stopped by the library to check out some books before they closed and still get her back in time. I thought of that razor and whish-pop. I doubted he'd really use it on me just for bringing her home late. He wouldn't, would he? You never can tell where dads and their daughters are concerned.

On the drive back to her place Carla said, "I'm sorry about my dad. He's really okay. He just likes to scare boy friends. He thinks it's his duty to protect me. He's so old world. But my mom's really cool. She's Brazilian, not real Portuguese like my dad."

I wasn't sure what it meant for her mom to be "Brazilian" or for her dad to be "real Portuguese," either. Carla was the youngest of the large Gomes family, and she was born in Sao Paulo, Brazil..

It was funny, genetically speaking, but she was the lightest of them all. The oldest, a son who was married and had been a partner on the peach farm with his dad until he started his own farm, was almost as dark as any of the Negroes who live in our town or over in Marysville. But Carla was fair: her hair was almost blond and her eyes are light green, sometimes bluish, depending on the light.

When I mentioned this to her she said it was a thing unique to Portuguese families. The more kids you had, the lighter they seemed to turn out. "The oldest kid is really Moorish and the youngest sometimes looks like Sandra Dee," she said. She couldn't explain it.

"Maybe the old man just runs out of bullets," I said. She giggled.

I devoted two all-night shifts working at lighting smudge pots in Mr. Gomes's orchards. It was colder than a well digger's fingers and toes. In between lighting pots, we hunkered down in our heavy coats, huddled around empty fifty-gallon oil drums they used for fires, trying to keep warm while drinking cups of really strong Brazilian coffee spiked with lots of sugar.

When we got there about dark the temperature was in the low forties. Within an hour it had dropped to around thirty-three. We sat there for a few minutes until the wind died down, everything got quiet and the mercury suddenly dropped again - to twenty-eight - and we scrambled to get the pots lit and keep them going all night with kerosene. I slept all the next day and didn't even shower to get rid of the black soot and stink of kerosene smoke before I fell into bed. I was beat. Mr. Gomes offered to pay us all, but we refused because Freddie and Carla were our friends. After that Mr. Gomes started being nicer to me.

* * * * *

Mom woke me for supper the end of my second day of sleeping after helping in the orchards. Allie had already finished her dinner – she's a fast eater – and was cleaning her plate at the sink.

"Alex, I got elected chairman of the junior prom and I insisted your band would be hired to play for us." Allie chose to attend classes instead of helping with the smudge pots. Most of the other girls in our school did, too.

"Thanks, Sis, that's cool. How much of a budget…?"

"And I've decided to run as a delegate to the Democratic national convention."

"Yeah, that's cool, too, but how much of a budget do you have for the band?"

"All you care about is money! You don't care a bit that I want to be a delegate. Screw you! And your band!" She stormed out. Allie can be moody.

What the heck's a delegate to a national convention, anyway? And how does that affect me? I didn't know Allie was a Democrat. She can't even vote – she's too young.

Allie had a budget of two hundred dollars for the band. After taking my usual ten percent that meant we would split the rest five ways. I know, I said there were only three guys in the band: Hugo Sargenti, Freddie Gomes, and me. Now there're five of us. Here's what happened:

Right after the fruit frost scare, there was an exchange talent assembly with Marysville High School. They came over and entertained us in our new, modern big gym, and then we went over and entertained in their old, tiny, cracker box of a gym. It's really small, crowded, and has no stage or any way of making a stage.

Bud (my Dad insists we call him Bud) tells a story of how he and a bunch of his buddies were students at Marysville before the War and they pulled a prank. Well, they *tried* to pull off a prank, but it didn't work *and* they got in really big trouble. Kicked off the basketball team. Expulsions. That kind of serious trouble.

In the old Marysville gym there are these two balcony things built on each side and above the basketball floor where the home fans, students, and the school band all sit on one side and the visitors sit on the other side during games or other events, looking down on the floor, and facing each other's side.

The basketball court takes up the entire floor. The player's benches are snugged right up next to the balcony. If you were on the lowest row of seats you could reach down and hit the players on the head, they're that close. There are steps leading up to both balconies off the playing floor. There are also stairs up the back way from the outside of the building. And that's where Bud's story begins.

There was a basketball game with another school, not ours, from out in the west valley somewhere – I think he said it was Arbuckle or Grimes or some other hick town. These visitors were *real* farmers – cows, pigs, hay, sugar beets, that kind of thing.

So Bud and his pals decided to taunt those farmers. They stole a live cow from some farmer out by the town of Sutter, and left her up in the visitors' balcony seating area. They sneaked her in during the night and tied her down so she couldn't get loose and wander around.

Next morning, the janitor opened the gym for first period gym class – girls P.E. – and this awful stink hit him in the face. Bossie had pulled loose from her tether during the night and jumped over the edge of the balcony onto the hardwood floor. She broke both front legs and must have died of the shock. But not before she crapped about a hundred pounds of manure all over herself and the floor.

They got the dead cow hauled off to the glue factory and the place cleaned up in time for the game. But in spite of buckets of Lysol, there was still a bad cow manure stink in the gym for the game. Word of the prank got back to the visitors before the game. They were not amused.

Neither was the Marysville High administration. Marysville's principal had some finks on his payroll and by game time they had fingered Bud and his pals, who were all on the basketball team – the whole first team, in fact. They were all summarily kicked off the team and expelled for a month. The coach had to put in his scrubs to play and Marysville lost to this little cow town high school from the west side for the first time ever. Marysville, a sure bet to win the conference! Bud and his guys were literally cow manure in that town for months after.

Good thing the War broke out so Bud could join up and skip town with dignity and honor restored. He served in Army Intelligence.

Anyway, when Marysville performed their talent assembly for us, this big teddy bear of a kid that I'd never seen before, with this big head full of kinky brown hair gets up on stage with just an acoustic guitar, no backup, and belted out a hip-twisting version of Buddy Holly's *Peggy Sue*. And he also plays a thirty-two bar bridge. All ad lib. He brought the house down. Afterwards, I went up to him and asked how he learned to play guitar like that.

His name was Gary Kinnersly and he had transferred to Marysville at the semester from Mesa, Arizona. His dad had died recently and he came to live with his mother and her second husband – Gary's new stepfather – who owned a dairy farm out towards Beale.

I asked him if he had ever played any jazz. He said he'd played with his school's jazz band in Mesa and that he'd studied classical guitar with a guy on the music faculty at Arizona State. I didn't even bother with the formality of an audition. Man, he was in my band from that day on. He picked up on our book just by practicing and jamming with us. And that's four out of five.

The fifth member of our band was the surprise bonus addition: Carla Gomes, Mr. Whish-pop's daughter. Allie informed me that the fine print in the contract for us playing the junior prom included letting Carla sing with our band. "I didn't know Carla could sing," I said.

"Duh. She sings in the girl's choir. Or didn't you notice?" Allie was referring to the fact that I pitched in and accompanied the girl's choir for Miss Phelps, the band and vocal teacher, when Janeen Brown took sick and had to drop out of school.

Janeen is kind of my nemesis. We compete for piano and organ jobs around town. She's pretty good, mechanically speaking. But musically I'm better. I was sorry she got sick – Diverticulitis – the trots. She had to stay home where she could be close to a bathroom at all times. Janeen would have to repeat her senior year as a result.

My part time job is playing organ for the Methodists and the Catholics. I make five dollars a week from each one. That's just for their church services – prelude, hymns, that stuff. If I'm asked to accompany their choirs I get another five dollars a week.

But I don't like playing weddings and funerals. Don't ask me to explain because I can't. I just don't like them. Actually, there is a reason, at least for the weddings: I get tired of people at weddings coming up and asking, "Can you play The Anniversary Song?" Or "Do you know The Tennessee Waltz?" Yeah, I can play them all. In waltz time, march time, four/four, and even my own jazz arrangement. But I don't enjoy it.

I got together with Carla and she introduced me to Brazilian jazz. I loved it.

"Where have you been hiding this stuff?" I asked.

"Nobody's been hiding anything. I grew up with this music. It's everywhere in Brazil."

"Well, it's not here in America," I protested.

Then Carla sang for me a little jazzy arrangement she said was in something the Brazilians called bossa nova style that she had written herself, while she strummed some great chords on her guitar.

The lyrics, of course, were in Portuguese, which I didn't understand, but were still beautiful, so she translated for me. The story was based on a Brazilian folk legend about a dolphin that turned into a man when the moon was full. This man was killer handsome and would wait until all the fishermen in the village left to go out in their fishing boats at night and he would turn into a really handsome guy, wade ashore and try to seduce the wives when the men were gone. If he made love to a woman when the moon was full, she would have a baby that was half dolphin and half man, just like him and the mother would some day lose her baby to the sea.

"I don't think the administration would approve if they really understood the lyrics," I said.

"How many of those old guys know Portuguese?" Carla asked, giggling.

She had a point. It was a beautiful song. And that's how I learned bossa nova.

* * * * *

Allie wasted no time getting down to business on her convention delegate quest. Within two days she had gotten her hands on a private list of all the known Democrats in our Congressional district, registered or otherwise. She got me working with her on a brochure she planned to mail out or hand deliver to all the Democrats on the list. "Why me?" I asked.

"You're a writer. And you owe it to me as my brother."

"But I'm not interested in politics," I said.

"Tough. Until I win, you're interested, Ducky." Right here I need to explain. *Ducky* is the nickname I inherited from her when I wore a duck's ass hair cut a couple of years ago. It was the style then and Bud did a good job of cutting and styling it for everyone, including me. Now I wear my hair short, like the Kingston Trio does. Allie started calling me Ducky back then, and the name stuck long after I quit wearing my hair that way. Anyway…

I helped her write a brochure and design a poster. We got a couple hundred of each printed, and she wasted no time getting stores and shops to put up her poster with her picture and her pitch. Because everyone knew and liked Bud, Allie got in almost every establishment in the area. I think only a few merchants turned her down and they were small gas stations or bars over in Olivehurst. The Olivehurst crowd doesn't patronize our town much or have anything to do with us anyway, so she pretty much wrote off that constituency, as she called them. I was learning about politics. It has its own jargon, the meanings of which are known mostly only to insiders and designed to baffle us outsiders.

"Why do you have to start now? When is this convention?" I asked.

"It's early July in Los Angeles and you're going with me," she announced.

"I don't like L.A.," I said. "I haven't liked L.A. ever since the Brooklyn Dodgers bailed and moved for the bigger bucks in Southern California."

"I don't care. I don't like L.A. either, but that's where it is and that's where we're going," she said. "What about the Giants? Didn't they do the same thing?"

Ouch! "That's different," I said. She gave me this look. It's the look that says "Gotcha!"

Mr. O'Farrell was the one behind this dream of hers. He had challenged the students in his civics classes to get active in politics. "Don't just sit there and let the grownups make all the decisions for your generation. That's how mine was treated," he said. "You're the future leaders of this great nation. In a couple of years you guys will be registering for the draft. You'll be expected to die for your country.

"Don't you want to have a say in your future? Then get involved. Pick a party – either party – and get involved. Get out and help register people to vote. You can volunteer to canvass votes. You can drive old people to the polls. There's lots you can do. Why, heck, you can even be a delegate to your party's convention."

"Isn't there an age limit?" someone asked.

"There's no age limit to be a delegate that I know of," he said. I read in the paper the other day of one girl in Iowa or Indiana or someplace back there, who's only eighteen, and she's planning on being a delegate to the Republican National Convention this summer. I think she's a Rockefeller supporter."

That's when Allie came home all fired up and determined she was going to go, too. And Kennedy was her man. Now John F. Kennedy was the topic of every meal time discussion in our house. Pictures of JFK were plastered on the walls in her room. Suddenly we had news clippings festooning the fridge door: JFK. "Bud, why don't you learn how to cut guys' hair like John Kennedy?" she asked one night.

"Actually, I had a kid request a JFK hair cut the other day. I think he's from Marysville, though," Bud said.

"Did you do it?" Julia asked, between bites of her delicious coq au vin.

"It wasn't that hard. I just used one of the photos Allie asked me to tape up in the shop and I followed the contours," he said. "Ivy's a big John Kennedy fan, you know. He says Kennedy will be the first white man in the White House to do anything for the colored man since FDR. He's predicting that if Kennedy becomes president, he'll have a Negro on his cabinet, too." Allie pumped her fists and cheered at that prediction.

Ivy is Bud's new junior partner at the shop. He's a Negro and recently retired as a Master Sergeant in the Air Force at Beale. Ivy was actually a cook in the service, but he started cutting hair because it used to be that none of the military barbers would cut hair for the Negro servicemen. Ivy had made an immediate impact on Bud's revenues because all the Negro guys in the area came to him for hair cuts, including many of his old Air Force pals.

Ivy is a big man, so black he's almost as purple as a ripening prune, with a grin so big it split his face in half. He likes to hum blues tunes while he cuts hair; I could sit and listen to his songs for hours. Ivy has a large family. Two of his sons and three daughters are already grown and gone, living out of state. One of the middle boys is taller than his dad, probably six foot six inches and was recruited hard by Coach Frye to transfer to our high school right out of his junior high over in Marysville to play center. There was a snag in this plan: the kid, Orly, didn't live in our school district boundaries, so a supporter came up with the idea of letting Orly live with him and his wife. Their kids were all gone and they had plenty of spare bedrooms.

Orly felt a little weird about being a Negro living with those white folks until his momma learned they were good Baptists and then it was okay. Orly made a real difference for our basketball team from the very first game he played in as a sophomore.

It looked like we were finally going to have a winning team. Shoot, we might even dream about beating our arch rival, Marysville, which we hadn't beaten in two decades. Everyone began thinking Coach Frye was some kind of genius.

I wasn't so sure Mr. O'Farrell was a genius. I doubted it was smart of him to give that why-don't-you-guys-get-involved pep talk.

As always, Allie took it as a gauntlet thrown at her feet.

CHAPTER FOUR

In mid-April I was invited, along with four other honors English students, to accompany Miss Jensdatter on a field trip to U.C. Davis – a poetry seminar, a symposium featuring a poet named Robinson Jeffers. He would be reading several of his poems and taking questions from the audience afterwards. Miss Jensdatter suggested that the two of us who were guys might want to wear a blazer and a tie. "Why?" I asked.

"I guess you don't have to unless you want to," she said. I ended up wearing my navy blazer, khakis, button down shirt and a repp-striped tie. I hoped it would make me look older, less of a high school student, more like I was in college.

The other guy in our group was Pat "Wick" Wickstrom, a real loner. I had never had much to do with Wick until the trip to Davis to hear Robinson Jeffers. Wick is large, marshmallow-soft, and has a bad acne problem. His clothes always look like he's slept in them for a week. He obviously doesn't care about clothes, popularity, or what other people think about him.

Wick only cares about one thing: studying. He always has his nose in a book, whether he's walking in the halls, eating lunch, sitting on the top row of bleachers at a football game – he was reading something. He drives the school librarian nuts with requests for obscure journals on science or medicine. His favorite subject is human physiology and anatomy. We all figured he'd become a doctor. Or maybe he's just a closet pervert, who really knows for sure?

On the drive down Wick opened up and briefed us on the research he had done into the life and writings of Robinson Jeffers. Jeffers was born into a religious home – Calvinists. His father, a strict man, was a professor of religion at a seminary in Pennsylvania. Jeffers had learned to read Greek by the time he was five. He studied science and medicine at several universities, including one in Europe (that appealed to Wick). He inherited a lot of money as a young man, married and moved west, to Carmel, California, building a rock home on a cliff overlooking the ocean.

He wrote of nature and man's relationship to nature. He wrote of the depravity of man (no surprise here, considering his Calvinist upbringing); of the certainty of death, with nothing more to follow. In his younger days he had been a mere imitator – of Shelley, Byron, Keats – but in his later years he began to see and experience an evolutionary development – a progression – in his poetry, from rational thought, through feelings and emotions, until he thought poetry could ultimately even become almost as pure as music. (That last thought appealed to the musician in me.)

We met in an upstairs lecture hall in the college of veterinary science building. The weather was mild and sunny and the drabness of the plain brick institutional buildings of this cow college – the poor relation of its bigger sister campus in Berkeley – was brightened some by tulips and daffodils blooming everywhere. That helped some to take our minds off the strange smells floating around that veterinary building.

Some professor of English from Berkeley, a friend of Miss Jensdatter's, was Jeffers' introducer for this three-hour symposium. This professor was a young man dressed in a tan tweed jacket and gray flannel slacks, a button down shirt and striped tie. He had a Kennedy-like mop of reddish-blond hair, a mustache, and smoked a briar pipe. The jacket had a lot of pinhole-sized burn marks in the lapels from errant tobacco coals. His name was Professor Harold Hill (I'm not making this up). He jokingly said that he wasn't the same famous guy from "Music Man" – that he had never been, nor would he ever be, a traveling salesman, nor could he sing. That got a few polite laughs.

Professor Hill spoke briefly about how the purpose of this seminar was in partial fulfillment of his master's degree in English and philosophy at Berkeley. He started out with a question: Did poetry still have any utility – or usefulness? What was the value of poetry in our modern society? He thanked his colleagues on the English faculty at Davis for their foresight in planning and arranging this symposium. Then he made a few introductory remarks about Mr. Jeffers, who, it seemed, was a friend of his. It seemed like Professor Hill had read the same biography that Wick had, because his remarks were almost word for word the same as Wick's. Hill ended by introducing Mr. Jeffers as "the Robert Frost of Carmel – our own native California poet."

Robinson Jeffers was in his early to mid-seventies, thin, stooped shouldered, with a shock of white, unruly hair that was thinning above his brows. The white hair did make him look like a skinny Robert Frost. He was dressed in a black turtleneck sweater and brown corduroy slacks with scuffed desert boots on his feet.

As he took his place at the lectern, he leaned against it for support. He apologized that he was just recovering from a bad cold; for emphasis he pulled out a big red hanky and wiped his swollen, runny nose. He seemed quite frail, as if something more was wrong with him than the common cold.

Jeffers said he had been asked to read a few of his poems and comment on them, perhaps to explain the elements of poetry, and techniques he utilized when he wrote. After that he would be willing to take questions from the audience. "Since I don't hear too well any more, could you please write them down and someone will collect them during the break."

He said he was reluctant to give too much self-analysis of his own poetry, but he would try to make some observations about what he was thinking or feeling at the time he had written them. He started out by reading a short poem entitled *People and a Heron.*

> *A desert of weed and water-darkened stone under*
> *my western windows*
> *The ebb lasted all afternoon.*
> *And many pieces of humanity, men, women, and*
> *children, gathering shellfish, swarmed with voices of*
> *gulls, the sea-beach.*
> *At twilight they went off together, the verge was left*
> *vacant.*
> *An evening heron bent broad wings over the black*

He went on and read several more short poems, then a few lines from his two most famous ones *Tamar,* and *The Roan Stallion.*

But my mind kept turning over the words of the first one. I imagined myself on a cliff above a beach. I'm there for the solitude, for the break from humanity and the stresses of living. I'm watching the hordes of beach combers talking silly talk and racing to see who could get the most sea shells or the prettiest or the most unique.

I saw the lone heron, blue-gray, thin, fragile, ungainly on land, but perfected beauty itself in flight. It spreads its wings and the evening sea air catches them like sails, fills them, and lifts him above the black ebbing tide. I could almost smell the salty sea spray and hear the hiss of the surf retreating down the pebbled sand and the smell of kelp and decaying shellfish. I could hear the plaintive cries of sea birds as they winged to their night rests calling to each other in the gloom.

I don't remember much about the questions and answers and I remember I was tempted to write down a question and submit it, but decided not to because I didn't need answers. I saw so clearly what he was trying to say, and it was in the words, the emotions, the imagery, the music of the poem itself, neatly contained in those few, short, perfect verses.

I didn't need to hear any explanations about what the poetry did or didn't mean.

I got it!

We finished the seminar in late afternoon and Jensdatter invited us to stop off for dinner at the Nut Tree, twenty minutes south of Davis in Vacaville. It was a bit of a detour, but nobody objected.

While we were waiting to be seated I went into the gift shop to look around. They had a rack of new neckties, Rooster brand ties, made by Ernst in San Francisco. I had seen an ad for Cable Car Clothiers featuring these ties in a recent issue of the *Chronicle.* They were made of raw silk, were square on the ends and had horizontal bars that looked like they were hand-painted. I bought two, one for myself and one for Bud. He likes to wear things that are trendier, not so traditional.

We ordered dinner - chicken salads, date nut bread, and the like. Wick embarrassed Jensdatter when he asked the waitress if they had peanut butter sandwiches with jelly. The waitress was nice and said she'd see what she could do "even though that item isn't on our menu, sir." What can you expect from a kid who has saved all his used gum since the fifth grade? I'm not making this up: Wick has this huge ball of already chewed gum that he keeps in his bedroom. We suspect he's going for some kind of record in the Guinness Book. The Nut Tree people actually made him a plate of peanut butter sandwiches. No wonder he has a zit problem.

We all had to write a report on the field trip for extra credit. I got an A.

* * * * *

Allie celebrated her new driver's license by borrowing the family station wagon and driving to a Kennedy rally in Sacramento the Saturday following the Robinson Jeffers symposium. She hijacked me into going with her, even though I had a lot of studying to do, plus a gig playing Saturday night over at the Elk's Club in Marysville.

She drove the speed limit – 55 – all the way, and hugged the right shoulder, as far away from the center of the road as possible. She insisted on rolling the windows down and it was really humid from the water-flooded rice fields on both sides of the highway.

Allie also insists on listening to her pop music. She plays it as loud as possible. I don't see how she can stand it, it ruins my hearing. "I hope this makes you happy," I said, not sincerely. Allie smiled quickly and fixed her eyes back on the road. "Relax, Sis, your knuckles are white," I said.

"So are yours," she shot back. I looked down and my fists were clinched. I tried to relax, but the Everly Brothers were wailing at about a thousand decibels about *There he g-o-o-o-e-s, he's Cathy's Clown...*

After that, the Hit Parade included sets of three tunes, followed by five minutes of mindless commercials: Coke, Coppertone, stock car races, zit cream, Wrigley's Double Mint gum ("Double your pleasure, double your fun: chew Wrigley's Double Mint Gum!"). Then we heard another set of three tunes: *Theme from a Summer Place*, by Percy Faith; *It's Now or Never,* Elvis Presley, and *Only the Lonely,* Roy Orbison.

"Can't we change it for a while?" I begged.

"Touch that dial, Ducky, and you're dead!" She didn't take her eyes off the road to glance at me. Her tone was warning enough. "After you drop me off you can listen to your jazz stations all you want," Allie said. "That was the deal."

She got out thirty minutes later at a big convention center and I took over the wheel. I remembered this place from the circus last summer where I played the steam calliope in the circus band. My good friend Jack Armstrong, who rides circuit all over three counties teaching music in rural schools, got me that job, and I made some really good money that day. It was a kick in the pants, too. "When do you want me to come back for you?" I asked Allie. It was nine o'clock. We coordinated our watches and I agreed to be back at one. "Have fun," I said. "Give Jack a big hug for me."

"He won't be here. This is just for all his supporters and delegates…"

"Which you aren't. Yet…," I reminded her. She frowned.

"If a Kennedy's there, which I was promised, I'll get some pictures to put in my campaign literature." So this was to be a photo op for Allie.

"Whatever," I said. "See you later."

* * * * *

Allie wasted no time in scoping out the big hall and deciding which seat closest to the podium was the best. She registered and asked where the reception was. "Over there," a worker pointed. "Follow that line." Allie got in line and in about a half hour made it into the smaller room that was crowded with an assortment of politicos, from Governor Pat Brown all the way down to state assemblymen, Congressmen, county commissioners, and ward bosses, all eager and hopeful to get close to the famous Kennedys.

The reception line consisted of Pat Brown and his wife, a Senator, a couple of Congressmen, and the Lieutenant Governor. At the end, standing about the space of one person apart, was Teddy, the youngest of the Kennedy brothers. He was movie star handsome, like both his famous older brothers, with a full head of the Kennedy strong dark hair, and the ever-present smile with dazzling white, perfect teeth.

A few paces away a gaggle of photographers herded together snapping

26

pictures of all the hand shakers, recording their moment in history. The line moved slowly. The rally was to officially begin at ten o'clock, and it was five minutes until the hour. It seemed hopeless that Allie would get her chance in line for the photo shaking hands with Teddy. She was two people away when a voice came over the PA system, "Folks, let's gather in the main hall. We need to get this party started!"

Allie made her move while heads were turned to the PA voice. She deftly slipped in line ahead of a large woman with fake red hair. "Sorry," Allie said as she grabbed Teddy's hand. "Hi, I'm Allison Rodgers from Sutter County just north of here, and I plan on being the youngest Kennedy delegate to the convention in LA in July!"

"How do you do, Allison Rodgers, from Sutter County. I'm Teddy Kennedy." (As if she didn't know!) "I'm sorry my brother Jack couldn't be here himself to wish you well. But on his behalf and everyone in my family, good luck. I'll see you in LA, then?"

Teddy turned and smiled for the camera as Allie moved in, and her photo has her clutching his arm and planting a big kiss on his cheek, all the while facing the camera full-on and wide-eyed.

While Allie was rubbing shoulders with the hoi polloi, I made a trip downtown to the Roos Atkin department store to stock up on some new shirts, ties, and socks. Roos had Gant oxford cloth button down shirts, the absolute in thing for every guy to wear. You couldn't buy them in our small town yet, so this trip was an opportunity for me.

I bought four, one each of white, blue, pink, and yellow (even though everyone said yellow was a fairy color and only queers wore them). I would need them in a few months when I started college. And I knew for a fact that in college, yellow was an okay color.

After the shopping spree at Roos, I dropped by the music store and picked over the charts in their section for big bands, jazz combos, and small groups. I asked if they had gotten in the theme for "Summer Place" yet. The salesman found it for me in the big band format (four saxes, two trumpets, two trombones, piano, bass, guitar and drums), but it also had a small combo version included, with words for either male or female vocalist.

I wanted to beef up our book with some of the newest hit tunes for the junior prom that was coming just a week away. If Gary Kinnersly couldn't (or wouldn't) sing the vocals, then I'd see if Carla could do it.

Allie let me drive home. She admitted that she was too pumped up with adrenaline from her rally; she babbled all the way back: "Bobby is Jack's manager for the whole campaign. They're kicking butt in the primaries, but they're getting a lot of pushback – dirty stuff, slurs and lies mostly – from Adlai (well, not the lies from him, he's too nice), but some from Hubert, and a lot from Symington and LBJ, so they need all the delegates they can get. They're taking nothing for granted. Teddy is also one of the Western States coordinators. Oh, Ducky, he's so young… and he's so drop dead gorgeous! I got my picture with him and I kissed him. On the cheek!" She reverently touched the now-sacred spot.

Maybe it was the humidity from the rice fields, but I had never seen her glow like that. I could swear she was in love. She didn't even notice that the radio was still on KGO, my favorite San Francisco jazz station.

* * * * *

We played the theme from "Summer Place" cold that night at the Elk's, without practicing it first, and it was a big hit. We got as many requests to play it again as we did for "Misty." Carla Gomes nailed the vocal the first time through, sight-reading it with us, and I loved her for her talent more than I ever had before.

28

CHAPTER FIVE

The week after the Sacramento political rally trip, Allie's softball team was in a championship game with Marysville for the league title. They'd beaten the Yuba City girls twice already in the regular season and were considered the favorites. That made us the under dogs and all bets were we would lose again. It was played on our field and this was a big game, so a lot of townspeople showed up. That's surprising. Even the boy's varsity baseball team hardly ever draws a crowd of more than fifty or sixty, usually moms and girlfriends.

But The Appeal-Democrat sports editor was famously biased in favor of Marysville. It always came through in his articles who he was cheering for. I think our whole town showed up in response to an article he had written bashing our girls' team.

Marysville was favored but we were hoping for a win. Bragging rights, yes. Title, hopefully. More importantly this year, we could rub that sports writer guy's face in it – give him back a little of the crap he constantly dishes out. I didn't realize what a big game this was for Allie until it was over.

The game was tight, extra innings. We were in the bottom of the eleventh inning with the score tied one-all. We had a great little third baseman named Molly Martinez who was faster than the Tokyo Bullet train. She managed to draw a walk and somehow moved to second on a wild pitch. That batter then struck out: down to our last out.

Then Allie came to bat. Marysville had a really hot pitcher and she had struck out Allie twice in the early innings. Our coach was flashing a very obvious hit and run sign, so Marysville moved their defense back, including the infielders, expecting Allie to try for the long ball, or at least a single that could try to score Molly from second.

On the two-one pitch Molly stole third and they let her go. A wild throw would score her and lose the game for them. Allie took the pitch. The call was a strike. The next pitch was a change-up, a ball. Count: three-two.

Our women's softball coach played in the big leagues at one time, but he had a drinking or drug problem and fell from grace. He ended up here, coaching girl's softball – the only job he could get because Mr. Sumsion was a friend of his and wanted to give Coach a second chance. Coach had seen everything there was to see in the game of baseball and he had a few tricks to call on. Now he pulled one out of the hat that nobody expected. The smart money tells you never try a bunt on a full count, right? The percentages of making it work are too low and the odds are too high against you, right?

Coach didn't believe in smart money. He believed in his players. He had managed in just one season to take a couple of talented players like Molly Martinez and Allie plus a bunch of scrubs, and through good coaching, hard physical training and discipline, turn them into a team of contenders.

As the Marysville pitcher released, Allie squared for a bunt. The crowd hushed; their defense froze, never expecting a Hail Mary move like this. How she did it, I'll never figure out, but Allie laid the ball down softly, perfectly, along the first base line. Allie was out of the box and streaking down the line to first.

The pitcher got to the ball too late to tag Allie, or to throw to first for the out. Her only option was to underhand it to home. As the ball left the pitcher's hand, Molly streaked to home and slid under the tag. She jumped up and the whole team was off the bench mobbing her to the ground. It looked like a Rugby scrum, but with cuter butts.

Game over. We win two-one. Championship is ours.

Allie told me two things later: they had practiced that play all week, everyone on the team working on laying down bunts until they had perfected it. And there were no less than six scouts from major colleges at that game. She really didn't care about that.

Allie's picture was featured in the next night's edition of The Appeal-Democrat and the sports writer actually laid on the praise for Allie and the entire team. The best part was that he mentioned that Allie was a candidate for national delegate and a Kennedy supporter. You can't buy publicity like that in our small community.

* * * * *

Junior proms take on a life of their own, and this year's was no exception. Allie wanted the theme of "The Lamp is Low." She got that from the title of one of the tunes on a Ray Conniff LP album at home. Her committee overruled her and came up with "Enchanted Isle" with the theme song of *Bali Ha'i* from "South Pacific." Apparently they didn't have a clue what it meant for the lamp to be low; however, Yuba City is a long way away from Bali Ha'i.

One of the girls on the committee had an uncle in Sacramento who was in the business of building swimming pools. He said he had a small portable pool with a waterfall that they could rent for only fifty dollars for the night. The waterfall and a pool filled with giant gold fish would be the focal point of all the decorations.

Finding the sheet music of the same title wasn't a problem for me. It was tradition for the band to play the prom's theme song about half way through the dance when the King and Queen and their escorts were introduced. The King and Queen would then lead off a solo dance number to the theme song. Don't get me wrong – I have a lot of favorite tunes from Broadway musicals. "Bali Ha'i" is definitely not one of them. But we were getting paid two hundred bucks and would do whatever we could to please the folks paying us.

Allie turned down three guys who invited her to the dance. She would be there all right, but she felt since she was in charge, she shouldn't be distracted by a date. "It wouldn't be fair for me to come with some guy and spend the whole night having to deal with other problems," she reasoned. I promised to break away and dance with her a couple of times if I could.

The waterfall/pool was a bad idea. It leaked badly and Mr. Warner, the head janitor, spent the entire night mopping up the darn thing until he finally convinced someone to shut it off - to save the giant gold fish, which looked pretty stressed by the time the night was over.

Another thing they did that was different this year: they didn't put the punch bowls out on the refreshment table, but faculty chaperones served the punch in individual cups from the cafeteria window. The reason for this was last year some of the guys on the varsity football team – including Sarge, I suspect – had volunteered to be in charge of the refreshments. They smuggled in several bottles of vodka and spiked the punch. Half the dancers were looped by the end of the night, including some of the faculty chaperones.

This dance was on a Friday night. Thursday, I had been contacted by a talent booker in Sacramento, wanting to know if I wanted to play with Ray Conniff and his orchestra and chorus Saturday night at a concert he was giving at Chico State College. Conniff's auxiliary percussion player – the one who played celeste and bells – had fallen sick. Apparently I had come highly recommended by someone. I asked who. It was my friend Jack Armstrong who taught music at several small rural schools all over the county and who had gotten the job for me to play calliope at the circus last year.

This presented a big dilemma for me: I was signed up to take the college entrance exams at Yuba College. The exams would last most of the day Saturday. I didn't think I could miss them. The rehearsal with Conniff's band would also take most of the day Saturday. And I didn't want to miss that chance, either.

I talked with Mom and Bud and asked their advice. Of course they told me it was a nice opportunity, but it was a one-time event. College was important for my future – the rest of my life would be pretty much based on college. "But it's your decision, mon petit chou chou," Mom said. Thanks a bunch.

I talked with my counselor, Matt Starrs, and he thought he could get the fees I'd already paid for the exams applied to the next test date – in late August. "Of course that will somewhat limit your choices for college," he said. "The results from the August exam won't be available until just before fall semester starts." I said I understood, but the Conniff gig was a big break for me and I'd probably regret it the rest of my life if I didn't get to play with this great band. He said he understood my dilemma. He hoped I would make the right choice.

After my English class on Friday I talked with Miss Jensdatter about what to do.

She told me a story about herself. She said she once had a chance to do something like that and had played it safe and done the thing everyone was expecting her to do. She regretted it ever since. She was working at Harrah's Club at Lake Tahoe making change for the summers when she was in college; there she met a lot of performers and famous people. She started dating one of her fellow workers, and by the end of the summer he'd asked her to marry him. She thought about it and asked advice from a lot of people, who advised against it. She turned the guy down. "He really loved me. I've regretted it ever since. Now look at me. I'm virtually a spinster."

"You're not a spinster," I said, disagreeing politely.

"You're kind, but honestly speaking, I *am* a spinster and I don't think I'll ever get another chance at marriage. Follow your heart, Ducky. You'll be happier that way. Life is shorter than you have any idea. Don't you get down the road another twenty years or so and have any regrets."

"I hope you get a second chance at love," I said. She smiled, took both my cheeks in her hands and squeezed them with her forehead touching mine.

I raced home and called Conniff's booker in Sacramento.

Mom drove me up to Chico early Saturday morning for the rehearsal. I'll be glad when I can have my own car. "Do your best," she smiled at me as she left. She always says that. "We'll all be back in time for the concert." I had four free tickets. Bud and Mom drove back up again later to the concert. I had also invited Freddie and Carla to come along and use the other two tickets, so they rode with Bud and Mom.

Conniff rehearsed us hard all day, with only a short break for lunch.

The concert was in the large auditorium and we (the band, the singers, Mr. Conniff) all filled the stage. We made a big sound with that many players. I had a great time playing with Conniff. I didn't have a very big part, true, but it was more fun than I'd ever had playing in a group. I didn't know that a big band could be so much fun.

His keyboard guy had me sit down and play a few tunes for him from their book during one of the rehearsal breaks. "You're pretty good, kid," he said. "Tell you what. I'll ask the boss if you can play keyboard on a couple numbers to spell me off. I've got a cranky case of arthritis in my thumbs and I could use a rest now and then."

I played "I Hear a Rhapsody" and one other easy number on keyboard. After the concert I asked Mr. Conniff if I could keep the piano scores and asked him to autograph them for me, along with a couple of my mom's LP album covers.

He told me he was reluctant to let me have the piano score. His policy was to never let his music leave his control. "My music is my legacy for my wife and kids," he said. But he did autograph the LP album covers for Mom, and thanked me for stepping in to play on such short notice. "I like to write bell parts in my arrangements because I think it adds a texture to the overall score. It's an important part of my music and you played it well tonight. Thanks."

He also said," You have a fine talent. I hope you keep playing all through your life. Even if you only play for your own enjoyment, do it."

I went home really happy. Someone great had noticed my talent.

CHAPTER SIX

May 1, 1960: *U.S. pilot Francis Gary Powers, flying a top secret U-2 spy plane, is shot down by Russians, held as a spy.*

May 10, 1960: *Kennedy sweeps both the West Virginia and Nebraska primaries.*

Allie was working extra hard at flunking spring semester because she was spending so much time working on her own campaign to get elected as a national delegate. I knew it meant a lot to her, but as her brother, I felt I had to say something. I took a break from my homework and went to her room.

"I know I'm spending a lot of time on this stupid thing! If I'd known it was going to be this hard…"

"Is anyone helping you, or are you doing this thing all by yourself?" I asked.

"It's just me, Ducky. I don't have any friends any more. I don't study, I don't do homework, I don't sleep. I don't have time to eat. I don't date. They all think I'm crazy, just like you think I am." She broke down crying, something she hardly ever does.

I put my arm around her shoulder. "You're not crazy. Well, maybe a little. I'm really proud of you. What can I do to help? I've got this last semester aced and I could probably coast until finals week. That gives us at least two full weeks. What do you want me to do?"

"I need wheels, a car. I need to get around and meet more people, the delegates to the county conventions."

"I'll go to work on it right now. I can get Hugo to let me use his."

Do you have to?" she asked.

"Why?"

"I know he's your best friend, but I can't stand him. He's too hands-on." She shuddered.

"He's not exactly my best friend, and anyway, what do you mean?"

"You didn't see him at the Junior Prom when he took a break from playing and danced with me? I had to keep taking his hands off my butt the whole dance. Ugh, what a worm!"

"You do have a cute butt…"

"You swine! You pervert! My own brother…!"

"No, I didn't see you dancing with him; I was playing, remember? Besides, we… *you* really need his car right now. You know the old story about beggars…?"

Allie reluctantly agreed that we needed Sarge's car. "I just don't want him to get any ideas that I owe him anything, any ah… you know…favors. Understand? Make that really clear to him."

I nodded. "What's next?" I asked.

Hugo Sargenti has a 1951 Mercury coupe that's really cherry: skirts, lowered in the back, twin glass pack mufflers, and painted a candy apple red. It's hot. Real chick bait. I didn't care about the chicks for now – that could wait until later. Allie needed my help. We just needed transportation and I got it for her. Turns out Hugo is getting a new car anyway, as a graduation gift from his parents, and he wanted an excuse to wheedle it out of them early. I provided him a convenient excuse. It helped that his old man was a Kennedy fan, too. Hugo had to call them long distance to make it all right to get the new car.

Sarge's dad and uncle are typical American success stories. They immigrated to America as teenagers and ended up in our community with about twenty dollars between them. They worked hard at any job they could find – it was the Great Depression and jobs were scarce, but they somehow managed.

They saved and eventually opened up a small deli near the new lake that was being built over in Marysville as a WPA project, Lake Ellis.

There were a lot of ethnic workers employed on the project and they appreciated the fresh salami, wurst, and other European meats, cold cuts, and sausages the Sargenti Brothers served up. Then the War came along and they became contractors to supply meat products to the government for Beale Army Air Base east of Marysville. They continued to prosper.

Now they have a big operation, employing over a hundred people and their meat products are distributed all over the West Coast. They're stinking rich. Hugo's dad and mom were on a long cruise through the Mediterranean and wouldn't be back in time for his graduation. They had sent a nice hand-tailored suit from Italy for him to wear at graduation. Pity nobody would see it under his robes. They also told him he could have any new car he wanted for his graduation. Hugo was the first Sargenti to ever make it that far up the educational ladder and they wanted to show the world how proud they were of his accomplishment.

Hugo had a new 1960 MG "A" on order. They came in silver, black, white, British racing green, Robin egg blue, or red. He chose red. I would have picked the green – it's more traditional. But then that's me.

Hugo picked up the new MG from the dealer in Sacramento, and I followed him home driving the Ford. Allie refused to come along, fearing he would make her ride with him. He probably would have, too. It's a good thing there was a gas war on that spring. The '51 Ford was hot, too hot. It drank gas like a thirsty alcoholic. And it had to be premium grade, not regular. Gas was twenty cents a gallon for premium and we could fill it up for a little more than three bucks.

I have to hand it to Allie She knocked on every door of every delegate to the county conventions in our district, which included Yuba and Sutter counties, and – thanks to a Republican-controlled state assembly that had no conscience about gerrymandering – parts of Colusa, Yolo, and Nevada counties, too. That's a lot of road time, believe me. I drove it while she shuffled three by five cards and checked people off her lists. She had three columns in her list of delegates: yes, no, and maybe. So far, she was running neck and neck with the guy who had gone to so many national conventions nobody could count. He was just an automatic shoo-in every time.

Allie was determined to change that. She got red in the face whenever anyone said they were thinking of voting for Homer Pratt "just like we always done before."

Homer Pratt was a political hack. He was a part-time farmer, part-time realtor from Loma Rica, and had been a candidate for just about every office possible, except governor. Homer had been a state assemblyman during the Democrats' glory years of the New Deal under FDR. Since then he had been a county commissioner on and off, when the political winds blew his way. In between, he had been on various boards. He was well-known by all the county delegates.

The question I asked Allie was, "Is he possibly too well known?" She looked at me. "I mean, Kennedy is running on a platform of change. He's promoting the idea that he'd become the first president born in this century. Youth. Maybe you need to insert those ideas into your pitch. Try it on this next person we visit," I urged.

She did and it worked. "I'm so glad to hear you are running on a youthful theme," the lady cooed. "I'm frankly tired of old hacks like that Elmer guy…"

"Homer," Allie interrupted.

"Elmer, Homer…whatever. You can count on my vote, young lady. I'm going to vote for you. But don't tell my husband. He'd be furious." Allie put her finger to her lips, winked and promised, and put a tick mark in the "for" column. Until then, the lady had just been a "maybe."

"It worked!" she yelled when we were a block away. It worked two more times that day. We could feel the tide swinging Allie's way. But the fight was far from won. The county conventions were the second week of June, right after graduation week.

* * * * *

I stood on the stage next to Jolene Herrick, winner of the Bank of Greater California Award in Liberal Arts. I stood there wishing it had been me – for English. I was the last recipient – I was awarded the Fine Arts category for music. Pat Wickstrom, to nobody's surprise, was awarded the General Scholarship prize, which meant he didn't have a life outside of studies. In some ways I envied him: he won five thousand dollars to be used at any school for any purpose he wanted. With that kind of money I could afford to enroll at Southern Oregon, no problem, and totally immerse myself in English literature and Shakespeare and poetry and writing and maybe surface for air once a semester and go on for a graduate degree at some cool place like Stanford or Berkeley.

Prize Day, the day before graduation, was when everyone who received any kind of scholarship, prize, award or recognition of any sort came to the all-school assembly and had a moment onstage in the limelight. It was a great day to skip school if you weren't getting any awards or prizes.

Janeen Brown should have rightly won that Fine Arts music award, but she had to drop out due to her Diverticulitis problem. She was totally involved in music; I was only a part-timer in music activities at school. I had become the default choice. She would for sure get it next year.

The prize came with a check for two hundred dollars, a nice letter of citation on parchment, and a large walnut and brass plaque. I was also awarded a general scholarship by the Kiwanis Club in the same amount. I guess all the times I played piano for their luncheons paid off for me. I could use the scholarship money at any college of my choice for anything I wanted to spend it on. Certainly not big bucks like Wick, but, I could still use it and I was happy for it.

As I stood up there onstage, I thought about how Allie would clean up on awards and scholarships the next year, most likely in athletics and student leadership. Good for her.

As Mr. Sumsion read off a list of colleges and universities that had already accepted members of my class for next fall, I figured I better start thinking about a choice for college. It was only three months away. The way things were going I would probably end up over the river at Yuba College. By default.

My parents asked me what I wanted for a graduation gift, and I told them I wanted some money so I could go on a three-day trip to San Francisco after graduation with my friends. They thought about it for a few days and then handed me an envelope with one hundred dollars and a nice card. I was glad they trusted me and didn't try to talk me out of it. I'm also glad they didn't give me a cheap Timex watch or a portable radio or something like that. Within a year or two the watch or the radio would be lost or broken. The trip would be a memory for a lifetime.

CHAPTER SEVEN

It was a tradition at our school that the senior class recipient of the Bank of Greater California award for Fine Arts-Music would also be honored at graduation ceremonies by playing a musical solo. I came up with a winner for my piano solo – I chose the theme from a current hit movie, "The Apartment." Hugo and Freddie agreed to play with me – after some arm twisting and bribes. Sarge was a little tight from secretly sipping screwdrivers from under his graduation gown. Gary couldn't play with us because it was his own graduation night over at Marysville High, so I also asked Carla to sit in on guitar.

"This might be our last time together as a group," I said to Gary, stating the obvious.

"Sorry, guy, but this is also *my* only graduation from high school and I really don't think I should miss it, with my mom and step-dad and everyone there. My older sister and her husband are even coming all the way from Mesa to see me walk across that stage…," he argued back.

Our PTA committee had put together its annual graduation party at the Elk's Club in Marysville. We didn't have any classy places in our town to hold an event that big, but the PTA always does a classy job and I didn't want to miss it.

Sure, most of the members of the Peachtree Country Club (again, located over in Marysville) were rich and lived in our town. But the Peachtree was too small for a bash this big, so it ended up at the Elk's, where I and my combo had played so many times in the past.

I felt a weird sort of sadness at the party that I couldn't seem to shake. I know you're supposed to cut loose and have a good time, but I looked around at all my classmates and realized that we would never be together again like this: happy, no worries, and nothing but the sweet future with all its possibilities ahead of us.

I asked Carla to be my date, but her dad wouldn't let her stay out past eleven thirty. The graduation party was an all-night thing, so that cut her out. I wasn't interested in any other girl and there were plenty in my class whom I knew and who probably would have been okay about going with me. So at the last minute I asked Allie to come with me. "You need a break from all that campaigning," I told her.

"There's lots of girls in your class that will be heartbroken if you don't ask them," she said.

"But I need you there to keep me from turning into a drunk, lecherous animal," I argued.

She gave me her best fish-eyed look. "I'll go if…"

"I know: 'Just keep Hugo away from me'," I mimicked her whiney voice.

But she agreed to go with me. I was glad she did. I don't know why, but when I'm around Allie, she lifts my spirits.

There's this older woman up in Oroville who has a big band – Betty something. I played a New Year's job with her once. They held it in the Oroville National Guard armory, up on the levee by the Feather River, as I remember. I made some really good money for that job. Betty has a fat book of tunes, over a thousand, I'd bet, some I never heard of. She has all the big band tunes from the 20s, 30s, and 40s, and even a lot of current pop arrangements for big bands. She plays drums and is about the only drummer I ever played with that can keep a steady beat.

Betty also has an ample butt; I get a big laugh when I look over there and watch her jiggling up and down on that little stool like a big pudding. As I said, she's a large woman, blond hair from a bottle, with fake eyelashes and lots of makeup. She wears these outlandish flowery dresses and loads of costume jewelry, too. But, boy can she play! Lucky for us the PTA hired her as the band for our senior night graduation party. She made it more bearable for me. She and Allie. But I still got sadder as the night wore on.

I was starving, so I made for the sandwiches, chips and dips. I was just into my first mouthful of roast beef sandwich when I looked up and saw her coming my way. "I know what you need, Ducky," Allie said. "I'm going to snap you out of this black funk you're in." Allie took me by the hand and dragged me across the room to a group of girls who had been invited by some of my class mates.

"These girls," announced Allie, "have been stood up by their guys. Those swine are off somewhere outside swilling down booze leaving these girls all alone and panting for lu-u-u-v!"

"Girls," she said to them, "I have a nice surprise for you. Now… who wants him first?" There was a lot of foot shuffling, humming, hawing, and quiet giggling. Then one girl stepped up and offered her hand. I had never seen her before. She introduced herself as Jackie Presser.

"He doesn't look like much. Not real bad, but I'll take a chance with him," she said, giving me an appraising eye.

"Do I know you from somewhere?" I asked.

"Maybe," she said sweetly as she led me to the dance floor. Her hand on mine was remarkably cool. Mine was hot and clammy. The band was just starting to play a new set. They started with the theme from "The Apartment" that I had just played at graduation a couple hours before; then it was "Georgia on My Mind", a new hit by Ray Charles – halfway through the pianist did a really nice solo. Next we danced to "Only the Lonely," a recent pop tune by Roy Orbison. They finished the set with Bobby Darin's "Beyond the Sea." By the time the last tune of the set was over, I had forgotten my sadness. Jackie and I held hands as we left the floor to find a drink. I suddenly felt hungry again, too.

"What about your boyfriend?" I asked, after we got drinks and plates of food and found a table and sat. She shrugged her slender shoulders; she was wearing a bewitching little black sheath dress and black patent pumps. And, yes, she had a simple string of white pearls. All class. We danced the rest of the night together and at midnight I asked her if she wanted to go for a walk. She gave me a straight look that said, "I'm not afraid when I'm with you."

There's a little island about halfway around the shore of Lake Ellis, just a block away from the Elk's Club. On the little island is a large gazebo – a band stand, actually, painted white and built in a round shape. It was used a lot in the old days when life was slower and gentler, for live band concerts on July 4th and Sunday afternoons and the like. There were other couples out walking in the cool night air, escaping the tobacco smoke and sultry heat inside the building, holding hands, moving in a slow rhythm, in no rush to get anywhere, wishing for that night to last, hoping the magic would never end.

We sat on the steps of the gazebo and watched the lights from the cars across the lake going by. I sat one step below her and laid my head back against her knees. Jackie had taken off her shoes. At the lake we didn't kiss or anything major like that – we just held hands and didn't talk much. Nothing needed to be said; it was like we knew each other's needs and thoughts.

Around one or so, I took her home because her curfew was one-thirty. She lived on the east side of Marysville, just off Highway 20 (the road that goes through Browns Valley, Rough and Ready, Grass Valley and Nevada City, and connects with U.S 40 high up in the Sierras). I had a sudden urge to grab her, throw her in Bud's station wagon, and drive all the way on that highway past her house, all the way to Reno, and marry her that very night. I felt I was in love for the first time in my life.

On her porch, I kissed her goodnight and she kissed me back, even though the porch light was on. Moths batted happily against the dull yellow globe. I asked if I could call her again soon for a date. She said yes.

"I'll call you just as soon as I get back from San Francisco. Two of my buddies and I are going to spend a few days there for fun," I said.

"I'm going to be in San Francisco myself," she said. "I'm competing in a fly casting tournament."

"A what…?" I asked.

"We cast fly rods – fishing rods." I nodded that I thought I understood. "For distance and accuracy. I compete in the junior division. It's a thing my dad got me started on a couple years ago. He builds fly rods for a living, and he's an avid fly fisherman, too."

There's no telling about some people, I thought. "Where will you be staying?" I asked.

I can't remember," she said, "but the tournament is out at the Golden Gate Park, if you have time... Where are you guys staying?"

I was suddenly embarrassed to tell her it was the Sir Francis Drake on Union Square. She whistled softly. "Do you know it?" I asked.

"I just hear it's expensive – and ritzy."

"One of my buddies is paying for everything."

"He must be rich."

"Believe me, he is. Write it down. Maybe you can call me there and we can get together if you have time…"

She said she could remember it. I told her that I really needed to know one thing, it was driving me crazy and I wouldn't be able to sleep until she told me: "Where have I seen you before?"

She was Marysville's pitcher in that championship game that Allie won with the squeeze play bunt. "I read your article about that game you wrote for your school paper. You're a good writer," she said. "Your sister's a great athlete. I've never seen anyone lay down a bunt better than that one. Jeez I hated to lose that game." We kissed again.

I skipped the early morning breakfast spread back at the Elk's Club soiree; I also passed on the traditional skinny dip in Leeanne Wilder's back yard pool and went home to get some sleep instead. It was past three when I rolled into bed, but I couldn't turn it off. I kept thinking about Jackie. The scent of her Chanel No. 5 was still swirling around in my olfactory senses, in my head. I groaned and buried my face in my pillow.

CHAPTER EIGHT

Hugo, Freddie and I got away late the next afternoon in the new MG coupe. We were headed for three days of fun in San Francisco. We drove all the way with the top down. I was parched and sunburned by the time we got to the cooling cloud cover of the Bay Area. Convertibles are highly over-rated.

Sarge had gotten us reservations at the posh Sir Francis Drake hotel – the bill was all on him (or most likely, his dad). We each had a separate room. "Charge everything to your rooms; anything you guys need or want, just sign it to your rooms," Hugo ordered. Okay with me.

I felt bad that Gary Kinnersly wasn't going with us. He still had two more days of school after their graduation night – a strange way to do it. I had told him to skip it; ten years later would he remember any of it? "That's easy for you to say," he said. "You forget that I just transferred to a new school halfway through my senior year. I don't know anybody here. By rights I should be graduating in Mesa. So… I have to make the best out of what God handed me to deal with. Understand?"

I understood… I think. "Well, if you change your mind you know where to find us," I said.

We got to The Sir Francis Drake, parked in valet parking in the Union Square garage and checked in at the front desk about seven. Sarge was so smooth and authoritarian with the desk clerk, it was obvious he had done this before. More than once, I'll bet. Having never done this sort of thing before, I would have been intimidated by all the marble columns, the Chinese rugs, the big bowl of fresh cut flowers in the lobby, the plush leather chairs and rich mahogany furniture everywhere, and the attitude of the guy behind the desk. Not to mention the snotty attitude of all the other help. I felt like I was being watched in case I should try to make off with a towel or something. I seriously considered snagging a towel, just to show them they weren't so hot.

"What do you guys want to do?" Sarge asked, after we were all checked in and the uniformed bell boys were standing by the elevator door in their silly little caps, our pitifully small overnight bags under their arms.

"I really don't care," Freddie said, "whatever you guys want to do," as the elevator doors closed.

"This sounds like when we talk about going out to eat," I said. "Someone says Mexican. Someone else says let's go to Mama's Place for Chinese. Someone else says he doesn't care. When the third guy gets pressured for a decision, he says either one will be okay. So where do we always end up going?" I asked.

"Mexican," Freddie said.

"Tell you what," I said. "I plan on ordering room service, taking a long shower, and afterwards I'm going up to North Beach and find some jazz clubs where I can hear live jazz. But you two are welcome to come with me, or you can do whatever you want. This is a holiday and we're here to have fun, remember?"

Hugo said something about maybe going along as far as North Beach, but he was looking to find some live folk music, like The Kingston Trio, or the Brothers Four, or The Limelighters if any group was in town. "Maybe even the Smothers Brothers…" We agreed to meet in the lobby at nine and take the trolley as far as we could and either walk or take a cab the rest of the way.

After the bell boy had showed me the closet (obvious) and how the TV worked (duh!), and I had tipped him for this valuable news, I checked the ads in my complimentary room copy of *The Chronicle* for movies playing in the local theaters. I had already seen most of the ones listed: *Psycho* (awesome! – a great date movie); *The Alamo* (The Duke – what else need I say?); *The Apartment* (chick flick), *Butterfield 8* (ditto); *Exodus* (Sal Mineo is too cute, and a little swishy; Paul Newman is cool, but the film is way too long); and *The Magnificent Seven* (Charles Bronson is sooo

Macho. Ditto that for Steve McQueen and James Coburn).

One movie was playing I wanted to see – if there was time between jazz club hopping and looking up Jackie Presser at Golden Gate Park: *Ocean's Eleven,* featuring The Rat Pack – Frank Sinatra, Sammy Davis, Jr., Dean Martin. The movie critic's write-up mentioned some music – a plus for me. But that could wait until tomorrow, maybe a matinee.

But tonight, jazz was on my agenda.

* * * * *

After we boarded the trolley, I asked the driver, who was a Negro, if he liked jazz music. He nodded and smiled broadly. "If you had a shot at some good jazz, where would you go?" I asked. He said there were really only two good places: Pier 23 at the Embarcadero, or Jimbo's Bop City in the Fillmore District. He didn't have any specifics about who might be playing tonight.

We three split up at the Embarcadero, in front of Pier 23. "This is my stop," I said. "Anyone care to join me?"

"I'm sticking to my original plans," Sarge said. "I'll catch you guys in the morning for breakfast, maybe a swim in the pool." He hailed a cab and disappeared on his great adventure.

"I'll come in with you," Freddie said. "Maybe they'll know some good Brazilian jazz tunes. If not, I may go out to find some Latin place with live music."

"Cool," I said. "I'll pick up the cover." There was some local group: piano, bass, drums, tenor sax and a guitar player who was plugged into an amp, and was really good when they let him take a solo. They played pretty much the standard stuff, with a few original tunes thrown in.

When they took a break to go out for a cigarette, or whatever they were smoking, I approached the piano guy and introduced myself. I told him where I was from and that I had my own group. I admitted I didn't know much about improv, but that I was planning on taking a couple of classes in college this fall.

"Yeah, kid, that all helps. But you really learn by just getting up there and playing. You have to learn how to play with other guys, listen to them and learn. These guys I'm with tonight? They're pretty regular here with me – it's really my gig – but sometimes I have to get another guy for bass

47

or drums, or lead horn. This young kid on tenor sax tonight? His name is Dexter Gordon, and he's sitting in for my regular guy, a trumpet player. You'll hear a lot more from Dexter in the future. He's more of a Bebop guy, but he can adapt to just about anything you throw at him. Get it? He's playing tomorrow night up in the Fillmore District at a place called Jimbo's Rock City, if you care to hear his other style. Well, break's over. Gotta go. Say, kid, you want to sit in on a number with us?"

"Uh… I'm not anywhere as good as you guys."

"Come on. You got to start sometime. Do you know Ray Charles's new tune *Georgia on My Mind*? Maybe you've got another number after that you can play with?" I said I did. "We'll lead off our first set with *Georgia*. Dexter can take the first chorus. You take the second, and everyone comes in for the third one or however many you all feel like playing. Then on your second number, just give the other guys a heads up on the name of it, what key, they'll all follow your lead when you take off with the melody. Don't worry, you'll do fine. I'll be out there in the crowd, circulating and listening."

I did some deep breathing to calm my jitters and the guy went onstage and introduced me to the patrons… and the band. "Ladies and gentlemen, Pier 23 is proud to present a young man on piano. He's now going to sit in with the band for a few numbers. As you all know, you who are regulars here, from time to time we like to introduce new musical talent. Here for your enjoyment then is Alex Rodgers, just graduated from high school and he comes from a nice little town north of us, Yuba City. He leads his own group up there, The Cool Standards Jazz Quintet. A big hand to welcome Alex!"

I nodded to the bass and guitar players and counted off the rhythm. They gave us a four-bar intro, and I picked up the melody line for a few bars to get us into the tune. Then Dexter took over.

Dexter Gordon: a young Negro, tall, thin, good looking, nicely dressed with a tan suit, white shirt and a striped Rooster tie. I suddenly felt self-conscious that I was dressed so casually. He came in so smoothly and sweetly you hardly knew he was there at first. I faded out and kept a soft under rhythm, just playing chords with the other guys. Dexter was so good and talented I forgot to come in. Actually, I lost count of the measures, so the guitar guy came in and took the first bridge. When he was a few beats from the end he nodded to me and I took over the melody for the second chorus.

I admit I was really timid at first. Then I began to feel the groove and flow of the melody and heard the words in my head. I found myself reaching for runs and chords and it was exhilarating to experience. What a rush when I finished my solo chorus and the crowd started clapping. I nodded my head to them in thanks. Was I grinning like a fool? I had just received my baptism into the church of real jazz!

The guys in the band all clapped for me when we were done with the first number. They stood there waiting for me to tell them what was next. I scratched my head and began running my fingers affectionately over the old worn ivory keys, playing it like a lover. It was a nice old Baldwin, the feel was a lot like my piano at home and it felt good to play.

I sort of played around, searching for the right tune for that moment. Then I remembered an old lady who had come into Shakey's one stormy Thursday night, soaking wet and looking really whipped. She asked if we could play "Look for the Silver Lining".

That was exactly the tune I was searching for. I started into the melody, slowly at first. By the time I got to the second line, I picked up the tempo and the guys followed me into a nice jazzy romp through happier days and happier times. I forgot to tell them the key was E-flat major. It didn't matter. They picked it up by themselves. We must have gone through the whole band, everyone taking a solo, even the drums, and we came back and did another run through it, the whole ensemble, probably four more times before Dexter led us down to a finish.

That was it. I was done. I stood up and took my bow, my hand on the old Baldwin for support; I was slightly shaking from the excitement, the adrenaline rush. That old piano had probably seen hundreds of pairs of hands more talented than mine in its days. The leader came up onto the stage, shook my hand and thanked me. He made me take another bow and I turned and thanked the guys in the band. "See you tomorrow night, kid?" the bassist asked.

"I'm going to Jimbo's tomorrow night," I said. There were a few good natured hisses and catcalls from out on the floor.

"I'll be there," Dexter said, and he waved me good bye, then lit up a cigarette.

I jumped down and looked for Freddie. "Man, that was good," Freddie said, as we left.

"Want to go find Sarge?" I asked.

"Naw, he's not at any folk singin' place, man. He's gone to find a hooker." From somewhere out in the Bay a ship tooted its mournful horn through the mists that were settling, slicking the pavement under our feet.

"You feel like walking back?" I asked Freddie.

"I'm feeling like a rich man tonight. Let's find a taxi," he said.

We didn't talk much on the taxi ride back to The Sir Francis Drake. I thought about Sarge going out to find a hooker. Why would a guy who was as good-looking and rich as he was want to buy sex, I wondered. "Why would a guy as rich and good-looking as Sarge need to buy sex?" I asked Freddie.

He just shrugged his shoulders and sighed. "I think that's the last we're gonna see of him for a while," Freddie said.

"Why?" I asked.

"He said something to me about wanting to do three things in San Francisco: One, have sex all night with a hooker. Two, get a tattoo…"

"Three…?"

"Join the Marines."

"What? That's… that's crazy! I can't believe he'd do it. The tattoo, maybe. The hooker, yeah. But the Marines…? Is he old enough to join without his parents' approval?"

"He just turned eighteen last week."

"I didn't know that," I said. "Gosh, we're friends, and he didn't even say anything to me."

"You intimidate him," Freddie said. That was another surprise to me.

"What do you mean? He's got everything and I've got nothing. How could I intimidate him, Freddie?"

"Okay, he's good looking and he's got money. But he thinks the only reason anyone likes him is because of his money. He's not really close to anyone, you me, anybody else. It's the money thing."

I thought about that and it began to make sense. Sarge did tend to be open with just a few close friends. When he did, he only shared his thoughts and feelings on his terms. Most of the other times he was a show-off, the class clown. The other thing I didn't get was why his parents seemed to be gone on trips all the time: New York, Italy, London, LA; always gone somewhere. Sarge, his sister and brother stayed home alone.

At least whenever we went on vacations, we always went as a family. True, we might want to kill each other by the time we returned after two weeks, but still… "I don't get it," I said to Freddie. "If he's so weird about people hanging on for his money, why is he always picking up the tab whenever we go out to eat after a gig? Why does he always insist on driving his car? Why is he picking up the tab for this trip? I have enough money to pay my own way. That was my folks's graduation gift to me."

"I don't know," Freddie said. "He's a mystery."

When we got back to our hotel I had two phone messages waiting for me. The first was from Jackie Presser. It said, "Alex I'm at the Seal Rock Motel on Lombardy. Number is 454-4545. Call me if it isn't too late. Jackie."

The second message was from my sister: "Ducky, call me. I need you. I don't care how late it is. Hugs & kisses, Allie."

I called Jackie first. I knew it would be a short call, and Allie would take all night – what was left of it. "Alex, hi," she said. "You're still up? I thought you'd be out club hopping all night. Hear any good jazz?"

"Yes, I'm still up. Actually, I just got in and saw your message. What time is it?"

"It's almost one. I just wanted to let you know where I'll be tomorrow. That is, if you're still interested in watching me compete…?"

"Sure, where do we hook up?" I joked.

"Ha ha! Nice one! The Reflection Pool at Golden Gate Park, eleven tomorrow. I'd love to see you… after I'm done competing."

"I'll be there. Thanks for asking me. I've never seen anyone fly casting before. Well… maybe I did once when we were on a family vacation in Yellowstone."

I said good night and asked the hotel operator to put a long distance call through to my home number in Yuba City. I figured Allie would be up waiting by the extension in her room. Mom and Bud would probably be asleep. They stay up to watch the Tonight Show with Jack Parr, and then pack it in.

I remembered one time, though, when I was about nine, I wandered into their bedroom late at night. I guess I was sick, or was thirsty or had a nightmare, or something. I didn't knock, but just opened their door and walked in. Their door was normally open, but that night it was closed. Thinking back, they must have been in the middle of having sex. I heard someone moaning when I walked in, and like I said it was dark, but I left the door open behind me and the hall light was on. Covers were on the floor, and Bud had a sheet on him only up to his waist. I said, "Hi, Bud, where's Mom?"

She was under the sheet and I heard her bust out giggling. Bud covered up in a hurry. "What do you want, Pal?" he asked. He was breathing hard and sweat was shining on his face and chest. Mom's face – actually, I could only see her face from her eyes up – popped out from under the sheets.

"I couldn't sleep," I said. "Can I get in bed with you?"

"Go back to bed," Bud said. "I'll come in and tuck you back under the covers in a minute, okay?"

"But I want to sleep with you. I'm scared," I said.

Bud climbed out of bed and turned his back while he pulled on his pajama bottoms. He was naked.

When Allie first got her periods, Bud and Mom sat us both down and talked to us about sex. After the pep talk I told Allie about what had happened that night in their room, what I saw.

"I know they were doing it," I said. "I saw them one night."

"Doing what?" Allie asked.

"Having sex," I said.

"Ugh, how gross!" Allie said. "I don't want to hear about it!" She covered her ears and closed her eyes. Two days later she asked me to tell her about it again, but with as much detail as I could remember this time. Telling it the second time didn't seem to gross her out, though.

"Hi," I said, when Allie picked up the phone after two rings. "You're up late."

"Alex, I need you." She only calls me by my real name when she wants something or really is scared or worried and needs me. We talked for almost two hours.

The bottom line was she felt her support was slipping and she didn't know what to do. I asked her a few questions and then I suggested she drop the Kennedy-Youth part of her pitch. "I read in The Chronicle yesterday that some of JFK's opponents – Humphrey, Symington, Adlai, LBJ – are now making his youth an issue. Jeez, who needs enemies when you have friends like those guys? You couldn't pay me enough to be a politician," I said.

"They're saying Kennedy doesn't have enough experience to be the man with his finger on the trigger – I guess that means the H-bomb," I continued. "They're saying he should think about the vice presidency and then come back and run for president in eight more years."

Allie was silent. I could hear her scribbling notes. "Yeah, go on," she said.

"That's it, that's all. I'd drop the youth thing for awhile and concentrate on how he looks like a president should look, how he's so articulate, and how he handles himself. He did really well in the primaries. He kicked Hubert's butt in West Virginia."

"For someone not interested in politics, you sure seem to know a lot about what's going on," Allie said.

"Force of habit. I read the papers every day," I reminded her.

"Ducky, the multi-county convention is in one week and I need you to help me write my speech. You always have such good ideas." I assured her I would be home in a couple of days and would jump right in to help in her campaign again. "I hear you and my friend Jackie really hit it off. She thinks you're hot. What have you two done so far? You can tell me."

"Nothing more than held hands," I lied. My sister didn't need to know anything about my love life – unless I wanted to tell her. "I'm seeing her tomorrow. She's here, or did you already know that, too?" Allie laughed and it was musical and reminded me of the night of jazz at Pier 23. I told her all about it and I could hear her yawn about the time I was finishing my monologue. "You're tired. I'll hang up." I could imagine her nodding. "I love you, Sis," I said, and I meant it.

"Love you, too, Bro," Allie said. Through the many miles that separated us, over the phone lines, I could feel she meant it, too. "Thanks for picking me up. I was lower than whale poop."

I started to hang up when she said, "One last thing. You know Mrs. Karnekis, our neighbor…?" I said I did. "She wants to talk to you when you get back. About her car – do you want to buy it? Her eyes are so bad now and she failed the driving test and says it's time to quit driving and she wants you to have her car. If you're interested…"

"Bet yer sweet… (I almost said a swear word) I am!"

CHAPTER NINE

I got to the hotel coffee shop just before they quit serving breakfast at ten. Freddie was already there, having a second cup and reading the morning paper. "Where's Sarge?" I asked, after I quickly ordered a breakfast of freshly-squeezed orange juice, toast, eggs and bacon.

"Haven't seen him," Freddie said.

"Have you called his room?" I asked.

He shook his head. "I'm guessing he's either still with his hooker somewhere, getting tattooed, or joining the Marines," Freddie said nonchalantly. "He's a big boy, remember, you said so yourself?"

"Yeah, but I can still be worried, can't I? I mean, if he doesn't show up when it's time to check out of this hotel, how we going to pay the bill? And what about his car? Are you proposing we just drive it home and let him hitch? Or do we leave the car in the garage, hitch our way home, and let him worry about us?"

"Why don't we talk about this stuff the day after tomorrow? We still got two more days of fun planned, and we can worry about the details later. Speaking of which, what's on your schedule today?" Freddie asked.

I told him I planned to spend the morning with Jackie and the afternoon was still open. Tonight I was going to go out to Jimbo's in Fillmore for more jazz. I finished my breakfast, signed the bill to my room, and excused myself. "You want to tag along? What you got planned?"

"The Giants are in town, playing a double header, and I thought I'd go early for the afternoon game and watch batting practice," Freddie said.

"Then I'll catch up with you tonight at Jimbo's, if that's okay."

"Sure," I said, "see you at Jimbo's, then." We were tossing off names and places like we owned this town. And for three days we planned to.

The day was foggy with a light mist sifting gently over everything. It made the sidewalks and streets slick. My taxi driver said it would probably burn off by early afternoon. "It's always soupy this time of year. But it always burns off by noon or so. Best time to be here is August and September. Man, ain't no finer weather. It's especially great when it's Fleet Week, when half the Navy's in town. Man, what a blast!"

As we rounded the corner and drove up Post Street to VanNess, an elderly lady, dressed in a formal suit, hat, and white gloves, was walking her dog, a pug. Business-men in suits or tweed jackets strolled casually along, some reading their papers, ob-viously in no hurry. Most of them wore hats. Many smoked briar pipes, the fashionable thing to do. This was a small big city, but well known for its attention to formal dress. Many visitors from Britain said that except for the hills, San Francisco reminded them of their own city of London in most ways. I planned to find out for myself some day. In spite of the fog I was in a good mood.

It took me a little while to find Jackie but it was worth the effort. She seemed happy to see me. "You actually came!" she said.

"Of course. You don't think I'd miss a chance to see you in shorts again," I said, even though she wasn't wearing shorts this time, like that championship game. She really did look good in shorts. Today she was wearing warm up pants and a nylon wind breaker with a team logo of some kind stitched on the back.

She scrunched her nose at me and said, "I have to go warm up. I start in a half hour."

I followed her to an area that was marked off with chalk. There were already a dozen or so kids her age practicing their casting. Jackie took out a beautiful bamboo fly rod from an aluminum case and put the three pieces together. She looked down the length of the shaft to make sure the guides lined up properly, threaded the line through the guides and flexed the long, limber rod a few times. She was totally focused, all business. I just took a seat on the lawn and watched.

I don't know anything about fly casting, but I know art and beauty when I see it. The object, I suspected, was to try for both distance and accuracy. Jackie and the others were trying to shoot their lines toward a target about a hundred feet distant. The target was a small circle of chalk on the grass, no more than two feet in diameter. There was a wind whipping in from the Bay, so you had to also gauge your cast across the wind to allow for this added vector.

The people around me were talking a foreign language. I heard talk about flex, and Leonard Tournaments, and Pezon et Michel's, and Grangers, and shooting tapers, and double-hauling, and semi-parabolics, and on and on like that. I figured I would ask and Jackie would explain it all later.

I discovered there is a rhythm to casting, almost a musical cadence. Jackie began the cast by stripping some slack line off the reel and letting it fall to the ground. She took a step forward and brought the rod back at an angle over her shoulder, but not quite level with the ground. The line began to float out behind her in a flat, tight U-shaped loop. She hesitated slightly until the loop straightened out and the forward motion began, but all in one smooth flow of liquid energy. The line shot out at the same time she stripped more line off the reel with her left hand in two quick jerks, all timed perfectly while the line was shooting forward. The silk line whistled softly through the thin little metal guides fastened by beautiful silk windings all along the bamboo shaft. The rod's lacquered finish glistened in the fog-filtered sunlight.

Jackie was all concentration, her muscles coiled, but her body was totally relaxed. I had never witnessed such controlled power in an athlete, for this was in fact an athletic event. All the other competitors were equally fixed on their work and as determined to win. I could tell how she was doing by the expressions on her face: a frown meant she wasn't satisfied with something, some little thing only she knew was happening or not. A grin told me it was all coming together.

As a tennis player, I could relate to this extreme concentration. She was in a zone, alone with her fly rod, and everything else was shut out for the moment. I was not there. The other competitors were not there. The dim sunlight bouncing off the reflecting pool, a ship's horn out on the Bay, ducks gabbling and muttering in the pool, wind whipping the tops of the ancient eucalyptus trees nearby were only present for me and the other spectators, not for her. Time stopped; all consciousness was fixed in the moment for Jackie.

Someone made an announcement over the PA system and Jackie hauled in her line, reeling up the slack, wiping down the long bamboo with a soft cloth. A man walked over to her and gave her a hug. They walked toward me and I sensed he was her father, I could see the resemblance in the eyes and nose.

"Alex, this is my dad, Peter Presser." I shook the offered hand, a firm handshake, the skin toughened from hard work, a craftsman's hand. "He built my rod," Jackie said with modest pride.

"That's a beautiful rod," I said. I don't know the first thing about what I'm saying, but out of habit, I tried to be polite. I want to make a good impression on this man. Fathers can be a little tricky to deal with, especially when you're the new guy in his daughter's life. They act a little suspicious and protective until you prove to them that you're okay and you're not going to hurt their little girl. Whish-Pop!

"It's a Powell rod. Dad works for E.C. Powell right here in Marysville. Mr. Powell's a really famous fly rod builder."

"Happy to meet you, sir," I said. I had no idea who this E.C. Powell guy was, but I nodded like I was in the know.

"Likewise, Alex. Well, Sugar, you ready to go?" he asked Jackie. She nodded and grinned tensely for a brief second. "That's my girl. You just focus and do your best." I think that's exactly what I would have said, too.

The competition was over around five. Jackie came in second and she seemed happy with that. She was up against some older kids who had been playing the game a lot longer than she had.

Mister Presser – Pete – seemed happy, too. He invited us both to have dinner with him on Fisherman's Wharf. We ate at Alioto's, the most famous and popular of the seafood grottos. I had filet of sole sautéed in sweet butter and slivered almonds and potatoes au gratin. I made a show of pronouncing the French words a little too loudly.

I was trying too hard to impress Jackie and it just came off wrong. Wrong place, wrong time, wrong people. The Pressers were obviously a lower middle class family, not that I was class conscious at this time of my life, but the man was plain-spoken, he dressed plainly, he was a craftsman – a working stiff, just like Bud – his grammar was not perfect, nor was Jackie's. I shouldn't even care about little things like that in such a great girl as Jackie, let alone notice those things. But I had let it bother me just the slightest and it continued to bother me throughout the meal and I was in a mild funk for being such a petty snob when we left the pier.

I asked Jackie if she wanted to go with me to Jimbo's for some jazz. "That is, if it's all right with you, Mister Presser."

"All my friends call me Pete, so you can call me Pete, too" he said. "Two questions: is it a safe place? What time will you guys be back?"

I assured him it was totally safe and we would be with some friends, a group. That is… if Freddie showed up after his Giants game, it would be a group. I wasn't sure about Sarge and I really didn't care if he showed up or not. He could be obnoxious where my girl friends were concerned. He either made a play for them or had to show off to impress. Either way, it always embarrassed me and made me feel uncomfortable.

"Don't I need to change into something more… nice?" Jackie asked. I told her it was a really casual place and she was fine with what she had on. I almost said she could wear farmer's overalls and a welding mask and would still look great to me. Instead, I told Pete that I would try to have Jackie back to their motel by midnight at the latest. He was okay with that.

"You guys go ahead and have fun," he said.

"Thanks, Daddy," Jackie said, as she pecked his cheek. I thanked him for letting her go, and for the great meal, too.

* * * * *

Jackie was curious about my hotel room and wanted to see it before we went to Jimbo's, so I invited her up. As we got in the elevator to go up the bell boys gave me that look that says, "Hope you score, man." Not a chance. I was really nervous about her being in my room alone with me, especially after I had made such an effort to prove to Mr. Presser – Pete – that he could trust us to be alone.

"Wow, this is really neat. I mean, compared to the cheap motel where we're staying, this is royal," she cooed.

I was pleased with her reaction but tried to act nonchalant about it. "I couldn't afford a place like this if it were just my own money. But my friend Sarge, I told you about him…?" She nodded. "He charges it to his old man's account. He does that, charges everything everywhere he goes. He's kind of nuts, you know, but even so, I like him."

59

"Nuts?"

"Crazy. He just turned eighteen and joined the Marines today, we think. We haven't seen him since we checked in here yesterday, so we don't really know for sure."

"If he's gone, what if the hotel won't let you check out until your rooms are paid for?"

"I'll worry about that later. Right now I could use a coke. Want one?" I treated us both to cokes from the mini-bar in my room. We sat on a little couch by the window and looked out at the city. A layer of fog had drifted in so we couldn't see much except some street lights and the headlights from cars driving up Post Street. I turned on the radio and found a station playing jazz, a slow tune was on.

"This is so romantic," she said. I nodded, put my drink down and put my arms around her. We started to move in time with the music, dancing really slow and close. I wondered if she would let me make out with her if I tried, but couldn't get up the guts to start. We kissed, long and slow, while we kept dancing. I don't know about Jackie, but I was really starting to feel something, something really right and good. Suddenly I didn't care if we went to Jimbo's or not.

"Do you really like jazz, or are you just saying that to make me happy?" I pulled back and asked.

"To be honest…?" I nodded, encouraged her. "I don't really get it. They seem to start out with a tune and then pretty soon everyone's playing their own thing that seems to be all made up and not following the original tune at all. Have I hurt your feelings? I have, haven't I?"

"Not at all. And you're pretty much right on with how they go about playing it. It's called improvisation. You just make it up, your own version, as you go along. It really takes a lot more talent than it sounds like. It's not that easy… What kind of music do you like, anyway?" I asked.

She stepped back, lowered her eyes and whispered, "Gospel music."

I was speechless. This girl was a genuine, God-loving church-goer, and I was caught in the act of trying to seduce her in my own room. Well, maybe not seduce her, but my thoughts had not been entirely pure and chaste toward her. I started to say something smart, but I was saved from myself when the phone rang and I pulled away to answer it. "Really?" I said holloly.

It was Freddie saying he was thinking of coming straight back to the hotel from Candlestick instead of meeting us at Jimbo's. "I guess I was lucky I caught you there. I mean, I thought you'd already be gone to the club by now. You alone or is *she* there?" The way he said "she" heaped on more guilt; by now I was feeling guilty enough already.

"Yeah, Jackie's with me, but I don't know if we want to go clubbing now. I mean now that you don't want to go. I'll ask her. Maybe we'll meet you downstairs for dinner. Just ring the room when you get here, okay?" I waited for half a minute, like she and I were discussing it. "Freddie...?"

"I don't know, it would be weird, man. I mean, you two together and me without a girl..." he said.

"C'mon, Freddie. We want you to spend the evening with us, don't we, Jackie?" She nodded. "She says yes, so call my room and we'll meet you downstairs when you get here. There's a piano bar and we'll talk and kick back and have some fun. That's why we're here, remember, to have fun?"

He hung up. The mood had passed and we didn't feel like dancing any more. And now that I knew she was a church girl I didn't feel it would be right making out with her. Some other time when the place would be better. I wondered what to do to kill the time until Freddie got back.

"I have an idea," I gaily said to Jackie, trying to lighten the atmosphere. "Have you ever been in a strange town and looked in the phone book to see how many people in there had the same last name as you?" She shook her head. "Let's do it." I pulled out the thick phone book and opened to the Ps. "Look at this." She looked over my shoulder and her short hair brushed my cheek; it smelled like the salt air and grass of Golden Gate Park. I ran my finger down the page of Ps and stopped.

"See, four Pressers. Now let's look and see if I have any relatives."

That game lasted about four or five minutes and an awkward silence set in again. I looked at this girl and realized she was a mystery – I really didn't know very much about her. Is this what it's like when you date someone seriously and you're maybe thinking serious thoughts, like maybe getting engaged?

I suddenly got scared. Jeez, I just graduated from high school a couple days ago, I'm not quite eighteen, and I'm thinking weird thoughts about getting engaged. At that moment I wanted to be with my sister, someone

I knew really well and who I could share secrets with and had so many things in common. Like the thing about religion that suddenly popped up tonight. I realized I would need to date a lot of girls before I could ever make a commitment to be with one person forever.

Maybe Jackie had the same idea or thoughts, because she interrupted the quiet with, "Maybe we should go downstairs and wait." She suddenly seemed nervous, edgy too, so I agreed. We took turns using the bathroom, took the elevator down, not touching, not speaking a word until Freddie arrived.

We had dinner in the hotel dining room and talked mostly about familiar things like the rivalry between our two high schools and people we knew and pop songs we liked and our big plans for the future. When we were waiting for dessert I went to use the house phone. I called Jimbo's to find out who had been there to play tonight. Over the crowd noise they told me it had been Lionel Hampton and his band, and Johnny Mathis. I didn't know he sang jazz tunes – he was a pop singer, wasn't he?

When I got back to our table I relayed this info to Jackie in case Pete asked her when she got back to the motel what we did and who had played at the club.

I put her in a cab, kissed her on the cheek and said I'd call her in the morning. I remembered to thank her for a really nice evening. "Thanks for coming up to my room. It was special… you're special," I said, as I closed the door. She blew me a kiss.

I went back in as Freddie was signing the dinner bill to his room. "Thanks for the dinner," I said. "What do you want to do now? Go to Jimbo's still? It's not too late."

"Naw, I'm beat and the mood for jazz has left me, don't know why. She's a fox, that Jackie."

"Keep your hands off," I warned. "So what you want to do?"

"I'm going upstairs, take a long hot bath, watch some TV and crash. See you in the morning," as he shuffled off to the elevator.

I felt crummy about how the evening had turned out. I was sure Jackie thought I was the biggest jerk around for hauling her clear down here and flaking out on the jazz club. It was obvious she didn't like jazz all that much and had just pretended to, to please me. Gospel music! Whatever.

Actually, I was getting tired of this trip and was starting to feel like going home. If it was up to only me, I'd leave tonight and drive back right now. I missed Allie and I was getting anxious to get enrolled at Yuba for summer school and start my college career. I wasn't sleepy yet, so decided to go into the bar and listen to the piano player for awhile to calm me down before I crashed.

CHAPTER TEN

Out of habit I moved toward the piano music coming from the oak-paneled bar. The woman playing was good, smooth in her improvs without being showy. Some of her chords reminded me of Amad Jamahl's style. Everyone was copying him it seemed. I stood in the doorway letting my eyes get used to the dim lighting. There were two people at the bar, a girl in a slinky green sheath dress, revealing lots of thigh, probably a hooker. Down the bar from her sat an older guy, doing a noble job of ignoring her. He was large and bearded, hulked over his drink, nursing a cigarette. I decided to sit next to him and see if I could schmooze the bartender out of a beer. Maybe the room was dark enough that I could pass myself off as legal age. I didn't know if I could pull this off, I'd never tried it before. As a last resort I could try to charge it to my room.

I sat down next to the older guy. He didn't even look my way. "What you got on tap?" I asked the bartender.

"Lucky Lager, what else is there in this town?" he said. He eyed me and said, "I don't know, you look marginal. Maybe I should ask for ID." I started to tell him I was a guest in the hotel, when the guy next to me spoke up.

"Won't be necessary," the man said. "He's with me. Run it on my tab."

I sipped my beer and after a minute or two turned to my host and said, "Thanks. I owe you."

"Not necessary. I could use some company." I was suddenly a little nervous. What if this guy was some kind of pervert, a pedophile? Had I made a huge mistake? I guess he sensed my worry, because he said, "Relax, you're safe. What you doing up this late on your own, if you don't mind my prying into your personal life?"

"My buddies and I came down here for our last fling together after graduation. One of them ran off with a hooker, got a tattoo, and we think joined the Marines. My other buddy spent all day at Candlestick, ran out of gas, and is upstairs taking a bath. I was supposed to go to Jimbo's tonight with my girlfriend, but she has to get an early start back home in the morning, so…"

"So you're bored and lonely?"

"Yeah. Sort of…"

"I'm not very good company, but I'll try. So you like jazz at your young age? Who are your favorites? Maybe I know some of them." I told him who I liked, and didn't like. I told him that I had sat in and played piano with the local guys last night at Pier 23. "So you actually play? Most people I meet seem to just talk about jazz, like they really know. I believe you need to really do something before you can talk like you know anything about it, see what I mean?"

I said I did. "What else do you do?" he asked. I told him I liked to write and I planned on going to college. I'd go tomorrow, if I had my way. I was anxious to get started learning the ropes so I could be a better writer. "Oh God, not another one," he moaned, finishing his Scotch, and motioning for another.

"What do you mean, not another one?" I asked. "You're a writer, aren't you?" Then I recognized the man I had been talking to. Jeez, not only was he a writer, but one of the best American novelists ever, and one of my downright favorites! And here I am sitting elbows to the guy and drinking his beer. I suddenly got tongue-tied, searching for something witty or brilliant to say, but I couldn't think of anything. "My sister back home, my twin, she's running for national delegate to the Democratic Convention in Los Angeles," I said.

"How old are you, eighteen? And she's only eighteen. That's a noble goal. Let's drink to your generation," he said, and we toasted my generation and sat in silence for awhile.

"Can I ask you a question?" I ventured.

"I'm guessing you're going to ask me about how I write, something like that? You doing an article for your student newspaper? No, I guess you wouldn't be now that you're starting college," he muttered. His sarcasm was keeping pace with the Scotch he was sipping. "Okay, just one question," he said.

I sucked up my courage, thought a minute, then "Okay," I said, "of all the things you've written, is there one thing that's your favorite, and if so, why is it your favorite?"

Steinbeck drained his Scotch, ordered another and thought for a minute. "That's not a fair question," he said. "Damn, you are a sharp one! Okay, you asked, so here goes: I like them all for various reasons, but my favorite – it might surprise you – is *Sweet Thursday*. For personal reasons better kept to myself. You're a smart kid, so you can work it out. Look, I'm beat and I want to go to bed, so I'll say good night and thank you for your company."

"I would have guessed *The Pearl*," I said. That stopped him for a moment.

"Why that one and not *Grapes of Wrath*?" he asked, a quizzical look in his dark eyes.

"I like its poetry and human pathos," I offered, thinking that maybe that had the same appeal for him.

The great man nodded, then heaved himself to his feet and tugged at the khakis bunched in his crotch. He walked toward the door, turned and came back. I took a few tentative steps toward him. "One more thing, if I can offer some advice…?" I nodded eagerly. "Don't write crap. Know what I mean?" I nodded. "You seem like a smart enough fellow, but smart isn't enough. You look and sound capable of writing good stuff, but first you need to go out and see the world, let it beat the shit out of you, and make you suffer with the rest of humanity. Have you read *The Grapes of Wrath?*" I nodded. "That's human suffering. Only when you've suffered like that are you qualified to write about anything worthwhile." He moved back toward me. "Now, you owe me for that beer and advice, and since that lady has quit playing, I'd like you to sit at that piano over there and play me something."

"Like what?" I asked, moving to the piano that the woman had abandoned.

"Play some of your favorites, anything except *Misty*," he grinned and had another Scotch brought from the bar as he sat down in an overstuffed chair, his back to the doorway. He seemed to draw within himself and shrink a little, as I started to play *Solitude.*

Steinbeck left after I played it followed by *In the Still of the Night* (his particular request). It was a nice piano, a polished ebony baby grand Steinway, one I certainly could never afford. After another half-hour's noodling around on the piano, I got tired, left the bar and went upstairs. Instead of going directly to my own room, I detoured to Freddy's. I knocked on the door and waited, knocked again. Maybe he had a girl in his room; but not too likely, knowing how shy he is around girls. I waited, and reached out to knock again when the door opened a crack and he looked at me through sleepy eyes. "What you want? What time is it?" he said, a hint of irritation in his voice.

"I don't know, but it's got to be sometime after midnight." He frowned and yawned a noisy yawn. "I been thinking," I said. "I don't know about how you feel, but I'd like to go home now, or at least first thing in the morning. This is more fun than I can stand and I'm worried about Mr. Worthless. What if he's ditched us and he doesn't show up when it's time to check out of this palace?" Freddie shrugged nonchalantly. "I'm really pissed that he ditched us!" I said with some heat. Freddie looked up and down the hallway, motioned for me to calm down. "Let's pack up, take his car and go home tonight. He can find his own way home. I've had it." I finished and waited for his response.

Freddie was a little pissed too, but at me, I could tell. "Go to bed. Can't this wait until morning? I'm really tired and need some sleep, and so do you. Tell you what, meet me for breakfast at nine and if he doesn't show up by eleven I vote we do it your way: check out, take his car and drive home. Hell with him!" he said. I think the swearing was for my benefit.

"Yeah," I agreed and started to return to my own room. Then I felt very tired, frustrated, lonely and wanting to be with someone. I suddenly did not want to return to my own room. Except for my room at home, if I was ever on a school trip away from home, I almost always bunked with someone else. I realized that this was some kind of childish thing I had and I needed to overcome it and grow up. I had just graduated from high school, making big talk and big plans about the future, that all sounded very grown up, but I truly needed to be with someone this night and I didn't want to spend another night alone in my own room.

I was beginning to have bad feelings about this trip: the expensive plush room, signing rich meals to our rooms, acting like we were big shots, riding in style in Sarge's new MG. The whole scene seemed so surreal, bizarre, and it didn't fit my life, the way I was brought up in the small town I was from.

I wanted to get back home to my small town familiarity and spend some time helping Allie. I sensed from what she didn't tell me on the phone was that she was in big trouble, sinking, her own plans going up in smoke. She definitely needed me. I wasn't even sure I should register for summer school. Maybe I would skip it as well as fall semester and help Allie with her election stuff and then I could load up on extra classes spring semester and beyond and eventually catch up with the rest of my freshman class.

"Can I come in, for just a while?" I asked Freddie. He stepped aside and I went in and flopped on the couch. "What you got to drink?"

"Just some coke and orange juice." Orange juice sounded good to me right now.

"Anything to eat?" I was also suddenly hungry.

"There's some cold pizza in that little fridge," Freddie said. I helped myself. "What's up, pal?" Freddie sat down in one of the big chairs in the conversation area. "You don't seem your old happy self." I shrugged, not in the mood to talk right then. I was content just to be there for now. I just chewed on a piece of cold pizza and swigged orange juice.

He waited patiently until I finished. "Freddie," I said, "I thought graduating from high school would be a liberating experience. Now we're free from the rules that made us go to public school for such and such number of years, and we can make some important choices about what we want to do, like do we go on to college, do we get a job, do we join the army, like Sarge?"

"Marines," Freddie corrected me.

"Right, Marines. Or... do I hitch hike across Europe, do I get married? Stuff like that." He nodded. "But I feel tonight like I'm tired of schooling for awhile and I'd like to just work with my sister on her campaign and have a little fun myself, maybe travel, spend some time in New York writing, that kind of stuff, before I jump into the meat grinder again. I'm thinking how just a few days ago we were sweating our *cojones* off with final exams and finishing school, and how much fun was that?" He shrugged.

"On the other hand I'm scared that if I get a taste of freedom from class schedules, studying, exams, papers, and stuff, I'll like it and will keep putting off the college thing forever. Know what I mean?" He nodded.

"What the hell! I'll deal with it tomorrow. I'm beat and need to sleep." I closed my eyes and must have dozed off because it was morning when I woke up with a bad cramp in my neck and I had been asleep all the time on his couch and Freddie must have thrown an extra blanket on me but I was still stiff and cold from sleeping all night almost upright.

After we had a quick breakfast in the hotel coffee shop and signed the bill to our rooms, Freddie and I packed our stuff in a hurry and slipped out of the hotel, avoiding the front desk which was fairly busy any way with a lot of people with their expensive leather luggage checking out that time of morning. There was a lot of confusion with bell captains barking orders at young bell boys, so we figured if Sarge ever surfaced he'd have to take care of the hotel and all the room charges, but with his balls he could deal with the stuffy guys at the front desk.

I had wakened that morning with an attitude hangover from my mood the night before and all through breakfast kept having this crappy feeling and Freddy noticed it right away and told me to chill out. Signing the tab made me feel even more like a low-class mooch and we didn't belong there and the sooner we got out of Dodge and on our way back home the better I'd feel. Walking out into the fresh morning air didn't help my mood like I hoped it would. There was something bad hanging over and around us. Was it that Sarge had ditched us, his supposed two best buddies? Where was he and what was he doing? The feeling persisted.

A few yards beyond the port-cochère of the grand hotel, we checked in with the valet parking captain, a kid about our age, maybe even younger. He was dressed in a short-sleeved tan uniform jacket with epaulets and lots of brass buttons and tan shorts to match that showed off his tan arms and legs. He had a snotty attitude like all the other guys who worked at this hotel. Maybe that was because he was Big City and somehow knew we were hicks from a small cow town. I didn't think it showed on us that much, but maybe you can never get away from the small town and it hangs on you forever. Or maybe it wasn't us, maybe it was just part of how they trained them: always ignore the customer, treat them like crap, and stare them down until the tip comes. And never under any circumstances act nice to the customers; they'll just come to expect it and then they'll treat you like crap, too. What a system.

"New red MG-A," I said casually, as I fished a fiver out of my wallet to prove we were big tippers. The valet gave me an all-over look and a smirk and stopped to talk with one of his friends for a full minute before he took the car keys with the little cardboard disc down from the peg-board, held them at arm's length like they were cat poop and started for the parking garage.

Five minutes later we could hear the new Michelins squealing down the sharp curves of the parking ramp before he roared up to us with the MG, stopping with a rubber burning screech. He went to the boot and popped it open for our small handful of overnight bags. "Jesus, Mary and Joseph!" he yelped, jumping backwards with his hand over his mouth, retching. The captain scrambled out of the little shack and got to the boot about the same moment Freddie and I got there.

"Oh, my God!" Freddie whispered. Jammed into the small boot, staring at us with vacant eyes was a very dead and bloated Hugo Sargenti, his death-darkened skin stretched abnormally tight, he was almost black. Sarge was dressed only in his under-wear, a fresh tattoo on his right forearm that was a partly furled American flag and under it the words *Semper Fi*. His throat was cut from just below his left ear and across the carotid artery. The blood was black and crusted on the wound and front of his tee shirt. The stench of death wafted from the boot, polluting the freshet of air. Whish-pop!

The smart-ass valet kid who brought the car was doubled over in the beautiful landscape shrubbery hurling his breakfast. "Don't touch anything!" the captain shouted. As if we would. "I'm calling the police!" He reached for the phone and dialed a number.

Freddie exhaled loudly, crossed himself and repeatedly whispered, "Nossa Senhora." He withdrew from the rest of us, turned his back and his head was lowered on his chest; he was again whispering something in Portuguese and it sounded to me like he was praying, maybe crying silently. I suddenly felt like crying, praying, too, but I didn't know what god I would be praying to. I mean, what god would let our friend, Sarge, get murdered like this on what was supposed to be our last fling as high school seniors?

* * * * *

The police came and took Freddie and me into a small room next to the hotel manager's office to interview us – question us. At first we were both together, and then, like good cops are supposed to do, they separated us to see if our stories stuck together or whether we gave different versions of the facts.

The cop who questioned me was an older guy with a ratty moustache who smoked Pall Malls constantly. In a short time I was sick from the smoke in the cloistered little space. He was overweight, dumpy-looking in a brown double-breasted pinstripe suit that looked like it came out of the Fifties. His skin was probably once dark but too many all-nighters, endless cigarettes and cups of coffee had turned it a sallow yellow. He drilled into me with his steely gray eyes, leaned forward and looked long and hard at me, wheezing his stinky tobacco breath every time he leaned too close as I answered one of his questions. Was he hard of hearing too?

I traced for him just about every minute of the time and what I had been doing, who I was with, since we left home three days ago, until the valet opened the trunk of Sarge's new car. Of course, I left out the details about having Jackie up to my room and the time I spent in the hotel bar with John Steinbeck. I knew he wouldn't believe me about Steinbeck.

After a couple of hours of this I badly needed to go to the bathroom – and get some fresh air; I was getting sicker by the minute, actually physically ill. "Can we take a break?" I asked, a pathetic whine in my voice. We did, and I used one of the pay phones in the phone bank of the hallway off the huge reception area. I made a collect call to Bud's shop. He picked up and accepted the charges from the long-distance operator.

"Dad...? It's me, Alex. I'm in some kind of trouble here." I explained how Sarge had ditched us from almost the moment we arrived in San Francisco and how Freddie and I had decided to come on home this morning and had slipped out of the hotel without paying the bill and had started to drive Sarge's new car home and then finding the body in the trunk and how it felt really creepy to see one of your best friends stuffed into the trunk of a car with his throat cut and stinking like death and I almost gagged from the too recent realness of the memory.

"I'll be right there," he said. "And don't admit anything to the police or even hint that you were doing anything wrong. Wait at the hotel until I get there and I'll get you guys out of this mess and back home. Ivy can take over here. How much is the hotel bill?" I said I didn't know for sure. "Whatever. I'll see you guys in a couple of hours."

* * * * *

It was late afternoon and the sun was sinking to the west below the Golden Gate Bridge when we finally headed east over the Bay Bridge, going home in Bud's 1957 Ford station wagon, the family car. It didn't take Bud long to get the cops to agree that we probably had nothing to do with Sarge's death and to let us go. Bud was all helpfulness and supplied them with contact information on Sarge's parents, who were on an extended cruise around the world and would be difficult to contact with the bad news. Mr. Brown Suit, who apparently was the senior cop in the group, noted this information in his little black greasy notebook and licked a stub of a pencil that looked like he also chewed the business end to keep a piece of lead to write with. Why do they do that, lick the pencil when they start to write?

Of course, the police said they'd have to keep the body and probably perform an autopsy, which gave me the chills. I don't care how I die, but just don't go cutting me open. But how unreasonable is that? When you're dead you're dead and it wouldn't hurt; you were beyond pain now, and where you were after death you didn't care anyway now. That is, if you believed in a life after death, which I still wasn't too sure about yet.

Earlier, before Bud got there, while the chain smoker was still questioning me in the little, closed up room, another couple of younger cops had been calling the local Marine Corps recruiting office and determined that Sarge had in fact applied to join the Marines. They also tracked down all the tattoo parlors in the North Beach area and finally located the one that gave him the tattoo on his right arm.

I guess the cops have their list of confidential street sources – snitches, informers – who they go to in cases like this one to try and track down information. Do they actually pay them, these snitches? Or do they keep something hanging over their heads to pressure information out of them? It took them a couple of hours, but they also located the alleged hooker who, when they showed her the black-and-white yearbook picture of Sarge that I had brought along with me for some unknown reason, told them yes, that face looked sort of familiar, like he might have been someone she met recently. That was good enough for them and it verified Freddie's story that Sarge had left us the first night to go get laid or whatever while we went jazz club hopping.

CHAPTER ELEVEN

R ush hour on the Bay Bridge. It took us a long time to creep over it in Bud's station wagon; the evening was warm and the humidity lay heavily on us pressing down the diesel fumes from the big trucks around us. Bud's car had no air conditioning and it did no good to open the windows. I was getting sick again.

We stopped again, a dead stop. Bud turned to me and asked, "You all right, Pal?" I gave him a small smile to let him know I was all right, but inside I was still badly shaken up. Through it all I had tried to be brave and tough, but when you're on the business end of a police investigation it can get your doubts going double time. I think Bud knew I was feeling bad, so he let it drop.

At last we exited the bridge on the Oakland side, turned north on the freeway and picked up some speed. The air cleared some and I opened my window a big gap, laid my head back and tried to rest. I drank in the cool moist air blowing towards us off the Bay; fresh air that was lightly scented by the eucalyptus trees and oleander bushes that lined the freeway.

"You guys hungry?" Bud asked. With all that had happened, we hadn't had anything since breakfast, a Danish and coffee eaten fast. We'd hardly had anything to drink, either. And I had had only one bathroom break – Mr. Brown Suit Chain Smoker was a ball breaker. I wasn't really hungry right now and I knew Freddie wasn't either; his face had a sallow color. He also had to be exhausted from the inquisition.

We passed a Ratskeller up near Richmond and I imagined huge roast beef sandwiches on sourdough buns, mayonnaise and brown mustard with potato chips and kosher dill pickles and sides of coleslaw salad. Then the vivid image of Sarge in that car trunk flashed through my mind again, turning off my hunger urges. I couldn't help myself thinking about Sarge. Where was he all that time? Or had he been killed the first night there when Freddie and I were at that jazz club, Pier 23, and Sarge had said he wanted to go on up to North Beach for folk music and was looking for the Kingston Trio or The Limelighters or some such?

I had asked the detective if he thought it was a professional job or just some random, senseless act. His curt reply was, "Just let me do the questioning here, *kid*." The way he said *kid* was a putdown and was intended to make me feel weak and insecure, or like I was some kind of undesirable, a leper from the streets of Calcutta, or worse. So I passed the time and endured his smoking and his stupid questions repeated over and over – always asked a different way, but the same questions – by asking myself my own questions.

Had Sarge been killed the first night? The blood was dried, crusted, black. No, it had to be either the first or second night, I reasoned.

But what about the tattoo, when did he get that? Do tattoo parlors stay open all night? I'll have to think about that one.

When did he find the prostitute, that first night in San Francisco when Freddie and I were at Pier 23, or the next day? The police probably knew because they had made contact with her, but they weren't letting us in on any of the other facts. They were out to build a case and our questions, stupid or otherwise, just got in their way. I'm betting he hooked up with the prostitute the first night.

Was she young and pretty, or an old skanky whore? Sarge could have afforded a high-class call girl that one of the hotel employees could call and bring to his own room, for crying out loud! Why go out to some dirt bag hotel and tumble with some dirty hooker? You think you know a guy...

And another thing: How and why do women get started in prostitution, anyway? What gets them going down a road like that? She had to be somebody's daughter, somebody's sister. But back to the questions about Sarge.

Did he get in a fight with the hooker's pimp over money and was he killed for non-payment? Or, did he flash a roll of big bucks and get killed for his money? Sarge had money, but I never remember him flashing it around. But maybe, far from home, he felt a need to flash it.

Then there's the possibility that drugs had been involved. Was he trying to do a drug deal and something went badly wrong and he got killed by the druggies? I can't recall Sarge ever using drugs, ever. Sure, there were drugs in our hometown, mostly marijuana, and we knew some kids, Mexicans mostly, who we could go to and make a deal with, if we wanted it. But we never did. Sarge's thing was sloe gin, if you can believe it. Everybody else went for beer, or, if they wanted hard stuff, vodka, but he raved about the virtues of sloe gin and how you could get a girl drunk easiest with that stuff than anything else.

When did the body get stuffed into the boot of his car? Who could have had access to the car keys, and how did they manage to stuff the body in by themselves? They must have had some help. My first thought was that it could have been one of the parking valets. In all the Perry Mason or cop shows on TV I ever watched, they say that fifty percent of the time, the first person to discover the body is the murderer. I'll go with that theory.

My head ached in spite of the fresh breeze blowing in the car window. Just after we passed the Nut Tree, Bud asked again if we were sure we weren't hungry or did we want to finally stop and get something to eat. The image was there again of that big roast beef sandwich, but my stomach rolled over as I saw Sarge in that trunk. Finally, partly out of desperation and partly to please Bud, who wanted badly to show his concern, we finally stopped and had hamburgers at an A&W in Davis. I had a hard time eating mine.

On the road again, and Bud asked me for the second time: "You sure you're okay? You've been really quiet."

From the back seat, Freddie summed it up: "Mr. Rodgers, until a person's been through it like we have with the cops, you don't really know what it's like." Bud nodded, smiling. "You ever been hassled, worked over by the cops, Mr. Rodgers?" Bud didn't say anything, just squinted down the road through his aviator-style dark glasses, his eyes crinkling at the corners.

Bud knew something about police and their methods and he said, "I've been through some bad stuff, and I know enough by watching, listening, keeping my eyes open and my mouth shut as much as possible. Our local cops'll come into my shop a couple times a week looking for someone or something - have I seen so and so or have I heard this and such. I have to be very careful about what I tell them… *if* I tell them."

I decided to ask Bud a few of the questions that had been on my mind. "So Bud, are we in trouble, do you think?" He shook his head no. That was positive. "Do you think they will ever find the killer?"

"Or *killers*," Bud corrected.

"You think there was more than one?" Freddie leaned forward, eager. Bud nodded yes this time. "Why?"

"Just a gut feeling, a hunch." He slowed down a little. "Look, I know this experience has you guys shaken up, but I don't think you should talk about it when we get home. I mean, you guys can talk about it with each other, with me. But if others ask questions, just say you're not supposed to discuss it – an ongoing police investigation, stuff like that. My opinion…?" We both nodded, eager for some closure, some confirmation from an experienced source. He continued: "My belief is that your friend Sarge got in a situation that was way over his head and he tried to tough his way out of it. He was your friend, and I'm sure he was a nice guy most of the time. But there were a few times when he came in the shop for a cut and he'd talk big and show off a little with his money. Maybe you saw that a few times with him. I had some doubts about the trip, his paying for everything; the whole setup bothered me and your mother a little. But, we reasoned, there comes a time when you have to stand on your own, make your own choices, learn from your own experiences. We figured this could maybe be a learning experience for you boys. See it from our perspective now?"

We both nodded. It now began to make some sense. "So was it… a learning experience for you?"

It was more experience than I cared to deal with right now.

CHAPTER TWELVE

I had done yard work for Mrs. Karnekis, our neighbor, since her husband died seven years ago. Every year, starting with the last Saturday in March, it was the same routine: mow the lawn and edge it with her old hand mower and edger; trim the boxwood hedges that lined the sidewalks and defined her yard in front, again with Mr. Karnekis's old tools; trim the gardenia and camellia bushes in the back yard, even if they really didn't need it. That gardenia bush put out the loveliest fragrance at night in the summer time when it bloomed profusely. She always had a single gardenia blossom floating in a brandy snifter set on a lace doily on the old oak table in her entryway in the summer time.

After I finished my small amount of yard work I would be invited in to have lunch with her, always the same thing: warmed up Chef Boyardee ravioli can with grilled tuna sandwich, potato chips, and fresh lemonade, followed by chocolate ice cream and her wonderful Tollhouse chocolate chip cookies with walnuts from the big tree in her back yard, the one that reached over the common fence that separated us, dropping part of its bounteous crop on us every autumn.

We didn't talk much while we ate lunch, but instead watched baseball – a couple of innings together of the San Francisco Giants on her old black and white Philco television set, the kind with the round screen. The picture was always fuzzy and the sound was too loud, a function of her failing hearing, I supposed.

But she was really into the game. She told me how much her husband loved the Brooklyn Dodgers (Roy Campanella was his favorite) and how he became so disgusted when the team sold out and moved to Los Angeles. Every time we watched baseball together, she had to tell me this story again, even though I'd heard it exactly the same way many times before. I never corrected her. But I really wanted to ask her if the same thing hadn't happened when the Giants moved from New York to San Francisco But I never argued with her. Do people repeat themselves more as they grow older?

We'd watch a couple innings and she'd shout in Greek (even a few cuss words, I suspected) at the screen and get angry if the manager left a pitcher in too long and he started loading up the bases with walks; she'd be happy, jump up like a kid and shout with excitement whenever the Giants scored a run.

Then she'd turn off the TV and say something like, "Well, Alex, you probably have better things to do than sit watching a silly, meaningless game with some kooky old woman." It was kind of nice, really, and I didn't mind sitting in for her deceased husband Russell for a little while, providing her with a little my company. It must be kind of lonely and quiet when you're the last one left in the home after the kids have all grown up and gone and your husband has gone, too, and memories are all around you still: pieces of furniture you bought in an earlier time; the family pictures, portraits on the walls, the certificates and awards, the potted plants, the pets that are getting older along with you every day that you hang on to life.

Then I'd help her clean up the lunch dishes and she would take out her old needlepoint coin purse and fish out a one dollar bill, which was my pay for the yard work, and hand it to me proudly. She was very independent and insisted on living alone in her old house despite attempts by her daughter in Stockton to have her sell the house and move into a rest home. Mrs. Karnekis's house was in the older part of town and had been there for many years, the very edge of town, until our new subdivision was added on.

"Are you sure you want to sell me that car, Mrs. Karnekis?" I asked for the third time.

"I can't think of anyone else I'd want to sell it to, Alex. You've been so nice to me taking care of me and my yard all these years since my Russell died, you know…" She got a little misty-eyed every time she or anyone mentioned the name of her dearly departed. They'd been married sixty-five years, she was proud of telling everyone. The way people divorced these days, that had to be some kind of record. Nobody seemed to stay married for very long any more. And if she had married at around twenty or twenty-one, that would make her eighty-five or more, wouldn't it?

"I just want to be sure you won't be changing your mind later on, wishing you hadn't sold it. I don't want you to regret this decision, Mrs. Karnekis," I said, and I really meant it sincerely.

"No, Alex, I won't be changing my mind. My eyesight is going, you see. They, the doctors, call it macular degeneration. My eyes will never get better, only worse and worse until some day soon I'll be completely blind, they say." She sighed a sad outpouring of breath. "And I can't have a license any more with my bad eyes because I can't pass the eyesight part of the driving exam. So it's just as well that I give it up. I have friends who can still drive me. Or I can have the bus come from the Senior Center and pick me up and take me wherever I need to go. Or maybe…" her watery eyes lit up and she smiled at me, leaning close enough for me to smell her violet-scented toilet water, "maybe once in a while you can take me for a ride in it, just for old time's sake."

I told her I'd be glad to do that for her any time she wanted, as I counted out the seventy-five dollars we had agreed on as the sales price, counting it out slowly in crisp fives and tens that I withdrew that morning from my savings account at the Bank of America office on Sutter Street.

I slowly drove Mrs. Karnekis with me when I went back to the bank for the notary public to witness her signing over the title. She signed the bill of sale and the back of the title in front of the notary, one of the bank's secretaries, a girl I knew who had only graduated from high school the year before.

And that was it: I had my first car, a shiny 1936 navy blue Oldsmobile two-door sedan with extremely low mileage. There were two jump seats in front that folded down, and it had a manual shift with three gears forward.

The back seat was huge! I figured the back seat was spacious enough that two couples could wedge in back there and we could try triple dating. It had huge whitewall tires and chrome moon hubcaps, giving it the appearance of something out of Elliott Ness and *The Untouchables*.

Mrs. Karnekis was truly the little old lady who only drove it occasionally to shop for groceries and to church on Sundays. After I drove her back to her house and thanked her again for the hundredth time, I got the thing registered in my name at the DMV and called Bud's insurance agent to get it covered.

Bud had a friend who was a mechanic who owed him a few favors. He looked it over and said that the only thing he could find wrong and needing immediate attention was the radiator. He scavenged around and found a good used radiator for fifteen bucks over in Olivehurst, and I helped him replace it the very next day.

Allie was pleased; she proclaimed we had dependable wheels to get her around for her politicking. I wondered to myself about the dependable wheels part; I also wondered if John F. Kennedy would feel he was riding in style if he ever rode in my car.

"Alex, thank you for skipping summer school at Yuba to help me," Allie said as she squeezed my arm. I looked over at her, young and fresh and eager in her blue jeans, Keds and tee shirt top, her summer tan just beginning, which always brought out her freckles. I smiled, glad she was my sister and that I was doing something good for someone. Life was truly short. Sarge had taught me that lesson. I didn't mind and who knew, I might just learn something from this political experience.

* * * * *

A couple of days after I got the car registered and insured, I decided to drive over and talk to Miss Jensdatter. I had been thinking a lot about my San Francisco experience and the fateful meeting with John Steinbeck and how I badly needed to get some focus in my life and settle down to start working on what I was supposed to be doing for the next forty years or so. I hoped she would push me in the direction of writing, a good hard push, because I was wavering.

I was already missing the old daily routine of high school: getting up early in the morning, choosing what I'd wear, looking at unfinished homework over Mom's breakfast; stopping at the bookstore to grab a free cookie freshly baked for us by Mrs. Hostetter, the bookstore lady and mother of one of our classmates.

Then there were classes, the learning something new, interacting with

81

the teachers you had grown to like and respect for their knowledge, each one very different in the way they taught a subject, but all of them similar in their desire to help us learn. Playing piano for the choir; working out in p. e., odors of sweaty young bodies, communal showers and the younger kids – the freshmen and sophomores – embarrassed, still not used to undressing in public, the last in the showers, turning backs, trying to hide themselves. The towel fights with buddies, snapping bare buttocks and leaving stinging red raspberry marks on each other, a test of manhood and your ability to take abuse and pain, release of more built-up testosterone.

Seventh period: trying to stay awake and one of your friends falls asleep with his face down on the desk, a pool of sleep-induced saliva ruining his open textbook.

Mercifully the final bell rings and the herd busts loose and you hang out around the lockers with friends or walk a girl home or stop by the library to check a book out of the reserve section, only to discover someone else beat you to it and it's not available. So you scan the New York Times or the Wall Street Journal before you head for home.

Just a lot of little routine actions that made for a satisfying day.

* * * * *

I loved my music and I hated the thought of giving it up. Our combo had been violently broken up by Sarge's death; it wouldn't be the same without him. Sure, he was a screw-off when it came to blowing his horn in our group, always wanting the limelight. And yes, I could probably find another horn player. I seriously toyed with going with a tenor sax player, a kid I knew over in Marysville who was really good. But Sarge was gone and I wasn't sure what to do now.

I considered the possibility of just Freddie and me and a vocalist, either Carla or Gary. Gary! Jeez I had neglected him and I felt like a royal jerk. Since I got back from the bad San Francisco adventure Gary Kinnersly had called a couple times and left messages for me to call him, but I wasn't up to it yet. I'd talk with Jensdatter and then decide what I wanted to do with my combo later.

Right now I'd committed to help my sister with her political stuff and I wasn't sure yet what that all meant and how deeply I really wanted to get involved. But I needed to focus on something to fill the void that

82

graduating from high school had left in my life. I'll call Gary later, I weakly promised myself as I pulled up in front of Jensdatter's apartment house.

As I climbed the stairs to her second-storey apartment I was thinking about the couple of times a group of us – some of her honors students – had been invited to her place to discuss literature over tea and cookies. Those had been mellow times. As I approached the door I could clearly see through a side window that the apartment was empty. Not only empty, but a for-rent sign was taped to the window.

I didn't bother to ring the doorbell but went downstairs to find the manager. Nobody responded to the door bell; I rang it several times and waited but no answer. I went around back behind the complex and found a woman who I rightly guessed was the manager hanging up wet wash on the clothes line.

The woman was short and flabby, pudding soft; I towered over her by a foot and a half. She had to be about fifty, but I couldn't be sure; from her hardened, wrinkled skin she could have been younger. Her greasy graying hair was still up in curlers in spite of it being mid-afternoon. She had a long filtered cigarette hanging from her lips and she squinted one eye closed as the smoke curled up. She was wearing a sloppy house coat with no sleeves, which exposed her fleshy upper arms; the fat jiggled as she reached to pin up a wet garment, further exposing her sagging breast in the large open armhole. Out of modesty (repulsion?) I quickly averted my eyes. The woman was unpleasant and shocking; I gulped and spoke.

"I'm looking for Miss Jensdatter – LaRue Jensdatter," I said.

"Don't live here no more," she said without looking up at me, hacking up wetness from deep in her throat.

"Do you know where she went, where she is, how I can contact her? It's really important," I implored, hoping to sound sincere. I also sensed she suspected I was a bill collector. Her guard was definitely up. The manager put down her arms, took a deep drag on her cigarette, exhaled slowly, blowing a smoke ring at the end of her exhalation as some kind of comment. I suddenly had a picture of her hunched over the penny slot machine at Harrah's in South Lake Tahoe, or worse, some smarmy dive out in the desert near Tonapah, sipping a watered-down complimentary highball, urging it to last longer, crunching ice between inhaling drags from her ghastly smokes. She squinted and eyed me, then hunched over her basket of wet clothes again.

"She eloped."

This news took me by surprise. "What? You sure about that? I truly expected this woman was playing with me, but she straightened up, put both hands squarely on her ample, sagging hips, and nodded for emphasis, when I eyed her questioningly.

"Couple of days ago. Gave me one day's notice, paid another month as a penalty and packed her stuff and gone. Took her about three hours to clear out," she concluded smugly. Of course she had always suspected this unremarkable, homely school teacher to be a closet floozy waiting for the first rich sucker to get her talons in and take her away from all this misery.

"Eloped?" I still couldn't believe what I was hearing. "Who… who'd she marry? I guess she married. I didn't know she was seeing anybody…" A new side of Jensdatter, a romantic bent (reading too many Jane Austen novels?) we students would never have dreamed of or imagined in her.

"Some guy, an officer from out at the air base." She inclined her head eastward toward Beale. "I hear he was some kind of military preacher or some such. Rumor was she met him through her church group." Another revelation: who would have figured Jensdatter was the least bit religious? But I guess with school teachers you don't really know the private side, only the public persona. I stood there stupidly not knowing what to do or say next as the washerwoman bent back to her task, waving a hand to fend off the offensive smoke curling up into her eyes.

"He's called a chaplain," I said pointlessly as I walked away.

* * * * *

The delegate-choosing convention was held that same night in the high school gym. Allie was nervous all day waiting for the moment to make her short speech. There were two other candidates for delegate, and each was allowed two minutes to make this final pitch for the job. Under the party rules the runner up was automatically elected as alternate delegate who would still go to the convention (but on their own nickel)to be there… just in case.

"What do you think your chances are?" I asked her for the tenth time in a week as we waited in the wings for her turn. She was so tense and I

84

knew this election meant a lot to her – it was a really big deal in her life. Chances like this don't come along very often, and Allie had made her own chance here. She had worked hard and had put in a lot of time. She would have also flunked spring semester if I hadn't done some last-minute cramming and tutoring her.

She looked at me and pulled a face. Tears came to her eyes and I knew it was just stress and emotions taking over. I put my arms around her and held her close. "You'll be okay," I whispered. She nodded and sniffed. I loaned her my handkerchief and she blew into it, stuffed it into her pocket. She was dressed in a light sleeveless summer dress, no makeup or jewelry, all business. Her hair was pulled back in a pony tail. Wrong, I thought. She ought to wear it down, less obviously youthful, more mature, businesslike. But it was too late to change and she would have thrown a major fit at me, so I let it pass.

Suddenly it was her turn. She pulled away, squared her shoulders and walked out onto the stage to polite scattered applause. At that moment I was prouder of my sister than I had ever been in my life.

Allie came in second by only four votes out of over two hundred cast. She would go to Los Angeles to the Democratic National Convention, only a month away in July, but not as the delegate. She would be the alternate, and would be duly seated on the convention floor with the rest of the delegates and alternates from the great state of California.

"I'm so mad," Allie fumed after the voting. "I was sure I had enough votes. So many people promised me! I can't believe I lost to Pratt, that old turd! He must have bought a lot of votes, that's all I can figure," as she choked back angry tears.

"At least you're going," I tried positively.

"That's another problem we have, Alex."

"Problem…?" I asked as we drove home.

"I need to ask you another big favor." I could feel Allie's big blue eyes in the darkness, pleading with me. Whatever she wanted, I was so proud of her tonight that she could have it. All she had to do was ask. Shoot, it was already too late to enroll for summer session at Yuba, my combo was now non-existent, and she owned me for the rest of the summer.

"What do you need, name it," I said.

"Well, I need three things: your car, some money, and you, Ducky."

"Car…?"

"To drive me to LA and to get around when I'm there. The convention is way down town and the cheapest motel I could find to stay at is way out in North Hollywood…"

"Okay, and the money…?"

"I'm broke. I've used up all my savings and I don't dare ask Mom and Dad."

"How much you figure on…?"

"At least three hundred, maybe a little more, but I promise to keep it tight and not go crazy with spending…"

"Tell you what: I'll be your treasurer and I can keep control of *my* money. Deal…?" We pulled up in front of our house. I killed the motor.

"So I guess you'll come with me? I really need you there with me. It was so comforting having you there with me tonight when I had my meltdown," she implored.

"Do I have any choice?" I figured I had just about three hundred in my savings account. Plus, I had the scholarship money.

Oh well… Kennedy just better win, was all I could think as I fell asleep to the soothing sounds of chirping crickets.

CHAPTER THIRTEEN

I woke up feeling that I needed to call Jackie Presser; I hadn't talked to her in over a week, since I put her in that taxi and sent her back to her cheap motel that last night in San Francisco. So much had happened and I had been so wrapped in my feelings about Sarge, then with Jensdatter leaving so abruptly, and now having committed to help Allie get through the convention in LA. I had been brought up with a certain ethic about the way we treat people. A decent person accepts responsibility for his actions and if he makes something bad happen he has the duty to stick around, tough it out and do his best to fix it, make it better. We weren't Christians, not even church-going people, but I think my parents did a fairly good job instilling a sense of right and wrong into us as we were growing up in their house. At least I take comfort in my memory that they did.

Well, I hadn't really done anything bad or lousy to Jackie. I thought we parted that night in front of the hotel with good feelings for each other. But she must have been a little confused about my feelings for her since it had been a week and I hadn't made the effort to even call and let her know I was back home. I let the phone ring five times and was about to hang up when her mother answered. "Mrs. Presser? This is Alex, a friend of Jackie's..."

"She's not here right now, she's at work."

"Uh, I don't think I have that number. Could you give it to me, please?"

"She's not supposed to get phone calls at work – it'll get her in trouble."

"I understand. Maybe if you told me where she works I could drop by during her lunch break…?" Long pause.

"Foster's Freeze in Marysville." She hung up without saying goodbye. I detected a certain coolness in her attitude. Maybe I should have told her I was a friend of her husband, Pete. Maybe that would have softened her.

I drove up to Foster's Freeze about a quarter to twelve and parked. I went in and Jackie smiled nervously when she saw me enter. There were three customers in a group she was taking orders from. She nervously pushed back a stray lock of her short hair. I melted at that slim, brown hand moving easily through her hair, suddenly wishing it were my hand touching her, remembering the softness of that brief, sweet time together in my hotel room. I stood in line behind the others and waited.

Another waitress behind the counter asked if she could take my order. I just nodded at Jackie and the other girls frowned. I waited. "May I take your order, sir?" she asked formally, the correct way she'd probably been taught in her one hour of training her first day on the job.

I looked at the large menu board above her head, avoiding eye contact. If I looked in her eyes I knew I'd lose control. The emotions of the past week had been building up inside me and the dam was about to burst. Fighting a lump in my throat, I finally looked at her and placed my order. "Yes, miss, I'd like a double burger, no onions, large fries, and a large coke. Please…" I hastened to add.

"We only serve Pepsi. I hope that's all right…" I nodded gravely, like world peace depended on it. She flashed me a smile, perfect white teeth. I wanted to jump over the counter, enfold her in my arms and tenderly kiss the breath out of her. My throat closed up completely; I was having a hard time breathing. "Your order's number seventy-two," she said and turned away to give the ticket to the fry cook. She turned back and I was still there. "Anything else we can get you?"

"I'd like some of your time, if you can arrange it during your lunch break…?" Why were we being so formal? She looked at her watch and I looked at mine. It was almost noon. She looked up at me and nodded.

"I'm off in a couple minutes. Can you wait?"

"I'm waiting for my order. I'm number seventy-two, remember?" She laughed as she unfastened her mustard and catsup-streaked apron, folded it and stashed it under the counter.

"Peggy, I'm taking my lunch break now," she said to the other girl, who frowned and looked at her own watch.

"It's still two minutes before noon," Peggy grumbled. Peggy was homely, overweight, wore glasses with twenty year-old frames, had a bad haircut and terminal acne. She also perspired heavily. It must have been a heavy burden for Peggy to work alongside a petite girl as nice and attractive as Jackie, who ignored her and joined me at my booth.

"Nice car," she said. I thanked her. Why were we both so nervous? Relax, Alex, relax... From my vantage point in the booth, I was facing Lake Ellis and could see couples out walking the perimeter of the lake, hand-in-hand, enjoying the pleasant summer weather. I nodded in the direction of the lake; Jackie turned and took it in. "I have an idea," she said. I read her thoughts. We took my order from petulant Peggy and walked across the street to the lake and found a shady spot to sit down and share lunch.

"There's no easy way to split this burger," I said as I offered it to her.

She shook her head. "That's okay, I'm all burgered out working in that place. Too bad there's not a taco stand close to here," she said. I didn't know she liked tacos; so did I. "So..." Long pause, as she looked at me evenly. "So, Romeo, where did you escape to for the past week, or is it a secret mission and you'd have to kill me if you reveal anything?" She leaned her head close to hear my confession.

I fought back tears that were suddenly close to the surface. "Do you believe in an afterlife?" I asked her.

"That's the funniest pickup line this girl ever heard." She laughed, but could quickly see I was serious. "What's happened? Something awful's happened to you, Alex, hasn't it?"

I chewed on the burger as I fought for control. I swallowed, went on: "I told you we had a friend, a very rich kid, who treated Freddie and me to the fling in San Francisco... You came to my room, saw how plush it was? And I told you he paid for it all..." She nodded, waiting. "Well, he left us that first night after we got there and we never saw him again. Until the third day and Freddie and I had already decided that morning to leave and go back home without him anyway, and as we started to leave, we found him in the trunk of his car. Dead..." The dreaded word hung in the air.

Jackie's hand instinctively reached to cover her mouth. Then tears formed and pooled in her eyes, she shook her head in disbelief. When she could finally talk, she said, "I read about a Yuba City kid named Sargenti who had died in the city under suspicious circumstances and the police were treating it as a homicide. And that his parents were out of town on a cruise somewhere and the police had a hard time finding them and letting them know about the tragedy." She reached a hand and put it gently on my arm. "I didn't know he was *that* friend. Oh, Alex, I am so sorry..." She put both arms around me, held me. She exuded an aroma that was a blend of jasmine, mixed with French fries and mustard.

* * * * *

It took the San Francisco police another week to wrap up their investigation. The autopsy by the overworked pathologist seemed to take forever, which angered Sarge's parents no end. When they docked in Athens, they caught the first flight home they could book. I can't understand why police have to keep a body that long when the family wants to bury their son, wants closure to the tragedy.

Since finding Sarge in that car trunk, I had been thinking a lot about an afterlife, life after death. I know a lot of religions believe in the afterlife. I was mixed up, confused, wanting to believe. But believing in the afterlife meant I would have to admit that a God really existed, too. I talked about it with Allie and I wasn't too surprised when she said she believed in afterlife and in a God, too.

I thought about some of my friends and wondered what, if anything, they believed. Freddie, being Catholic, would naturally believe in both God and an afterlife. Else what was all that stuff about Purgatory and Hell about? Why else did they light candles and say prayers and hold masses and all that stuff?

Adelman had once told me that Jews didn't believe in afterlife - at least he didn't think they did. But then he admitted he and his family were *Reformed* Jews, whatever that meant, as if that explained everything. Big help.

I sort of assumed, from what I'd half listened to in the sermons when I was playing organ for the Methodists that they also believed in afterlife. And after Jackie told me she was religious – when she said she liked gospel music best – then I knew she must be Christian and believed in God and some kind of afterlife, too. But the confusion in all this for me came with

90

wondering what this afterlife (assuming it existed) was really *like*?

Where was it? Was it nearby or was it floating somewhere out there in space, like an undiscovered planet? Was it anything like the stories you hear about pearly gates, streets paved with gold? Was there really a frowning, crabby St. Peter standing there checking over his list of good guys-bad guys as the line of newcomers backs up into the clouds, waiting to know if they'll qualify?

Once you're inside, is there really eternal harp playing and hymn singing? What about other kinds of music, like the stuff Bach, Beethoven and Copeland wrote? And will there be any other musical instruments to make music with, other than the harps and the organs and the choirs of angels?

Will we recognize our family members and our friends (again, assuming we all qualify for entrance), and will they recognize us? What about little kids who die young? Will they still be little kids in Heaven or will they be full-grown? If they're just little-kid angels, who takes care of them? What if a family all got killed together, say in a car crash or a tornado or something, would the parents raise their little-kid angels?

What language will we speak? Will everyone speak English, or will it be some ancient Biblical thee and thou and thine kind of speech?

Will there be animals there, and birds, fish, and insects? Will there be flowers and trees and plants? Will there be weather and changes in climates like here on earth?

What about food? Do they have food there, what kind, and did you get to eat anything? Or do you need to eat anything if you're just a soul or spirit?

What about sleep and rest – did you ever get tired playing harps and singing all the time, and did you get to have some rest or sleep? What about physical relationships – were you allowed to touch each other, hug, kiss, hold hands, rock babies to sleep, assuming you had the physical ability to do those things? Do you have feelings, emotions, like anger, fear, love, hatred, happiness, hunger, greed, lust, and so on? Were married couples allowed to live together privately in their own homes or apartments and could they, you know, *do it* once in awhile, like maybe on special days like birthdays, Christmas, Easter, wedding anniversaries?

Did they even have Christmas and Easter? Did the Jews get to celebrate Hannakah

and Passover? And did they remember birthdays – did you get a party with cake and

candles and ice cream? Did they play games there like baseball and volleyball and

tennis? What about card games – were they allowed? I could just picture Bud and his

buddies sitting around in white robes playing poker every Thursday night, smoking

stogies and drinking Lucky Lager.

But now I'm getting even more confused, because when you die your body goes in the ground, doesn't it? Or you're cremated and your ashes scattered, but that complicates things even more. That's why they have funerals and why there are morticians and funeral homes and people are cremated or buried and they have grave stones and caskets and big sprays of flowers and you go to the relatives' house after for ham and scalloped potatoes and sandwiches and drinks and cakes and brownies, and everyone talks in really quiet voices and says what a good guy he was.

But what happens to the other part that's not your body – your soul? – is that the part of you from earth that goes on to Heaven? But then the Christians bring in the thing about Jesus and Easter and the Resurrection and the promise that someday we will all be resurrected – body and soul put back together –and all will live happily forever with God and Jesus in Heaven.

So I poured all this out to Jackie as she hugged me and patted me and whispered quiet soothing shh sounds in my ear and told me that she understood and I softly cried but couldn't help myself every time I stopped for a breath as my hamburger and fries got cold and the drink got all watery. "It will all work out. You'll see, I really believe and I'd really like to tell you about why I believe some day," she soothed. And I wanted to believe her, I really wanted to.

We didn't even get around to talking about Jensdatter leaving. As she held me, I thought about Rose of Sharon and the final scene in *The Grapes of Wrath.* Somehow, though, Jackie holding me and comforting me like that made me think of graham crackers and milk, which I hadn't thought about since kindergarten.

CHAPTER FOURTEEN

The congregation was seated, waiting expectantly, with the Sargenti Family – Sarge's parents, brother and sister, uncles, aunts, cousins – taking up the first twelve rows of pews. Directly in front of the family was the casket, a bronze box covered with a huge spray of white roses. The Sargentis had opted for a closed casket, even though they had dressed their son in a newly-tailored dark gray suit they had made for him in Italy while they were on their cruise, the same one he wore to graduation just a couple of weeks ago. Mrs. Sargenti refused to let people, strangers, gawk at his body, "looking to see if they can spot that ghastly scar!"

Father Bevan, the priest, dressed in green vestments, and his assistants, dressed in white lace cassocks, entered the chapel. He's a large bear of a man, Father Bevan, with muscled forearms like bundles of steel cables; he has a large bald head fringed with frizzy gray hair. His eyes are dark and brooding, but his entire face can suddenly crinkle into deep grooves when he laughs or smiles, which is often. You always feel comfortable around Father Bevan; he's like your big brother, or your favorite uncle or granddad all rolled into one package.

Jackie sat on the side of me next to the aisle, dressed in a demure white linen suit with navy trim, shoes, gloves and wide-brimmed straw hat all in matching white. Allie and Bud sat on my other side. Julia - Mom - had already left town with her annual tour group to France. Down the pew from Allie and Bud sat Ivy, looking perfectly smart in a light brown suit, white shirt and Rooster striped tie; next to Ivy sat Freddie and Carla

Gomes.

Father Bevan faced the congregation, an overflow crowd that was filled mostly with former classmates and curious students from our high school. The church was bulging that day, and they probably could have moved the services to the high school gym to accommodate everybody. Half the town was there, at least. He raised both arms Heavenward in supplication; the organ music stopped and the funeral mass began. If I had expected to get some answers about an afterlife for Sarge, it would have to wait. The mass portion of the services was totally Latin and I didn't understand a word. Thank goodness for the printed program to guide us through the formal part.

After the prayers, hymns and liturgy, the program invited anyone who wanted to make a brief statement in remembrance of the deceased, Hugo Sargenti, to come forward to the microphone and speak.

The first to step forward was Brian Bork, one of Sarge's football-playing buddies, and an all-around popular guy in our class; also known as "Peaches". Brian made the usual comments about what a nice guy Sarge was – had been – and how much he was going to be missed and how bad it was to see such a promising life cut down at such an early age. He mused about how Sarge was now up in Heaven playing his horn with the best of the good trumpet players and cracking ethnic jokes about Poles, Italians and Jews with all the other angels. This brought a nervous shuffling from the congregation, and a loud harrumph from Mr. Sargenti.

Undaunted, Peaches then launched into recalling how several guys from the football team used to go out after home games and get drunk together, and that Sarge could hold his booze right there with the best of them. They would take turns buying the illegal stuff and they had to resort to all kinds of devious plans to get their hands on it.

One night Sarge's turn came around to buy. Sarge waited outside Mug's Liquor Store in the darkness until a lone wino came along and Sarge talked him into buying the booze with a bribe of an extra couple of bucks for the wino to buy his own jug of Thunderbird. The scheme worked and they all got good and drunk, thanks to Sarge's genius.

"Then there was graduation night just a couple weeks ago. Sarge came up with the brilliant plan for a bunch of us to wear bed bottles, you know, those old fashioned rubber bags under our graduation robes, strapped to our legs. We filled the bags with screwdrivers, fixed them up with stoppers and long rubber tubes that Sarge stole, uh borrowed, from biology lab. The tubes went clear up to our mouths and we could suck on them any time we wanted a drink. Ha ha! That was brilliant. Nobody knew what we were doing!"

The priest stood up and whispered into Brian's ear. He waited with his head cocked to the side, nodding and grinning stupidly. "Father Bevan says I should end and give someone else a chance to say something." He nodded to the priest, who hung around to see if Brian would take his seat. "But I want to tell just one more story – about Sarge's love life. He was a great lover, at least in his own mind."

I held my breath as Peaches, that big oaf, turned back to the mike. Father Bevan hesitated, looking worried, then just shrugged and sat back down. Brian went on with yet another story. I hoped and prayed it wasn't the one about when Sarge used another old wino to buy him a dozen Trojans from Mr. Anderson's Rexall downtown before he and Peaches and a bunch of the guys went off to visit some cathouse in Marysville, one of the many we all knew existed next to the levee, over by Mama's Place. Mercifully, Peaches refrained from telling about that adventure; instead, he told one just a little bit more in good taste. But just barely.

"I just wanted to tell about the time Sarge and me double-dated to the Junior Prom last year. His date was Janet Ulrich. You all know her father, he owns the funeral home, he's the mortician… There he is in the back of the room." Peaches waved and said, "Hi, there, Mr. Ulrich! Nice to see you! Well, back to the story. Sarge goes in to pick up Janet and Mr. Ulrich meets him at the door, all dressed up in his usual black suit, just like he's wearing today. Anyway, Sarge asks Mr. Ulrich 'How's business, Mr. Ulrich? Pretty dead, I'll bet!' Ha ha!"

By now, Peaches was the only one laughing. "Well, I'll just end by saying he was a good friend and I'm really gonna miss him."

That's all Brian could think of to say and he actually wiped at a tear as he sat down to thunderous silence. Mr. Sargenti loudly harrumphed again as Mrs. Sargenti launched into a fresh outbreak of wailing, her head leaned on her oldest son's shoulder, rolling from side to side. No amount of patting or soothing caresses could comfort her. It was pathetic.

Mercifully, Father Bevan took back the mike and made as if to cut short the testimonials for Sarge, when a lone figure stood from behind the organ and made her way forward to the podium. From back where I sat, I couldn't make out who this person was. Then she took the mike, turned, and I was surprised to see an extremely thin Janeen Brown standing up there before everyone, bravely facing us. She had lost a lot of weight through her year-long illness. I thought of grainy black-and-white pictures of those survivors from the Nazi POW camps– mere skeletons.

Of all people, Janeen Brown was the last person you would think of as catching Sarge's eye. She was quiet, plain, bookish; she was not cool or popular. Janeen was definitely not the kind of person Sarge gravitated to and mingled with. We all leaned forward, wanting to catch every word from this waiflike girl's mouth. She started quietly, almost a whisper, a hush fell over the congregation while everyone strained to hear her.

"When I was in eighth grade we all had to take dance classes, it was a thing that was just required, so there was no escaping it. Some of you may remember: *Oh, Johnny, Oh* and *Virginia Reel?*" I remembered it well.. "And then we moved on to waltzes and the fox trot. I was always the last girl chosen, partly because I was tall back then and all the boys except for a couple of future basketball stars were still shorter than we girls were. I wasn't pretty in eighth grade; I'm still not." She made a gesture with her hand, pointing to herself. A few nervous, polite chuckles.

"I'll never forget the time when Hugo – he was still Hugo back then, that was before he entered high school and became known as Sarge. Hugo came over to me, held out his hand like a regular gentleman, and asked me if I'd like to dance with him. I actually stopped breathing. I was so surprised I didn't know what to say. I thought he was doing it on a dare; that his gang of buddies had put him up to it, like, 'Come on, Hugo, betcha don't have the guts to ask weird old Janeen for a dance!'

"But I truly believe, to this day, that he did it out of the goodness of his heart. Because he was then, and still is today, basically a decent person. He had back then, and still has now, a good heart." Then Janeen got personal. "And I'm sure, Mrs. Sargenti, that you can take some comfort in knowing your son – the gentleman - asked a homely, shy, lonely girl for a dance, and that she's never forgotten and will always remember that act of kindness."

Janeen sat back down in the organ loft. Slowly at first, then erupting into thunderous applause, everyone in the place stood and clapped and cheered. Mrs. Sargenti was radiant and with fresh tears streaming down her cheeks smiled her thank-yous to Janeen. I suddenly had a new sense of admiration for this shy girl who I had always viewed as my competition. She was now one of my heroes.

Mrs. Sargenti had asked me to play something on the piano for Sarge. I asked her if she had any favorites and she came up with some of the usual lame, sappy tunes they always seem to play at funerals that I hate playing, so I suggested *he* might like hearing *Vocalise* by Rachmaninoff. I assured her it had been one of his favorites. *Liar*! I said to myself. I had never played it for Sarge, and I doubted, if pressed, he could even tell me who Rachmaninoff was. I hadn't played it in a long time and managed to squeeze in a last-minute hurried practice. I got through it okay with only a couple of small mistakes that my frowning face probably gave away, then sat back down, relieved it was over and I was safely back with Jackie again.

Father Bevan thanked me for that nice musical number and thanked Brian and Janeen for their "kind remarks". Then he announced the ceremonies would now remove to the city cemetery for the interment at the family grave.

Overnight, the weather had turned from mild and pleasant to ferociously hot and overcast; the air was soppy with humidity and rain threatened at any moment. The humidity dripped from large-leaved trees and a perceptible fog hung in the air. I asked Jackie if she'd had enough, and she wisely decided to skip the cemetery. I told Allie and my parents that I was driving Jackie home because she had to work the evening shift at Foster's.

I was really grateful to Jackie for coming with me, and I told her as we drove over the bridge to Marysville, how it had helped me get through the ordeal. I apologized for those stories that were in such poor taste. "Sounds just like the guys I know at Marysville High," she laughed.

"I'll call you later," I said, as she got out. She leaned back in and kissed me with a brushing of innocent lips on my cheek. I touched the spot and it felt warm as I drove out to Gary Kinnersly's house.

Gary's real father died just a couple years ago and his mother had quickly remarried a family friend, maybe he was even a distant relative, a man named Arlo Haycock. Mr. Haycock owned a small dairy farm out by

Beale and Gary had joined his mother only recently after staying for over a year with an older sister in Mesa, Arizona, after his father died. From the few comments Gary had made he was having a hard time adjusting to the new life on the farm and working for his step-father.

Gary had been a city kid most of his life and farming was a hard life, a totally new way of living: up before dawn to milk a herd of thirty cows, mucking out the barn feeding the cows, back home right after school to milk again, homework, and falling into bed half-dead before the sun was really down. It was exhausting, killing work. It totally consumed the farming family and left very little time for social life or sports or musical pursuits, which was Gary's one great love in life.

You'd think that due to his circumstances, Gary would be down, depressed, rebellious. Not so. He was a big, garrulous kid with an unruly mop of curls that crowned him like a reddish-brown corona. He had rosy cheeks, freckles, and an infectious laugh that seemed constant. When he laughed, his cheeks would merge with his squinty eyes and laughing tears would roll down his cheeks. If you could look past his slight pudginess, you'd see that he was actually verging on handsome.

Everything delighted Gary; nothing daunted his spirit. And he lived to make music with his exceptionally beautiful voice. Gary was a great mimic: he could imitate anyone's singing voice – Pat Boone, Harry Belafonte, the Everly Brothers, Buddy Holly, Elvis, Johnny Mathis. You name the voice, Gary could imitate. He was a great hit at parties, loved by all, guys and girls alike. The guys liked him because he never made a play for the girl they brought to a party, like some guys'll do, especially when they get drinking a little booze. The girls liked Gary because he seemed so sympathetic to them. Some would say he was bordering on effeminate, but I can swear he was hetero, all the way.

It was early afternoon when I got there after leaving Jackie, too early for milking time, so I knew Gary would be available to talk. He answered the door in outlandishly huge boxer shorts festooned with pairs of big, red lips, and a wife-beater undershirt. He was carrying his guitar in one hand and a can of Dr. Pepper dripping with sweat in the other. "What…?" He deadpanned when I looked at his boxers and made a face. "It's bloody hot out there!"

Gary sprinkled his vocabulary with British phrases every chance he got. He had gone on a trip to London a year ago with his sister just before he moved here from Mesa, and he never got tired of telling you how the Brits had a new type of rock and roll and how it would some day invade America and change everything in pop music here. We mostly ignored his hyperbole and chalked it up to wanting to sound superior because how many of us had even been outside California, let alone across the Atlantic? He was a genuine world traveler, so he must know what he's talking about, especially in all things musical, right…?

"Sorry I haven't called sooner," I began apologetically.

He shook his head and grinned. "Don't worry, dear boy. I heard through the grapevine what happened when you guys were in San Francisco. To think…" his voice trailed off.

"What…?"

"I was nearly *there* with you, don't you remember? But for my own graduation getting in the way, I would have witnessed it, too…"

"Yeah…" was all I could think of to say. "So, what's up?" I asked.

"I have an idea for us, a new thing we can do together!" He was all enthusiasm, like a puppy playing with a new toy.

"What's your idea?" I asked, playing along.

"Sit down and I'll tell you! Want a Dr. Pepper? Take off that bloody tie and jacket, get yourself comfortable, dear boy!" I did as I was commanded. Over an icy can of Dr.Pepper, Gary unfolded his new idea of the two of us forming a duet and singing together.

"What kind of songs?" I asked, a little suspicious because I was a piano player, not a vocalist like him.

"Wait!" he said and left the room. He was back in half a minute wearing a new red blazer over his wife beater. "How do you like it? It's our new outfit!"

"We're going to sing for fox hunting parties?" I laughed.

He laughed, too, and said, "No, we're going to sing folk songs, like Joan Baez. Like Belafonte or the Kingston Trio or the Limelighters! You'll need to get a blazer for yourself, but isn't it a capital idea? What do you say?" He turned around and struck a GQ pose for effect, then strummed his guitar. I laughed and agreed to do his silly thing. If…

"If we can add Freddie on bass, then we'd have a group just like The Kingston Trio, or the Limelighters…," I said.

"But without a banjo," Gary hastily added. "I really don't like banjos all that much." I nodded my agreement to appease him.

I figured singing with Gary would help fill in the time between working with Allie, spending time with Jackie, and what else…? I didn't have a job, not a real job where you report to work at a certain time with certain duties like most of the guys I know who work summers at the Wilbur Ranch prune dehydrator, or the Del Monte cannery, or in the orchards, or at a grocery store, then check out by the clock eight hours later. The only other thing I could think of that occupied me was practicing piano, something which I hadn't done much for several weeks.

Before I left, Gary got a commitment out of me that I'd get going on learning to play guitar. I thought of Carla. Maybe she could help me get started. As I drove back home I thought about getting a job bagging groceries at the new Lucky Store. I also thought about finding some graham crackers and milk when I got home.

CHAPTER FIFTEEN

June 27, 1960: *In the very last of the state Democratic conventions held today in Helena, Montana, Senator Kennedy adds more delegates pledged to support his candidacy for President of the United States. Now, on to the convention, as he takes a commanding lead in delegates heading to the nomination in Los Angeles, when the gavel will hammer the delegates to order on Monday, July 11th. The actual voting by delegates is scheduled for Wednesday evening, July 13th.*

For the first time in over forty years California would be hosting a national political nominating convention, the Democrats. The convention would be staged in the newly constructed Memorial Sports Arena in Los Angeles, barely completed in time for the grand event. It was modern in design, circular, constructed with a lot of plate glass and tile floors throughout; it boasted the latest in communications facilities, including accommodations for television broadcasting. The three major television networks, according to a study commissioned by them, claimed that this would be one of the most closely-watched events in modern history. Over forty million American homes now had television sets, and it was hoped that a good many of them would be watching the convention.

Governor Edmund G. "Pat" Brown had won as the favorite son in the California primary, meaning the delegates were pledged to him in the first round of voting. Thereafter, they could be released to vote their own conscience or political preference. Through some clumsy last minute-political maneuvering, Pat Brown had tried to cast himself as some sort of dealmaker, had courted favor with the operatives in the camps of both front-runners, Adlai Stevenson and John Kennedy. Brown essentially lost control of his delegates, who would ultimately end up voting their favorite candidates anyway.

All of the candidates and their staffs – Stevenson, Symington, Johnson, and Kennedy, had arrived in Los Angeles several days ahead of the opening day of the convention and set up command posts in the massive Biltmore Hotel, the heart and nerve center of the real action outside of the convention site in the Sports Arena. The candidates and their people were well-organized and ready for the fight. But the best organized by far was the Kennedy campaign.

Senator Hubert H. Humphrey, of Minnesota, had already bowed out of the race after losing badly to Kennedy in West Virginia. Out of funds now, Humphrey released the members of the Minnesota delegation who had been pledged to support him. They could now vote their own consciences, thus creating a wild scramble for their votes..

For several weeks, pressure had been mounting for Adlai Stevenson to actually come out and declare himself committed to fight for the nomination. Stevenson remained reluctant, aloof, but his backers, all the forces opposed to Senator Kennedy, were maneuvering to hastily put together a stop-Kennedy movement.

As the delegates and their families (who could resist the chance to bring the family for a trip to the new Disneyland in Anaheim?), an estimated forty-five thousand strong, descended on Los Angeles, the high-and-mighty, and the well-heeled delegates also took up residence in the Biltmore. The others, less blessed financially, took other accommodations.

Because Allie was an alternate, not an officially certified delegate, she had to make her own financial arrangements for a room. She booked a double room for us in a little motel out on Laurel Canyon Boulevard, in North Hollywood, a good hour's drive to the downtown convention venue, but it was only twenty dollars a night and gas was cheap – there were price wars everywhere, even in L.A.

We planned on staying five nights, Sunday through the next Thursday. We would attend the acceptance speeches scheduled to be held in the

Memorial Coliseum, after which we would hit the road and take turns driving all night back home, saving us one night's motel bill. Allie found the room through one of our local travel agents, who really didn't know much about the place; she just looked it up in some listing book travel agents have for those things, I guess. The place was called The Nile River Motel. The name should have given us a clue. The weather report was at least favorable: clear skies, moderate temperatures, overall balmy Southern California for the entire week.

* * * * *

When I got back home from Gary's, Allie was in a frenzy.

"What's up, Sis?" I dodged a pair of jeans and some dirty socks that flew out of her room through the air into the hallway.

"I have to get ready to go. The Convention's only two weeks away and there's not enough time to get done everything that I need to be ready to leave." She straightened up, blew a stray lock of hair out of her eyes. She fished a piece of paper out of her hip pocket, handed it to me: a list of things for me to do. "Here, you can get started helping me."

Job 1:   Get car in shape to travel

Job 2:   Travelers' checks from bank

Job 3:   Camera, plenty of film, ditto flash bulbs

Job 4:   Snack food, plenty of it! (We have to save money on food)

Job 5:   Ice chest filled with ice and plenty of canned drinks

Job 6:   Coppertone, in case we get a chance to go to the beach. Plus beach towels

Job 7:   Plenty of note paper and ball point pens

Job 8:   Keep track of my official credentials

Job 9:   Extra medications like aspirin, band aids, merthiolate, etc.

Job 10: Your own suitcase, extra underwear, shirts, etc.

Job 11: Extra can of gas and cans of motor oil in trunk in case we run out

Job 12: Anything else I can think of later

* * * * *

103

The day before we were to leave for LA, Allie got a very special letter:

John F. Kennedy Committees:
Massachusetts Labor and Public Welfare
Government Operations
𝔘𝔫𝔦𝔱𝔢𝔡 𝔖𝔱𝔞𝔱𝔢𝔰 𝔖𝔢𝔫𝔞𝔱𝔢

June 30, 1960

Miss Allison Rodgers
93 Toledo Street
Yuba City, California

Dear Miss Rodgers:

I sincerely congratulate you for earning the right to represent your party in the forthcoming National Nominating convention scheduled to begin in just a couple of weeks.
Although you are an alternate, and not an actual delegate, I hope you will look upon this as an honor and feel the weight of responsibility accorded to this position. Who knows but what you may be called upon to step in if there is an emergency,
I also understand you are somewhat younger than the usual age for delegates. No matter, the youth of this country may look to you for inspiration and come to realize what your generation can accomplish when they set goals and work hard to achieve them.
Again, congratulations, and I hope to be able to meet you in Los Angeles.

Sincerely,

John F. Kennedy

* * * * *

Day One: Sunday, July 10, 1960. Allie and I got away at about six o'clock in the morning. "It's going to be hot driving south and we might as well leave while it's cool," Allie reasoned. She hadn't slept all night for excitement and nerves. We left under a thin cloud cover. Bud was in his pajamas, hugging us, wishing us bon voyage, and I could see him through my side mirror as we pulled away, waving stoically. Julia was still in France on her tour; she wasn't expected back for a few more days.

The Olds was stacked to the gills with mostly Allie's stuff, except for the trunk, where we packed the extra gas can, oil, and the ice chest. Allie had used some masking tape to plaster a JFK campaign poster on the trunk, plus two smaller ones on the rear side windows, in case people passing us on either side hadn't seen the big one in the rear, she argued. We were missionaries on a mission.

We got as far south of town as Tudor, when Allie quickly fell asleep. I clicked on my new car radio (actually slightly used, only cost twenty-five dollars, but I had to have my music), and found a station that played mostly popular stuff, and settled in for our big adventure.

The car began heating up between Stockton and Lodi, and I stopped to check the radiator. It was steaming some, so I let it cool off before I took off the radiator cap. Steam whooshed out and I jumped back to keep from getting scalded. When the boiling died down enough, I refilled to the top with water and we were on our way again. Allie only woke up for a minute to ask what was the matter, turned the other way and was back asleep.

This was not good. I wondered if I could keep limping along under fifty and stop to let it cool about every half hour. That worked okay until we reached Merced and the thing was really hissing and steaming like the boilers of hell. I stopped at a Signal station that stayed open on weekends for travelers like us and asked the pimply-faced kid behind the counter if they had a mechanic on duty. He said they did, but the guy was having a lunch break at his girlfriend's house, and winked a big knowing leer, nudging an imaginary rib with his elbow.

"When will he be back?" I asked.

"Depends…"

"Depends on what?" He smirked and laughed. I swear it was more like a whinny.

Allie woke up to use the bathroom and we had a sandwich and a mostly cool canned coke from the ice chest that had been sitting in the trunk too long in the sun. I felt a little better after we had some lunch. "What's happening - why are we stopped for so long?" Allie asked as she looked around. The kid kept sneaking looks at her butt and her boobs, which made her very nervous. "I don't like that guy," she said quietly, more of a threat if he made any moves on her. Allie did not like being touched by guys.

Romeo finally returned. He wasn't much older than the other kid, but had a few dozen less zits. He took one look at the radiator and said, hands in pockets, pushing dirt with his toe, "I think I can fix it by flushing it out."

"How long and how much?" I asked.

"About an hour and probably twenty bucks, my best estimate, can't be sure until I get into her."

An hour and twenty precious bucks later we were on our way again. He had added some kind of gunk to help seal up any pinhole leaks, which he was sure would be there in a radiator this old. "But you got yourself a grand old dame there," he complimented, patting the hood as I handed over the cash. "Take good care of her and she'll last you a good twenty years or so."

We rolled down the windows for fresh air, and I nudged the speed up to sixty-five. It felt good to be rolling along with a good set of wheels under your butt, the fragrance of freshly-mowed alfalfa hay from fields along the highway, and one less thing to worry about now. *She* was a grand old dame, and I silently thanked Mrs. Karnekis for trusting her to me. She was a solid car and we rolled smoothly along in spite of the ancient concrete highway surface with all its cracks and little potholes.

President Eisenhower had started a new major highway construction project called the Interstate Highway System, and I was told it was like nothing we'd ever seen before: two lanes each direction, bypassing most towns, but with plenty of access on and off, so you could travel faster. I couldn't wait to see what it would be like to drive on one of these new highways. The work on the section over Donner Pass in the Sierras was already starting. How long before they finished the one between Sacramento and LA? Not soon enough for this trip.

We arrived at the Nile River Motel just after dark, and my heart sank when I saw this dump. Allie was cheerful, as usual; after all, it was her choice and she was a big enough person to accept the consequences, good or bad.

As I stepped into the reception office to register us the smell of curry hit me. A dusky woman in a sari came out from somewhere in the bowels of the motel offices, and sullenly, without a word, pushed a form toward me to fill out: name, home address, car make and license plate number, contact name and telephone number; number of days we plan to stay and number of guests. At the bottom of the form in bold letters was NO PETS!

I was truly disappointed to see her; I had expected something else. Driving down, to help kill time, Allie and I had played a game imagining to each other what our experience would be like, our motel room, the food, everything. I had described our motel manager to Allie as someone from Egypt, definitely Egyptian, I insisted. He would be big, burly, dark and swarthy, with a florid black, shiny handlebar moustache. He would sweat a lot, and would be wearing a red fez with a black tassel to cover his premature baldness. His name would be Habib, or Abdullah, or Achmed. Whatever his name, he would hide his shifty eyes behind his dark glasses, while his three wives cowered in their harem in some tacky back room.

Mrs. Patel was no Achmed. "That will be one hundred dollars," she said in the singing lilt of the Sikhs; she proudly wore a vermillion dot prominently painted in the center of her forehead.

"But it's only twenty dollars a night," I argued, my eyes glued to her red dot.

"All cash in advance," she looked down at some spot on the counter, no eye contact. Had I offended her ethnicity, stared too long at her dot?

I was tired, grumpy and I suddenly didn't care about her or her feelings. I had driven a long way, had almost had a serious car breakdown, and I was being pushed into a very bad argumentative mood. "I'll pay for one night plus a one-night deposit. I'll pay you daily, as we go. Otherwise..." I started for the door.

"Okay," she said, pouting, holding out her hand for the cash. I counted out four tens and asked for a receipt. She wrote out the receipt, handed it to me with the key.

"I need two keys, please..." I asked politely, checking my rising temper, fighting against the strain of our trip. I was normally a nicer person than this and felt ashamed that I had gotten snotty with her. I had too many friends back home of different races and ethnicities and my parents had taught me better.

"Room six," she said as she handed me a second key and went back to her curry.

"This is very nice," Allie cooed. I didn't have the heart to regale her again with descriptions of the opulence of my room at the Drake in San Francisco. "Just look at that nice antique pattern of wallpaper. The fly specks blend in so nicely! And the curtains, how they do help the ambience! Don't you agree, my dear?"

"Oh, yes. And I wonder how many of the Plagues of Egypt we'll experience while we're here," I said, getting into the spirit, catching her infectious optimism. "Why, just look at those nice beds, and those antique chenille coverlets. I'll bet they're home to at least several hundred families of cockroaches!" Allie laughed and socked me on the shoulder. I started laughing, too, and fell on the bed, exhausted, choking from the release of pent-up stress and worry. "It's going to be all right, Sis," I assured, as I covered my eyes from the one bare bulb overhead whose brilliance made me hurt. Too many miles driving and staring at the road ahead. And I thought again of Jackie and how she had held me by Lake Ellis and cooed in my ear the day I had my own meltdown and assured me quietly that everything was going to be all right.

I had to admit that since I made the decision to be Allie's right-hand man and had essentially signed on for the duration, whatever that may entail, I hadn't focused so much on myself and what the future was going to bring. And my other worries, like why wasn't I enrolled even now over at Yuba College, and all those other major issues that had worried me so much just a few weeks ago.

I suddenly had another craving for a cold glass of milk with graham crackers.

CHAPTER SIXTEEN

Monday, July 11, 1960: *As the Democratic National nominating convention in Los Angeles prepares to open today, officials report there have been some attempts by unauthorized persons to enter the Sports Arena, site of the convention, using apparently forged passes, which have been confiscated and turned over to the Los Angeles police for further investigation. The officials, who requested anonymity, refused to speculate how this is possible, or who may be manufacturing the bogus passes, but assured that more scrutiny will be made of all persons entering the venue.*

I was in the shower and didn't hear the knocking on the door at 7:30. Allie opened the door and Mrs. Patel, the curry-making woman in the silk sari, summoned Allie to the office to take an urgent phone call. Although there was a Los Angeles phone directory in our room, along with a copy of the Gideon's Bible, we didn't have a phone, for some strange reason. But we did have an old black and white TV.

I was dried off, in my boxers and fresh tee shirt, redolent with Brut cologne, pulling on a clean pair of Levi's and a dark green Izod polo shirt, when Allie burst into our room, her face flushed with excitement. "Guess what? Never mind, you'll never guess, so I'll tell you: I'm now officially the delegate! Isn't that neat…!? Old Pratt left last night and went back home with a sudden illness. So that means I have to get my butt down to the convention ASAP and report to the Credentials Committee to get seated. And I get to take his room at the Beverly Hills Hilton and it's all paid for, including meals! Isn't it exciting…!?"

I had to admit, her excitement, as always, was infectious. That's why she's so popular and always on everybody's list to join committees for some do-good cause or another. "Is there a phone in our room at the Hilton?" I asked. Allie frowned, shrugged… like, who cares?

Mrs, Patel, our hostess, didn't share in our excitement. She was obviously all too relieved to have us gone; but she stood pat on keeping the twenty dollar deposit. Oh well, as Allie later reasoned, we'd have spent that much on gas driving back and forth between The Nile River Motel and the convention center.

"Nice wheels, man," the parking attendant, leaning down at my open window said, as we pulled in front of the Sports Arena. "Looks like something out of The Untouchables!" I nodded; I'd heard this before and I'd probably hear it again and again.

"I'm just dropping off my sister who has to go inside and register," I explained. "So I won't need to park. I just need to find a place to turn around…"

He waved me to the curbside where I pulled behind a long line of black limos and let Allie off. "I'll take the shuttle back to the Hilton," she said. "Are you going to watch on TV?"

"Wouldn't miss it," I said. "Be sure and wave if you see a TV camera in your face, okay?" She grinned and disappeared with the stream of conventioneers shuffling into the entrance of the Sports Arena, carrying her oversized, bulging straw shoulder bag. "Take lots of pictures!" I yelled to her receding back. She waved a hand in acknowledgement. She was dressed in Bermuda shorts, rope sandals, a sleeveless light blue shirt, her wild blond strands secured in her trademark pony tail.

I was relieved that the Hilton was providing shuttle service to the convention. Allie could ride in an air conditioned bus and I could park in valet parking at the hotel, kick back, lounge around the pool and work on my suntan without feeling guilty about her comfort. When I got tired of the pool, I could play tennis or turn on the TV in our room, order room service food and watch the proceedings at night when the networks would be broadcasting.

"Nice wheels, man," the valet said, as I pulled into the hotel parking ramp. He started to say something else, like, "It's like some...," when I interrupted.

"I know. You were going to say 'like something out of The Untouchables'...?"

"You're a mind reader, my man!" He grinned, flashing white teeth. He was dressed in the ubiquitous parking valet's uniform: safari suntan shirt with a brass name tag declaring him to be Corey; he had matching khaki shorts – big baggy pockets – and gold braided epaulets on his uniform shirt. He had a mop of sun-bleached blond hair, cut in the now-popular Kennedy-style. Corey was in obviously good physical shape from all the jogging back and forth to fetch his customers' "wheels".

I had a sudden thought: "Are you a tennis player?" I asked. He certainly looked like he could be.

"Sure, why?" he asked, surprised at my off-the-wall question.

"I'd like to play some tennis while I'm here, you know, pass the time, and I could use a partner..." He nodded, waiting. "Any chance we could play a game after you get off?

"Sure, man. What's your room number? I'll phone and let you know when I'm off."

"Actually, we're in one of those cabanas..." I pointed to the group of stucco-pink cottages clustered under lush groves of palms and pine trees, set back and reached by a winding landscaped pathway, away from the main hotel building: private, secluded, oozing richness and privilege. Pratt had at least scored a home run on the room reservations, even if he had only gotten to stay the one night. "Can't remember our cabin number, but the name's Rodgers – Alex Rodgers."

There was a pink piece of paper, a phone message, on the stand beside my bed, next to the phone when I got back to the cabana. It declared the message as EXTREMELY URGENT. I called the hotel operator and identified myself.

"Mr. Alex Rodgers...?" she asked sweetly. I said I was he. "There's an urgent message for you to call a Mr. Tate, in Marysville, California, at the Appeal-Democrat newspaper. He needs to speak to you as soon as possible. Do you have a pencil? Good, here's the number... ready?"

The switchboard operator at the newspaper put me on hold. A half-minute later a husky male voice (another chain smoker?) growled:

"Roscoe Tate here.!"

"Alex Rodgers here, Mr. Tate. I'm in Los Angeles. I got an urgent message to call you."

"Alex, glad you called back. I'll get right to the point: I'm the editor at the Appeal-Democrat. I've read some of your columns you wrote for your school paper over in Yuba City, and I liked what I saw. We don't usually do things this way, but, well, this is a very unusual situation. Our reporter who's supposed to be covering the Democratic convention…" He covered the mouthpiece to talk to someone briefly, and was back again.

"Well, the stupid jerk took a side trip down to Tijuana, in Mexico, busted up a bar, roughed up some locals. Got himself locked up and the police won't let him out until someone pays his bail. They want a thousand bucks, if you can believe…Highway robbery! Anyway, I'm in trouble and I need a big favor – I need someone to cover the convention and file daily columns. Actually, Alex, the way I look at it, it's a favor to me, but it's a hell of an opportunity for you to break into newspaper reporting. If you're interested…"

Was I interested? "When do I start?" I asked, and wondering whether this would turn into a permanent job. He hedged a little about the job thing, saying he'd keep an open mind, depends on what kind of reports I sent him, we'll talk more later when I get back, crap like that.

Roscoe Tate quickly got back to the job details: he told me to report immediately to the Press Room at the convention where I could pick up my credentials and my Press Corps badge. He'd already phoned his friends there and arranged for everything for me. He wanted me to call in to his direct line, collect, twice daily, and would expect my first column that night. Approximately eight hundred words, no more than a thousand.

"I don't want a lot of girlie crap like what Mrs. Kennedy was wearing, how was she doing with her pregnancy, how was Mrs. Humphrey dealing with her husband's defeat in the primaries, soapy fluff like that. Get inside the candidates' headquarters, talk to their staff, get out on the floor, talk to the delegation bosses, dig for the best dirt, anything, local color's always good." He wanted me to do an interview with my sister first thing, whom he had learned was "without a doubt the youngest delegate to the convention, period."

I would write my column, then call it in and dictate it over the phone to one of their expert teletypists, and the editors would take it from there. It sounded all too easy, and I couldn't wait to get off the phone and catch the shuttle bus that left every hour on the hour from the Hilton to the Sports Arena. I was anxious to get my credentials, hit the floor, find the California delegation and share with Allie my... *our* good fortune.

Roscoe Tate told me to keep track of my expenses – long distance calls, parking, trip expenses like taxi and bus fares or gas for the car; food, bar tabs ("but you're probably too young to drink, thank God, so forget that item"), tips, supplies like pads and pens, etc. etc. – and I'd get reimbursed when I filed my expense voucher back home. We'd also take care of the employment paperwork when I got back.

"Don't forget, Alex, call my private line twice a day. Without fail!"

I told him yessir. I was now employed, at least for the next five days. Forget bagging groceries for Lucky Stores.

This job paid one hundred dollars a day!

* * * * *

I quickly changed my Izod polo shirt for a white Gant button down, grabbed a striped necktie, but kept on my Levis and Sperry topsiders, made a quick call to valet parking to put off my tennis game with Corey. If I hurried, I could just make the next shuttle to the Sports Arena. I grabbed a cold can of coke from the minibar and sprinted for the bus stop, notepad in my hand and a couple of pens in my pocket. My throat was tight with excitement and my hands shook just a little from the adrenaline pumping through my system.

As I rode into the bowels of downtown LA, I began to see things again – not just notice – but really see things like I thought a reporter should. I saw stray dogs, abandoned junker cars, street people, tall palm trees limned against the milk blue skies, swaying easily in the light breezes above the tattoo parlors, taco stands, and Army/Navy stores. Trash was everywhere, papers in gutters lifted by the breeze, swirling little dirt devils, women's skirts lifted above tanned bare knees.

I began to regret that I hadn't paid more attention to little details of life all around me. I should have drunk in more of San Francisco when I was there; I should have painted a better word picture of the red sun sinking below the horizon beyond the Golden Gate, pelicans gracefully bowing to each other as they glided in the Reflecting Pond in Golden Gate Park; the way Jackie's jaw set in fierce determination as she cast her fly rod that misty day and the graceful arc of the bamboo, bending – near breaking from the vectors demanded of it – but without splitting, tough as iron.

I had promised Mr. Steinbeck as he left the oak-paneled bar that night that I would not write about our conversation until he was long dead, or fifty years, whichever came last, almost in legal terms, it seemed. I ached to write a first-hand piece about that one hour with him, my impressions, how it might have influenced my life as a future writer, and so on, but I still hadn't written it down the way I knew I could. I still hadn't gotten it. Would The New Yorker publish a piece like that? Would it be believable enough for their editors?

Well, now I had my shot to prove I was a writer. Hemingway got his start as a reporter, a war correspondent, and he went on to bigger things. I could follow that path. With the missionary zeal of the newly converted, I vowed I would be good: I would write truly and cleanly, and my columns would put the readers' butts into the hard seats in the Sports Arena, smelling the human odor of large crowds pressed close together. They would hear with me the roar and noise of the mob as their candidate took the microphone to exhort; they would see through me the color and pageantry of politics. I would make the people – the girls in their summer dresses, straw boaters and red-white-blue bandoliers – come alive. The readers would see through my eyes the banners, posters and placards: UNIONS & LBJ ALL THE WAY!; GEORGIA FOR KENNEDY; ADLAI IS A LOUSY GOLFER! SYMINGTON- A MAN FOR THE 60s. I would eat, sleep, live and breathe the Convention for the next five days. I pledged to myself I would skip meals, forego sleep, go anywhere, do anything, talk to anyone I needed to for my stories.

The bus pulled in line behind the black limos disgorging the powerful and famous in front of the Sports Arena. As the sweating, heavy, middle-aged men in dark suits exited the sleek cars they were mobbed by small armies of campaign workers, mostly pretty young girls about my age, waving placards, passing out leaflets, pinning on badges to whomever stopped to pay attention; exhorting, cajoling, pleading for their candidates.

Mingled among this crowd of seething campaigners were the other exhorters: the REPENT – THE END IS COMING people; the JOHN

3:16ers; the lone woman waving her sign – STOP KILLING WHALES; a group of three bearded young men dressed in ankle-length burlap robes repeatedly chanting their mantra, "EAT WHEAT, NOT MEAT!" Another sign proclaimed WE WANT A PRESIDENT WHO SAYS NO TO THE POPE! Another: WE NEED A NEGRO IN THE CABINET. And another: STOP THE EXECUTIONS! There was no end to the exhibitionists and others espousing their pet causes, and the ever-present roving eyes of TV cameras caught it all for the folks back home. Above the rumble and din of the crowds I could hear bands playing rally music.

I saw and heard all this as I waited my turn to get off the shuttle. I took a deep gulp of oxygen and set my foot on the sun-bleached pavement, nearly stepping in a big wad of gum someone had spit out. None of the pretty girls swarmed to solicit my vote; they had rightly pegged me as a non-delegate, nobody important enough to waste time, badge or leaflet on.

I joined the stream of humanity moving slowly toward the main entrance. Directly ahead of me was a small man in a light blue seersucker summer suit, white button down shirt and neatly tied bowtie. He patiently fanned himself with a handful of leaflets as we ambled along. The crowd stopped and I leaned forward, eager to begin my reporting assignment. I tapped his shoulder and he turned, a trim moustache above his smiling mouth. "Sir," I started, "I'm a reporter and would like to ask you a few questions…" He nodded, still smiling. "Are you a delegate, and what state do you represent?"

"I'm proud to say I'm a delegate from Missouri."

"So, being from Missouri, you're probably committed to Senator Symington?" He nodded, pointing to his lapel badge. I scribbled notes. "Do you think he has any chance of getting the nomination at this point? I mean, it seems to me that Mr. Kennedy has it pretty well locked up. Would you agree with that assessment?"

"We'll just have to see what the first round of voting brings, won't we?" At the mention of Kennedy, the man's smile tightened; he turned away as the crowed surged forward again.

I gained the entrance and was stopped by a uniformed man who asked to see my ticket. "Do you have a ticket?" I shook my head. "It should look like this," he said, as he pointed to a poster showing the red-white-blue official ticket that looked to me very much like one for a rock concert or sports event. I explained that I was a news reporter and needed to find the Press Room to claim my credentials and pass. He reached inside his blue blazer and fished out a temporary pass, entered the date and time, scribbled his name and handed it over. "Down that concourse and to your left at Door 14. Next…!"

The young woman behind the folding table/counter with a name tag that gave her name as Cindy helped me fill out the forms and issued my credentials and pass, a plastic-covered card with my name, suspended on a cord to hang around my neck. She showed me where the message center was; I already had an inbox with my name and the newspaper I represented written on a strip of masking tape pasted below the box. Roscoe Tate wasn't kidding; he knew people and he worked fast. My box was already crammed with press kits from all the candidates. Cindy gave me a complimentary cotton shoulder bag to carry all of this stuff, courtesy of The Los Angeles Times and said I should check my box a couple times a day for messages; otherwise how would people be able to get in touch with me.

Except for the camera, which Allie had with all her stuff, I was ready to begin work as a real reporter. I planned on taking a lot of pictures, but I wasn't too sure what I would do with them or how I would get them back to Roscoe and his staff to use in the newspaper.

It occurred to me that it might be a good idea to read up on who the candidates were, their positions on issues, background facts that might be useful to know before I started pursuing a story. I found a folding chair along a wall and sat down to read through all the press kits. I could wait awhile to locate Allie and retrieve the camera; I would need it now more than she would. As I read the press kits, I kept my eyes and ears open to observe other reporters and news people, who they were, what papers or magazines or news organizations they worked for, and what they were like. I had this image of reporters as a hard-bitten bunch: hard working, hard drinking, hard-swearing, carousing types in dirty shirts and three-day stubble on their faces, who carried around a cynical view of the world and humankind. I don't know where I got that image in my head, but there it was. So it came as a surprise when I began to see that many were well-groomed, dressed in suits, polite, soft-spoken and businesslike, serious about getting to the truth of a story; and as the week would play out, that image gave me a greater respect for this new profession I had just joined.

I went down to the floor where the convention would be gaveled to order in just a few more hours. I wanted to find Allie and get the camera. Workmen were everywhere, frantically making last-minute changes to lighting, laying communications cables, adjusting delegation signs on the floor, tweaking the sound system ("testing, testing!"); others were draping colored bunting or hanging campaign posters. It was total, happy bedlam.

A few delegates were clustering in their assigned areas, huddling, their faces set with a determination to perform their civic duties. I spotted the sign that marked the large California assigned seating and headed for it, hoping to find Allie, or at least someone who'd know where I could find her.

As I half expected, she wasn't there. Only a few scattered delegates had taken their seats with still several hours until the convention opened. An elderly woman who busied herself with some knitting kindly gave me the information I needed: there was an informal caucus of the Californians over in the Biltmore Hotel that their leader, Governor Pat Brown had called. She had skipped it, she said, because it was too far to walk at her age in this heat; and besides, she had already made up her mind on her candidate, was firmly committed, and she wasn't going to have her arm twisted by Pat Brown or anyone else. I admired her sharpness at her age, as I thought of Mrs. Karnekis and her slowly-diminishing faculties. How much longer before the daughter from Stockton won the battle and Mrs. Karnekis was warehoused in some rest home, I wondered.

My mind had wandered and I missed something the nice lady was saying. "I'm sorry, what did you say? The noise in here…!" I gestured around.

"I see you have a press pass around your neck." I nodded proudly. "You look mighty young for such an important responsibility." I nodded again proudly. "I used to work for a newspaper, in Fort Worth, Texas, before I met my husband and we moved to Southern California for the work in the airplane plants. That was during the War. Probably before your time… But we had a nice home in Rosemead, real close to his work at the plant. The plant's gone now, but I still live in the same house with a banana tree in my front yard. It's really close to the Hollywood-Burbank Airport and the planes come and go at all hours. There are even jet airplanes now!" She went back to her knitting.

"May I ask you a rather personal question?" I ventured. She looked up, narrowed her eyes, waiting for the ultimate question. "Who are you voting for?"

"Now that's a secret between me and my Lord Jesus Christ," she said. "I pray every day, twice a day, in fact. And He directed me how I should vote. Do you pray, Mr. Alex Rodgers?" She was looking at my pass hanging around my neck.

I sort of nodded and made a quick exit, feeling guilty that I wasn't much of a praying type and had sort of lied about it. I needed to get on with my job and I was feeling like a failure; two quick interviews and two turn-downs. No story.

* * * * *

The Biltmore Hotel, the nerve center, brains and true heart of this convention. The Sports Arena would witness the official agenda unfolding and the business to be conducted there, but the Biltmore was truly the headquarters of power, where the action was, where the eyes of the entire world were focused now.

The major contestants had each reserved a wing of this majestic old hotel, which would be their command posts and communication centers for the coming week. I knew Allie would be only interested in anything Kennedy and I quickly learned that the Kennedy camp was settled in the 8300 wing. The lobby was totally packed with people, a repeat of the crowds milling around the entrance to the Sports Arena. I finally made it to the elevators; there was a long line waiting in front of each elevator, so I figured it would be faster to take the stairs.

The stairwells were also packed – both upstairs and coming down – and progress was painfully slow. I finally shook loose from the herd on the 8th floor and slowly made my way toward the Kennedy nerve center. The halls were packed with people; tobacco smoke hung over and around everybody and saturated my clothes as I fought for air and pushed my way to…to where? I had no idea where I was headed, so I relaxed and let the crowd move me along.

CHAPTER SEVENTEEN

Monday, July 11, 1960 – "Who Goes To Political Conventions?" *By Alex Rodgers, reporting on the scene for the Appeal-Democrat:*

Day One of the Democratic National nominating convention. As I approached the newly-built Sports Arena in Los Angeles, site of the convention - a massive modern structure made of plate glass and tile – I was impressed first of all by the outpouring of patriotism all around me. Everywhere I looked – inside and outside – people I saw, people I interviewed, were outwardly showing renewed enthusiasm for the political process. Why is this? Why do these people get involved? Why do they come? I asked.

The signs tell part of the story, signs everywhere the eye looks: "VOTE FOR ADLAI." "KENNEDY IS OUR MAN!" "LBJ ALL THE WAY!" And so on. The First Amendment of our Constitution guarantees the Right to Free Speech, and the convention also attracts many non-delegates, eager to press their pet cause: "SAVE THE WHALES," "THE END IS COMING," "VOTE UNION LABOR," "SAVE THE DAIRY FARMS OF AMERICA – DRINK MORE MILK!" And so forth.

I look around the convention floor as the delegates gather for the opening gavel that will call the convention to order. What kind of people do I see, what are they like? They appear to me just like the folks I would see on a typical day walking down the streets of Marysville or shopping in the groceries of Yuba City, or working in their fields or teaching in our schools, policing our streets, fixing our teeth or cashing our pay checks.

Here's a typical profile: Male, white (I see very few Negroes), middle-aged, tending to be solid family men, hardworking at various professions and jobs; the kind who want a home, a family, enough to eat, who want stable, safe governments, who turn out to vote and try to influence their friends, families or neighbors to vote for their causes and candidates; who drive a Cadillac, Olds, Buick, Ford, Chevy or Plymouth – cars made in America. Mostly church-goers – Protestants, Catholics, Jews, Muslims – even a few avowed Atheists, all thrown tightly together into this arena to produce their party's standard-bearer by week's end.

They keep their lawns mowed and pay their taxes; they regularly attend church and PTA meetings, support their home teams and pretty much mind their own business while expecting other citizens to behave the same way. They relax by grilling hamburgers over charcoal in the back yard or down at the lake; Saturday night is reserved for watching The Lawrence Welk show; Sunday night is for Gunsmoke and The Ed Sullivan Show.

Typical would be two people I interviewed: a man from Missouri, dressed in a natty blue seersucker suit and bow tie. I'm quite sure he was a Symington delegate, but he kept mum and refused to openly commit his preference. Then I interviewed an elderly woman who knits to fill the hours; she's from the small community of Rosemead, a suburb north of Los Angeles, near Hollywood. She lives alone and still keeps her little cottage with a real banana tree in the front yard. Who will she vote for? That's between her, her Lord, and her conscience, she said.

But there's one delegate from our own community of Yuba City who deserves special attention: my own sister,

Allison Rodgers, at age eighteen, apparently the youngest delegate to this convention. Allie was elected from our district first as an alternate, barely losing to another well-known local, Mr. Homer Pratt, who had to leave the convention due to a sudden illness, allowing Allison to step in as the credentialed delegate.

Allison's high school civics teacher, Mr. Tommy O'Farrell, deserves some of the credit for this success story. He gave his students a challenge last fall to get involved in politics. Even though she isn't old enough yet to vote in a general election, Allie took the challenge and decided she would be a delegate to the Democratic National convention. She worked hard, put in the time, traveled a lot, met a lot of our local citizens, nearly failed spring semester in school, but gained their confidence, garnered enough votes, and here she is!

Allison is not shy about proclaiming her favorite candidate: Senator John F. Kennedy, from Massachusetts. Why Senator Kennedy? "Other than the obvious – he's young and gorgeous and has a really cool wife – I like that he wants to take the country in a new direction, and he wants the youth of America to rise up and be part of the process...I think Kennedy will demand a lot from us, and he believes that all of us – young and old, rich and poor, black and white – have a lot to offer our country," she states. "That's why I'm here and that's why ho has my vote."

It's quite late now, and this opening night the convention has to deal first with the bread and butter matters of Rules, seating all the delegations, certifying the hundreds of individual delegates, procedures and the like; mostly boring stuff, except to political scientists.

Tomorrow night the real action begins with Senator Henry "Scoop" Jackson as the Keynote speaker. The gloves will come off and the sparks should start flying shortly after that.

* * * * *

I phoned in the report late that first evening; Roscoe got on the phone and said he wanted to cut the reference to Homer Pratt going home due to a sudden illness. He didn't want to have any political repercussions on a local level to deal with later, would I please just leave the subject alone? "Just let's drop the Homer Pratt matter, okay?" Okay with me, but it did leave me wondering what was going on that my editor was even slightly concerned about some two-bit local political hack.

I found Allie as she was coming out of a very crowded caucus room on the sixth floor of the Biltmore. Her straw shoulder bag was stuffed with campaign literature and her arms were loaded, too. She introduced me to a new friend of hers, a young Kennedy floor manager named Jeffrey. We shook hands. I noticed he was carrying a walkie-talkie about the size of a brick, which he spoke into often, interrupting our brief conversation several times.

Jeffrey and another guy were assigned to cover the California delegation; he went with the members wherever they went and stayed close by when they were on the floor and the convention was in session. He had strict orders to call the Kennedy headquarters on the 8300 wing every hour; he was to be denied sleep, and would virtually eat any meals on the run for the entire week. That was some pretty tight control over floor operations, I observed. I doubted the other candidates had as tight an organization.

I had already heard one complaint that the Stevenson people had lodged: the Kennedy walkie-talkies had some high-powered radio frequency that continually interfered with their own communications equipment. I never heard the outcome of that kerfuffle.

On the shuttle back to the Hilton, Allie filled me in on the California caucus: Pat Brown was demanding that the entire delegation remain pledged to him through the first round of voting; after that they could vote their own preferences. When he was questioned whether he stood for Adlai or JFK, he had hedged and waffled, and Allie thought he was trying to be a deal broker of some kind, most likely for all the personal political advantage he could gain. Rumors had started to fly around the caucus room that Pat Brown was angling for a Kennedy or even a Stevenson cabinet position and would hold out the entire California block of delegate votes until he got some kind of guarantee from the two leading candidates to secure his position.

"Do you believe them, these rumors?" I asked her.

She frowned and said, "I don't know anything about how this game of politics is played, but I'm sure learning fast. It sure looks to me like Pat Brown is holding out for some kind of deal that benefits himself, and I don't think that's fair or ethical. We'll see what happens tomorrow; we're supposed to have another caucus and JFK is supposed to speak to us. I can't wait."

She leaned against me and fell asleep before we got back to the Hilton. I didn't have a chance to tell her about the weird phone conversation I'd had with Roscoe Tate about Homer Pratt. I guessed that would wait until breakfast.

CHAPTER EIGHTEEN

The convention organizers had shown some foresight in planning the best possible communications for the press corps, including not only the printed press, but especially in allowing for the hundreds of radio and television reporters who would descend from all corners of the earth to cover this convention.

I was faithful about checking my inbox for messages twice a day, picking up sheaves of mimeographed copies of the latest press reports from the candidates at the same time. I glanced through them, looking for anything that might make it into my daily report, discarding ninety-nine percent of the stuff as campaign hype aimed at the delegates.

The organizers had brought in a bank of about fifty new Royal typewriters, each one set up on an individual table, every table supplied with extra paper, pencils, carbon paper, just like a little writing office. Each desk was numbered one through fifty, and you were supposed to sign up in advance to reserve one of the typewriters. I wished that they had installed the phones on the little writing desks, too.

The phone bank was on the wall opposite the desks. There were only twenty phones available, wall phones, and they were monopolized twenty-four hours a day. There was no sign-up system for the phones and you had to stand in line on a first come, first served basis.

The first day, when I had checked in to get my credentials and press pass, I had asked one of the girls behind the folding table counter in the press center when was the best time to get a phone. She said I should try either very early in the morning – before seven – or late at night, after midnight. But she couldn't guarantee anything.

I figured I would stretch my luck with Roscoe and try phoning in just at midnight, which I'd done successfully that first night. But he did say he wished I'd try to call in a little earlier next time so he could put the paper to bed and go home and try to get some sleep himself. I couldn't see the big deal - wasn't it an afternoon paper? Why not try to call in the report early in the morning and save both of us some sleeping time? He grouched, swore, and ordered me to keep getting the reports in, "but try to call before goddamn midnight, will you!"

* * * * *

Through Allie's new friend Jeffrey in the Kennedy camp, I scored a real coup: He arranged to get me inside the control room, Suite 8315, for a two-minute interview with Bobby Kennedy. I climbed the stairs again to the eighth floor, avoiding the packed, slow elevators. God help us if ever a fire broke out on one of the top floors.

Bobby was in full operational combat mode: a phone stuck to each ear, grabbing sips of coffee from a mug in between bites on a sweet roll; his shirt sleeves were rolled up past his elbow, his tie was loosened and his gray plaid suit trousers were hopelessly wrinkled and hung limply as he strode the room, calling out orders, taking notes handed to him, scanning them quickly, nodding yes or shaking no in stride, his voice a staccato of hoarse barking into the phones, his famous tow-headed mop of unruly hair in disarray.

He kept cradling one phone under his chin, then the other, brushing rogue locks out of his eyes with the freed-up hand, but all in vain. There were creeping strands of gray sprinkled throughout his head.

Robert Kennedy: lean, wiry, tense, yet relaxed; his gray eyes were darting around the room, taking in everything happening around him. He was my height, and I'd bet he'd make for a merciless opponent in tennis. I secretly wished I could invite him to the Beverly Hills Hilton for a game with me one evening under the lights so he could relax a little for just an hour.

Jeffrey introduced us. Bobby put down one phone in its cradle, shook hands perfunctorily, stabbed at his hair, running his hand through the mop;

125

he cleared a stack of morning papers and offered me a seat as he signed off on the other phone. "Sorry for the confusion," he grinned shyly. "What can I help you with? Want some coffee?" as he glanced at his watch.

I thanked him but said no thanks. I knew time was too short for social niceties. I plunged in with: "I only have one question: From what I hear around the floor," I gestured lamely, "you seem highly confident your brother has the nomination locked up. Why is that?"

Bobby didn't miss a beat: "Seven hundred. That's the magic number. We believe we have at least that many delegates locked up and if they hold with us and we can make it to at least seven hundred delegates towards the end of the first vote, say by the time we get to Pennsylvania, we'll have the momentum to go all the way." He looked at me with those cool gray Kennedy eyes, studying me, my reaction. "You can print that; it's no great secret," he grinned as he pointed to my unused pad. I hadn't even lifted my pencil to write a note.

"But..." he added, "we're not resting, as you can see. We Kennedys believe in running hard, all the way, not conceding even one vote! As we speak, my brother Jack is out meeting with caucuses, still pitching for votes. It's not over until we top eight hundred five." We got interrupted by another brief phone call that he handled with a yes, no, and another yes.

"When?" I asked. "When do you calculate you'll hit eight hundred fi?"

"Washington, we hope, but at least it has to be by Wyoming, or..."
"Or what...?"

"I don't want to think about it." He offered his hand; it was soft. Our interview was over. I thanked him, I thanked Jeffrey. As I walked away, Bobby called after me: "I hear your sister is the youngest delegate here..."

I turned and it was my turn to grin as he gave me two thumbs up.

* * * * *

"You what?" Allie shrieked. "You met Bobby?" I nodded yes and she hugged me. "What was he like?"

I told her about the interview, as she munched on a hamburger I had brought her and drank from a warm bottle of coke, her eyes never leaving mine, nodding, alternately grinning or frowning.

"Thanks to your friend for Jeff setting us up," I finished. "Look, Sis,

I'd love to stay, but I got to go, people to see." We hugged goodbye and I asked her when JFK was supposed to address their caucus. I hoped vainly that Jeff could squeeze me into the room, but the pooling arrangement hadn't included me in this drawing for press spaces.

"You'll fill me in later with details?" I asked her.

* * * * *

Tuesday, July 12, 1960: *WE WANT ADLAI!*

Day Two, the Democratic National Convention, Los Angeles, California, By Alex Rodgers, as reported from the scene for the Appeal-Democrat.

I was privileged earlier today to have a brief, but exclusive, interview with Robert Kennedy, younger brother of the candidate, Senator John Kennedy of Massachusetts. Robert Kennedy is the national campaign chairman for Senator Kennedy. Robert exuded the confidence that his brother would win the nomination, which confidence has been the hallmark of the Kennedy campaign thus far.

The Kennedys' magic number seems to be seven hundred: if they can surpass that number of delegates in the first vote, they feel they will get the rest of the votes needed for the nomination. In this case, they will have to have eight hundred and five to lock it up.

But in the meantime, the Stop Kennedy movement continues to work nonstop against them.

In another recent development: Governor Pat Brown appears to have lost control of his California delegation. From a reliable source close to the governor, who requested anonymity for this interview, I learned that the governor, who considers himself close to Senator Kennedy while trying to remain an admirer of Adlai Stevenson, left the California delegation earlier this evening after a tense, loud caucus with them. It appears most all of the delegates have bolted from being committed to vote for Governor Brown on the first vote, and they now seem to be evenly divided, with about thirty each for Stevenson and Kennedy, and a scattering of others for

127

Symington and Johnson.

But can Kennedy be stopped? Going into the nominating speeches tonight, the Stevenson bandwagon does appear to be gaining some momentum. What looked last night to be a small scattering of "WE WANT ADLAI" poster-carriers-chanters outside the Sports Arena, has swelled today into a much larger outpouring of support. I saw a veritable small army of Adlai supporters outside as I reported to the convention center today, probably as many as two, possibly three thousand strong, chanting slogans, carrying placards: "WE WANT ADLAI, AN HONEST MAN, THE DECENT CANDIDATE," "WIN WITH ADLAI, THE THINKING MAN'S CHOICE," and so on.

But the verbal part of the crowd chanted over and over as they marched arm-in-arm: "WE WANT ADLAI! WE WANT ADLAI! WE WANT ADLAI!" It's like this late effort was designed to start a panic among the other candidates, a calculated effort to try and stampede delegates into bolting from their candidate in favor of Mr. Stevenson.

The business of nominations was the agenda for the convention this night. Mr. Kennedy was given a rousing nomination by his friend, Senator Henry "Scoop" Jackson, of Washington. There was a great outpouring of verbal support and demonstrations for Mr. Kennedy, including the convention band playing "Happy Days Are Here Again" repeatedly. It took the chairman over ten minutes of gavel-pounding to calm the crowd, restore order, and continue with the agenda.

But the dramatic high of the evening was when Senator Eugene McCarthy, of Minnesota, nominated Mr. Stevenson. The high point of his very eloquent nominating speech was his plea to the delegates: "Do not reject this man who has made us all proud to be Democrats. Do not leave this prophet without honor in his own party."

Senator McCarthy was interrupted numerous times during his speech with shouts from the galleries: "WE WANT ADLAI! WE WANT ADLAI! WE WANT ADLAI!" while tons of red, white, and blue confetti were showered over the conventioneers.

Is the stampede having an effect - is it working? Or is it now just a case of too little, too late for Mr. Stevenson? We'll have to wait and see what tomorrow brings: the voting for candidates is set for tomorrow night.

* * * * *

Roscoe was out when I called around midnight; apparently he went home to nurse a sick headache, so I just dictated my piece over the phone to a very phlegmatic teletypist.

* * * * *

I went back from the press room and found Allie down on the convention floor, being interviewed by a BBC radio reporter who had discovered Allie was the youngest of the delegates. The reporter was young, blond, pretty, and had a bewitching way of slightly flinging her mane of golden hair at the end of each sentence or question.

She was assisted by a small crew of a sound man and her producer, both skinny, unwashed young men who projected an odor of several days without showers. I was instantly smitten by her very precise Oxford accent, and now I could see why Gary Kinnersly was so taken with the Brits and their culture. I wanted to go there someday. Soon. In the meantime, I tried my best to get Amanda Robinson, as she was named, to even notice me, but she was totally focused on Allie.

"And this is Amanda Robinson for the BBC, live from Los Angeles in California at the Democratic National Convention site, where I have with me a young lady who is perhaps, as far as we can determine, at age eighteen, the youngest delegate to this political convention. Her name is Allison Rodgers. Miss Rodgers, how do you do…?"

I quickly handed Allie a note that said I'd see her back at the Hilton, and beat a retreat to the Press Room where I needed to make another call. I realized that we hadn't called home to tell Bud we had arrived all right and let him know what was happening.

"Allo…," a very French voice answered our home phone.

"Julia…? Maman…!" I shouted. I had forgotten that my mom was supposed to be home that week; I was glad to hear her voice. We talked for several minutes in French – she rapidly, and I much slower. I asked all

129

about her trip, how it had gone, and how much we missed her. I told her all about Allie and how she was a *real* delegate now, and how I had actually interviewed Robert Kennedy earlier just this very day.

I paused for breath, and she told me that in France it seemed everyone was in favor of Jack Kennedy winning. The French thought he looked so presidential. Well, that was the French way of seeing things: how presidential did the man look, act, or speak? And besides, Jacqueline – Jackie – was so widely admired, almost adored, for her good manners, such excellent taste in clothes, her classiness, and the fact she spoke fluent French, which weighed heavily in her favor – and her husband's, too. There was a very live rumor over there that if elected, the Kennedys intended to hire not one, but *deux* French chefs for the White House kitchen! Zut alors!

She told me she had read my one article for the Appeal-Democrat and was very proud of my budding skills as a writer. I asked to talk with my father. Bud had already gone to bed, so I asked her to give him our collective love, and we kissed and hugged over the phone. My throat tightened and I fought back tears as I made my way to the shuttle. I missed her terribly.

CHAPTER NINETEEN

The press corps gallery in the convention hall was ideally situated to watch people, especially the famous and powerful. From our vantage point we saw:

Unions: the AFL-CIO's Walter Reuther, and Abraham Ribicoff;

Actors (Why was Hollywood so attracted to politics and vice versa?): The Las Vegas "Rat Pack" (Frank Sinatra, Sammy Davis, Jr., Peter Lawford, Joey Bishop, and Dean Martin): Jimmy Stewart, Marlon Brando, Henry Fonda, Kim Novak, Marilyn Monroe, and Sidney Poitier; John Wayne and Ronald Reagan; Spencer Tracy and Katherine Hepburn; and two more of Hollywood's s darling couples – Paul Newman and Joann Woodward, and Bob Wagner and Natalie Woods;

The musicians: Andy Williams, Eartha Kitt, Harry Belafonte, Julie Andrews and Robert Goulet; band leader Louis Prima and his young wife, Keely Smith; and a newcomer, Joan Baez;

Political bosses: Pat Brown (California), Richard Daley (Chicago), and G. Mennen "Soapy" Williams of Michigan, and the venerable John McCormack of Boston, lank and angular. From New York, Robert Wagner, Averell Harriman, Carmen DeSapio, and "Boss" Pendergast. Mrs. Eleanor Roosevelt, not a Kennedy fan, also made an appearance.

The NAACP was represented by Thurgood Marshall, along with several other Negro politicians – Dr. Martin Luther King, Jr., and two more young stars, Julian Bond and Jessie Jackson.

Comedians: Dickie and Tom Smothers, Bob Newhart, Jonathon

Winters; Dick Van Dyke, and Phil Silvers;

TV personalities: Walter Cronkite and Curt Gowdy;

Athletes like Arthur Ashe, football star Rosie Grier, several members of the U.S. men's Olympic hockey team and Carol Heiss and David Jenkins, the Olympic gold-medal figure skaters.

There were a lot of other politicians of all stripes, lightweights as well as heavyweights. I saw all of the candidates, their nominators and seconders, including Scoop Jackson, a possible running mate for JFK, and a young congressman from Arizona, who had also been whispered as a possible dark horse running mate with JFK, Morris Udall.

With a great deal of curiosity we watched many members of the large Kennedy clan, young and not-so-young, as they assembled on the podium.

And, of course, we witnessed first-hand the activities on the convention floor. Operatives and floor managers for the candidates moved constantly among the delegations, screaming into their walkie-talkies to be heard above the constant din.

The Kennedy hospitality girls, pretty in white gloves and matching heels, strings of pearls, red-white-and blue striped dresses, straw boaters, and broad chest ribbons with their candidate's name in gold lettering on them, moved in groups of threes and fours up and down the aisles, smiles permanently in place, carrying posters and passing out literature and buttons.

Heads of delegations chomped on cigars or chain-smoked while trying to keep their charges in line. Delegates fanned themselves in the constant heat and humidity, fighting fatigue and boredom, waiting for the clock to wind down to the exact moment their individual vote would be called for. Would it really make a difference after all, or was it a wasted exercise?

* * * * *

Wednesday night, and the time for exhorting was past, the time for counting votes was here. I tried to spot Allie in the large California delegation, finally seeing her blond pony tail bobbing excitedly. Her face was quartered away from me, but there was no doubt it was my sister. I felt a tightness of pride in my throat and my heart started racing from the buildup of anxiety and adrenaline.

The big question on everyone's collective mind was: Would the

Kennedys pull it off? Did they in fact have the votes they claimed? Could Adlai, could anyone, stop the Kennedy bandwagon with its huge head of steam? Was it still possible, or was it too late? We'd soon see.

One seasoned reporter for the Chicago Tribune who had befriended me shared some inside politics as we sat together sipping cokes in the gallery. He said – on good authority – that very morning Adlai, as distasteful as the game of politics was to him, and against his will, had given in to reality and tried repeatedly to phone his old friend, Mayor Richard Daley of Chicago, who controlled the Illinois delegation.

"If Adlai had any snowball's hope, he knew he had to be realistic and beg for Daley's help. My source tells me that Dick played rope-a-dope with Adlai most of the day, until finally this afternoon, the mayor couldn't avoid it any longer, and had to deliver the bad news to his old friend. He finally took the call and told Stevenson: Except for just two Stevenson faithful, the rest of the Illinois delegation – 59-1/2 votes- were being delivered to Kennedy. End of the line for poor old Adlai. Sure, I respect him; he's such a decent guy. And brilliant. My God! But he never really had a chance against the Kennedy Machine, did he?"

At eight o'clock, the meeting was finally gaveled to order, the band stopped playing, the din settled to a mere undercurrent of voices and a few scattered noise makers. Let the games begin!

"Alabama?"

"Mr. Chairman, Alabama casts twenty votes for Johnson; Kennedy, three and a half; Stevenson, one half; Symington, three and a half."

At New York, the count for Kennedy was just shy of five hundred. Pennsylvania put Kennedy just over the six hundred-fifty mark. Not quite the seven hundred Bobby had so confidently predicted to me.

Washington cast its vote and the count was now safely over the magic mark at 710. West Virginia added another safe 15 votes, won in the earlier primary, and Wisconsin with 23, to make it 748. It was now so close.

Wyoming was next. Wyoming could do it.

The audience became eerily quiet; everyone strained forward to hear this historic moment:

Wyoming's national committeeman leaned into the microphone from their place on the floor and said, "Mr. Chairman, Wyoming casts all fifteen votes for the next president of the United States, John F. Kennedy!"

The convention erupted, the band began playing again, tons of colored confetti and streamers rained down on the conventioneers; placards and straw boaters were tossed in the air. The spontaneous demonstration lasted for a full ten minutes before order was restored. Acknowledging that Kennedy now had it all but won, Favorite Sons released their committed delegates and the voting quickly wound down to the inevitable conclusion: 806 for Kennedy, electing him as the Democrats' nominee for president of the United States

* * * * *

I hung around, everyone hung around, waiting for Kennedy to appear from his secret hiding place where he'd spent most of that day watching, listening, and resting – a place known only to his family and a few close associates and top staffers - to make his grand entrance into the hall and claim his party's top prize. I kept glancing nervously at my watch, seeing the minutes tick down perilously close to midnight. If I didn't phone in my report and file soon, Roscoe would have my butt and I'd probably get fired.

To everyone's great relief, sometime right around midnight, we heard sirens, and outside the Sports Arena, the victor's motorcade arrived in an advance wave of blinking red lights.

I waited just long enough to see a well-tanned, slim figure, tailored in a dark navy suit stride (actually, he seemed to bounce like a boxer) to the podium, brushing back a straying forelock of glossy reddish-brown hair with one hand, grinning widely, waving to the adoring crowd with his other hand. It was John F. Kennedy's moment to savor, while his defeated enemies stepped forward one by one, eager to share the reflected glory of the rostrum, to shake his hand, pat his shoulder and make obeisance while flashbulbs incessantly popped and flashed, lighting up the night.

I raced to the phone bank in the press room, stood nervously in line waiting for one to be freed up, needing badly to also find a rest room.

And that was essentially the report I filed over the phone to a grumpy, sleep-deprived teletypist that night.

Except that I didn't include anything about the interviews Allie had had that day with *Time*, *Newsweek*, *Life*, The *Wall Street Journal*, the *New York Time*s, who had all apparently picked up on my little byline in the

134

Appeal-Democrat about her being the youngest delegate. Plus the radio interview with the BBC gal Amanda hadn't hurt, either. News travels fast and Allie became an instant celebrity, the convention's poster child, the darling of the news media all over the world.

CHAPTER TWENTY

When I signed on with Allie several weeks ago, I made a philosophical treaty with myself that, who knew, maybe I would learn something valuable about politics from this experience. As I lay on my bed at the Hilton unwinding, listening to pleasant breezes worrying pine needles in the tree outside my open window, unable to sleep for all the excitement and drama, I mentally went back over my notes and concluded that, yes, I had learned firsthand a lot about our political system: how it works, how things get done, how people vote and why; how candidates get elected. I knew I still had a lot to learn, and I suspected that my tour with Allie wasn't over yet.

In her interviews with the press that day she had boldly stated that if JFK got the nomination she would be working hard to deliver for him a majority of the votes in our congressional district come Election Day in November! That took my breath away and gave me a bad case of the heebie-jeebies.

First, for obvious reasons, it was a daunting task she had set for herself. We live in a rural district that tends to vote Republican. Not always, not every election, not overwhelmingly. Sometimes Democrats have a better than even chance in our district if they work hard and spend the necessary money – a big IF. But all other things being equal, usually the Republican wins.

Second, Allie had her schooling to think about. At least I hoped she was thinking about it. I doubted they would just let her drop out for fall semester while she helped run a political campaign. "Sorry, Mr. Sumsion. I won't be dropping by for classes today. Got important work to do for my candidate Jack Kennedy. You know him? No? Well, I do. I met him at the convention; he personally shook my hand and thanked me for the work I was doing on his behalf. Here, have a JFK button, on me."

No, Allie's work for Kennedy would definitely have to be evenings and weekends. How would she manage? I worried about how tough she was mentally, emotionally, for this giant undertaking. I'd already seen how her efforts just to become a delegate had almost put her in an institution last spring. I remember vividly her reaction when she narrowly lost to Pratt; she was convinced that so many people on her list were going to vote her in, only to find that the privacy of the voting booth does strange things to people you thought were your friends that you thought you could count on.

What would happen this fall when she discovered, like the proverbial Little Red Hen, that she was ending up having to do everything all by herself? I could just see it: it's early Saturday morning at the local Kennedy campaign headquarters, somewhere downtown on Sutter Street. Allie fumbles with keys to unlock the door, her hands full of donuts, coffee, campaign literature waiting to be stuffed into envelopes for mailing. One hour, two hours, three hours later, she's still all alone stuffing; nobody shows up to help. She breaks down and cries her heart out, swears a streak, throws a chair through a window, and storms out screaming, looking for something alcoholic to get totally wasted on…

And I could also see Alex – me – juggling a part-time job with classes at Yuba, gigs with my combo, singing in this new thing Gary wants to try, attempting to squeeze in a date with Jackie. All the while being expected to back Allie as her lieutenant, second in charge, her shoulder to lean on, cry on, someone to yell at or blame when things got really crappy;, if there was one thing I had learned already about politics, it's this: things can turn to crap in a big hurry.

Still, in just the few days I had hung around the convention, I had come to enjoy the drama, the intrigue, the crowds, the glamour, the noise, the bull crap, the adrenaline highs, the deadlines, the life of a reporter. In the end, I knew I would cave in and support my sister and her dream, even though I wasn't too clear yet on what her dream was or where she thought it would eventually take her. She was family, and in our home the rule was: always support family.

I also learned a few other valuable lessons about politics:

Like, to the victor flow the spoils of victory.

And its corollary, politics has no time for the losers. After Kennedy arrived to acknowledge his victory, the entire press corps swept him up, loved him, adored him. Nobody spent another second on Adlai or Stuart or LBJ. And Hubert had been chopped liver for weeks now.

Like, politics does indeed make strange bedfellows. It was an interesting study in human nature how just a few hours before Kennedy's victory, all the others were pillorying him and running him down like a rabid coyote. Then, just a few hours later, they were all sucking up to him, craving the smallest share of the limelight, kissing up for second place on the ticket: the vice presidency. Or, at the very least, a future Cabinet appointment.

As I drifted off to sleep I remembered it was now Thursday. Given his habit of working, running hard to the end, Jack would probably be up already, huddling with Bobby, wrestling with one of the most important decisions of his political career: who gets the number two spot on the ticket?

I'd be up in a few more hours myself, sleep-deprived, caffeine-driven, pretending to be the hard-bitten reporter digging into the story of the day: Who would Jack Kennedy tap for his running mate?

The Reno odds-makers were already betting heavily on Scoop Jackson, with Symington a close second. Mo Udall was the dark horse, the long shot. I kind of favored Humphrey; I liked his enthusiasm. The Happy Warrior, he called himself. I wondered how happy he was today.

* * * * *

Way too early, the alarm went off; I forced myself out of bed. I was double-dog tired with an adrenaline hangover and would have given anything to turn over and sleep until noon. As I sat on the edge of my bed the phone rang: Roscoe Tate in a foul mood. Was he a drinker; did he have a major hangover headache? If so, I hoped he had already had his first good slug of Scotch or vodka or gin or whatever poison he took.

"Kick your girlfriend out of bed and get dressed," he slurred. Yep, hung over. "You got work to do, boy!" Before I could protest that it was

138

seven o'clock and I was already on my way out the door, he continued, "I have inside info that says Kennedy is going to pick LBJ, if you can believe it. My sources are saying Kennedy can't win without the South, and only LBJ can bring in the southern voters. That and the unions…"

"But I thought the unions liked Kennedy," I interrupted.

"Ha! Boy, have you got a lot to learn. Listen to me! Quit thinking and get the facts. The unions are still mad at Jack's snotty little brother Bobby for the way he kicked Jimmy Hoffa's butt in those hearings. Those union guys got long memories. Anyway, LBJ's the guy. Get the story!" He rang off.

Once again I found myself skipping breakfast, making the agonizingly slow, sweaty pilgrimage up the back stairs to the 8300 wing of the Biltmore. The stairs were jammed with news people of all stripes – print, radio, and TV crews lugging bags of gear, cameras and sound equipment; cigar and cigarette smoke making it impossible to breathe in the fetid air, everyone shoving and grunting for breath as they worked their way slowly upward. I got the feeling that Roscoe wasn't the only editor in America thinking he had an inside scoop on the LBJ rumor. We finally busted out on the eighth floor; there wasn't an inch of space to move toward Suite 8315. The halls were hopelessly jammed with humanity.

I said to myself I was screwed and turned to force my way back down, when I was met by a phalanx of LAPD personnel in blue uniforms. They had orders from the County Fire Marshall or someone else with authority to clear out the place because of fire code violations or vague fears the mass of people would somehow cause the flooring to collapse. Someone next to me griped, "Tthe floors are made of concrete and if any uniformed baboon cared enough to pull back the wall-to-wall carpeting he could see for himself."

We did as we were ordered and inched our way back down the way we came with no news, no breaking story. In the crowded lobby of the Biltmore we were met by Kennedy staffers handing out pre-printed mimeographs of a press release stating that the nominee had in fact asked Senator Lyndon Johnson to be his running mate, and the big Texan had graciously agreed; John Kennedy would be holding a press conference at 4:30 to make it official.

In spite of a letdown feeling bordering on anti-climax, I was relieved that I could file the story as printed on the official Kennedy release but with maybe just a little personal drama thrown in for background color. So I stood in line for the shuttle back to the Hilton; I deserved a swim, possibly a game of tennis, if Corey was available and still willing. My watch showed it was late afternoon; I had been in that blasted stairway going up and down for the better part of the day without food, drink, or even a toilet break

I had another pink phone message in my room when I got back. It read: YOUR RED BLAZER ARRIVED. CALL ME, GARY. I laughed as I changed into my white tennis togs, envisioning myself in a red blazer, strumming a guitar and singing "Day-O!"

Corey beat me two games out of three. I think he purposely spotted me the first one, then just ran my butt ragged the next two. My excuse was that I was out of shape and hadn't played any real tennis since the conference championship games in late May.

Mostly out of morbid curiosity, I asked Corey what the gossip was around the staff at the hotel regarding Homer Pratt and the abrupt way he had left. He promised me he'd check on it and report back if he learned anything.

* * * * *

Allie joined me for chicken and watercress sandwiches with lemonade by the pool that evening, the first time we had spent together since our drive down on Sunday. She looked pale and drawn from the strain, the non-stop sessions in bad air indoors the past four days.

It was a good time to just sit together, not really talking, each in our own thoughts, memories and impressions of the recent events of history of which we, in our own individual way, had been part in the making. We were witnesses to a major historical event, and I would always have that in common with my sister, regardless of where the future took us or how our lives diverged. I thought of the times when we were kids and she and I would sleep out back in the summer under our sweet-smelling Kumquat tree, swatting mosquitoes, and talking about what we were going to be, what we would do, when we were grown-ups.

"Remember when we were kids and we used to sleep out back in the summer?" I asked her. She nodded dreamily. "Remember what you said

140

you wanted to be when you grew up?" I asked.

"I said I wanted to be a fireman," she said.

"And I said I wanted to be?" I asked.

"You wanted to be a school teacher."

"So what's to become of us, Allie?" I asked. "Where will we be and what will we be doing in ten years? It will never be like this again, never be this sweet."

She nodded, seemingly distracted by something, so I dared ask: "What? What were you just thinking about?"

"I don't want to be a fireman, not anymore. I don't want to see people hurt or their homes burned out. I want to do something to help people, true, but I don't think I can stand all the pain and suffering."

I was surprised; I had never heard my sister sound so eloquent or express such deep, tender feelings. I felt much the same way; I wished we could still be kids and sleep in the back yard under the Kumquat tree and swat at pesky mosquitoes.

"You'll find your path," I reassured her. I thought of Jackie at Lake Ellis patting me, stroking me, whispering in my ear, softly telling me that it will all work out somehow. I reached over and took Allie's hand in the mellow darkness and we held on to each other that way for a long, sweet silence, before I remembered my story and went inside to phone it in from our room.

Friday morning early we were awakened again by the harshly ringing phone. It was Bud. "What's up, Bud?" I asked, rubbing sleep from my eyes. My muscles ached from yesterday's tennis.

"I hope you're both having a great time." I assured him it had been grand and we were anxious to come home tomorrow. He continued, "Listen, I hate to spoil your fun, but it's your grandfather. We... well, the doctors... they're sure he's dying. He's in bad shape and they don't think he'll last through the weekend." Long pause while I slowly let out my breath; I didn't know I had been holding it. This was the bad news you knew would come some day with a cancer patient, but that you never really expected to hear. Bud went on: "Look, I know it's a big sacrifice on you, yours and Allie's part, but do you think maybe you could cut it short and come home? Today?"

We discussed the logistics, the timing, and I said we'd try. I needed to talk with Allie; after all, it was really her big trip, not mine, and she was still sleeping. I said I'd call him back later with a decision. There was really no decision; I already knew the outcome. Bud was not really that close with his father, my grandfather, but it was family, and we always supported each other. Always, dammit!

* * * * *

We silently packed and called the front desk for a bell boy to drag our few pieces of luggage out to valet parking. Valet parking! Here we go again, I thought. This time, I silently prayed, please let there be no stinking dead bodies in my car.

Corey brought the Olds up to us, washed and shiny new, the JFK posters, except for the host of dead bugs peppering them, mostly still intact. Jack, young and confident, smiled at us. Corey bounced out of the Olds and congratulated Allie on JFK's stunning victory. She thanked him. Feeling like a big shot, I fished a twenty out of my pocket and handed it self-consciously to him. "Hey, man, look me up next time and we'll play again," he said. I nodded, got behind the wheel.

Corey leaned in and told us confidentially that his sources around the hotel had told him "By the way, your guy Homer Pratt was sent home by the party bigwigs because Sunday night he'd been caught with a male prostitute in his room."

"In *our* room!?" Allie shrieked. "Our room, you said? Oh, how gross! I can't believe I slept in the same bed!" She hid her face in her hands; I was afraid she might retch.

"Nice wheels, man," Corey said and patted the car, as I waved goodbye and pulled out into the stream of afternoon traffic heading west on Santa Monica Boulevard.

I knew what he was thinking: just like something from The Untouchables.

CHAPTER TWENTY-ONE

Allie was in a deep sulk. She was missing the big convention wrap-up, Kennedy's acceptance speech, scheduled to be held tonight in the Memorial Coliseum, which seats between eighty and a hundred thousand. The Sports Arena could only hold a paltry thirty thousand. The convention planners wanted all the coverage and exposure they could get for the event.

I tried my best to make peace by playing her pop music on the car radio. I found Elvis singing "It's Now or Never," followed by Chubby Checkers doing "The Twist." They couldn't shake Allie out of her deep funk. The signal faded out badly when we climbed into the Tehachapi Mountains, and Allie whined about that. I told her that we would probably be able to listen to the speech on our radio when we got to the flat lands. She just shrugged and stared vacantly out at the jumble of drab gray rocks, star thistle, greasewood, lizards, and cactus whizzing past us.

"In fact," I said, "I have an idea. You should probably drive later on so I can take notes on Kennedy's speech. Then I'll call in my last column from somewhere along the way." I calculated that would be somewhere around Stockton, barring any major event or car problems to slow us down.

We came down the last long grade, the road flattened out, and we cruised smoothly along between endless fields of cotton, wheat, and alfalfa hay stretched out to the distant mountain ranges on either side of the highway. Massive irrigation sprinklers, a new invention, softly rained on future crops. Allie turned and fell asleep; I turned off the radio and listened to the hypnotic hum of spinning tires, the music of the open road, alone with my thoughts. I kept an ear cocked for any car noises; that's one of the best ways I know to keep awake. Any strange clunk, hum or whirring sound coming from somewhere under the hood or the rear end is as good as caffeine for me.

Alone with my thoughts. First, it was obvious to me that I should get some kind of part-time job and start getting ready for college; fall classes would start in less than two months. I'd resigned myself to spend fall semester, maybe a year at Yuba, then I'd transfer to somewhere else. My first choice, based only on sentimentality, was UC Berkeley. I knew they had a superb English program.

My second choice, based on the single visit I had made to their campus, was Southern Oregon, also for their English program. I made a mental note to add to my list of Things to do When I Get Home: check on college entrance exam – does Yuba College require?

I thought about friends and classmates from my graduating class - who was going where to school, who was getting married, who had already joined the military (mostly to escape Yuba City or a rotten home life or conflicts with parents), who were just working, filling time while they tried to figure out their life, wondering what to do next.

I knew for sure that Freddie Gomes was headed for Cal-Davis and studies in agronomy. That had been mandated by his family since before he could remember. He was their great hope to help them build an empire in agriculture, using the vast store of knowledge he would pick up in college. Then he would apply all that book-learning to tap into Mother Nature's mysteries locked away in the sun, rain and soil. In practical terms, what Freddie would learn most about being a successful farmer is this: find a good banker and stay on friendly terms with him.

Duane Andersen had jumped to the head of the line in the joining-the-military crowd' he had signed up for the Air Force weeks before graduation and had left for his basic training two days after the ceremonies. Why did guys join the armed services?

Yeah, I know: to get away from home, to travel to foreign countries, for adventure, for possible combat and getting to shoot lots of expensive weapons Maybe to get away from a clingy (pregnant?) girlfriend. Maybe they thought they just looked great in the smart uniforms. For some, a feeling of national pride or patriotism. I'll give them that.

Someone else said it was because deep down, they had a psychological craving for the discipline the military life provided that was lacking in their home life. Maybe. Someone else had a sick idea: because they liked the idea of taking showers with other guys.

I never was interested in military service. The pay was lousy. You got yelled at and put down by seniors in rank every time you turned around. You had to do crappy jobs all the time, like KP duty, or scrubbing out latrines with a tooth brush. Then you got yelled at for doing it wrong or not well enough for the likes of your drill sergeant. You got to roll out at 4 a.m. and do exercises and run for miles and miles before breakfast in all kinds of crappy weather.

They lured you into signing up with the promise of travel to exotic places. They did their damndest in boot camp to turn you into some kind of cretin, an animal, a non-thinking killing machine; then you got the privilege of maybe getting a bullet in your butt in some stinking jungle far away from home. Exotic travel, my eye! Not for me.

We passed a small town and there was another branch office of the Bank of Greater California. They were everywhere! My thoughts turned back to the day I stood to receive my Fine Arts award and scholarship from them. I could hear Mr. Sumsion, giving the honor roll call of names from our class, and where we were all headed to college:

"...Annette Atkinson, Brigham Young University...

...Rose Marie Biehle, Yuba College...

...Brian "Peaches" Bork... football scholarship to University of Nevada, in Reno.

...Ron Del Pero, San Francisco State...

...Jerry Duncan..." Jerry, where are you headed...? But I couldn't remember; my mind was drifting badly in the late-afternoon heat. I couldn't remember where he was going after high school, but didn't Sumsion say something about Jerry wanting to be a lawyer...?

"...Patsy Ethington, Yuba College...

...Claudia George, Yuba College...

...Homer Hankins, Yuba College...

...Jolene Herrick, full-ride academic scholarship to University of Oregon...

...Merilyn Mallory, Yuba College...

…Melvin Oliver, Humboldt State…

…The Phillips Twins…" What was it? Didn't he say nursing school…? I was getting dangerously sleepy from the heat. I rolled down my window; hot air scented with freshly-mown alfalfa blew in, revived me some.

"…Darlene and her brother, George Ross, Yuba College…

…Hugo Sargenti, San Jose State…" That was only a month ago, before… I forced myself to shut out that gruesome image in the MG's boot.

"…Robert Teja…" I forgot where Bob said he was going. Yuba…?

"…Leeanne Wilder, Brigham Young University…"

And on down the list: classmates off to Chico State, Sacramento State, Cal-Berkley, Stanford, and so on…

Mr. Sumsion never called my name because I hadn't stated a preference for a college yet. By default, though, I just knew I'd be going to Yuba. My deal with Allie had sealed it.

What else to do for the next couple of months until college classes started?

I swerved to avoid a roadrunner making an angular sprint across the highway, packing a huge lizard in its beak; the lizard was squirming for its life. Allie woke up and frowned at me, turned back to her window and harrumphed herself to sleep again.

My thoughts turned to Gary; I laughed as I remembered his message about the new red blazer. Tally ho! In the rush of leaving L.A. to get back before my grandfather shuffled off his mortal coil, I had forgotten to call Gary. I'd call him first thing tomorrow for sure.

And I made another mental note: call Carla Gomes to arrange for guitar lessons. I would humor Gary and try my best to help him make this big idea of his a success. I had never been much into folk music, but it was growing in popularity – all the pop music stations played it now – and I often found myself humming folk tunes when I was mowing Mrs. Karnekis's lawn, or doing other odd jobs.

*　*　*　*　*

On the outskirts of Bakersfield I felt the call of nature plus growing hunger pangs fighting each other for supremacy. It was now late afternoon; we hadn't grabbed any breakfast or lunch before we left and our stash of snack foods had all been eaten on the trip south. I spotted a McDonald's and pulled in; McDonald's always had clean restrooms.

I accidentally bumped into a concrete parking barrier, rudely jarring Allie awake. She scowled at me; she can be as mean as a mother bear when she's roused out of a sound sleep. There were pink and white stripes, indentations on the side of her face where she had slept against her fingers. Moist hair matted on her forehead that she tried vainly to brush back with the hand that she'd slept on. "Ow! Stings like a thousand piss ants biting me! What are we stopping for?" Her hand flopped clumsily, independently, as she shook it awake.

"Potty break and something to eat. What do you want...?"

"Whatever you're having. Want me to drive for awhile...?"

"Are you awake enough?" She sleepily nodded her head, yawning.

* * * * *

The sun was sinking in the west when we finally found a radio station that was sending a clear enough signal so we could hear Kennedy's acceptance speech from the Coliseum. Allie had taken over the wheel while I took notes. I held a flashlight between my teeth and began writing as fast as I could. I could only get down a few cryptic notes and phrases:

...times are grave...

...stakes are high...

...not curse darkness but light a candle...

...world is changing...

...old ways will not do...

...we stand on edge of a new frontier...

...frontier of unknown opportunities and perils...

...I give you not a set of promises...

...a set of challenges...

...the promise of more sacrifice, not more security...

...a race for mastery of sky, rain and ocean... (What the hell...??? The radio cut out; too much static.)

...give me your help...

...give me your hand...

"Holy crap cow!" I yelled, dropping the flashlight I'd been biting, as the car swerved sharply to the right, brakes squealing, sliding on two

147

wheels, nearly tilting over before Allie righted us and we slammed back down on all four, coming to a dusty stop on the verge, ten feet short of a concrete bridge abutment. "What just happened…!?"

"Sorry…" Allie was leaning against the steering wheel, softly crying. "I swerved to miss them…"

"Who…miss who?" I was looking around through the dusty twilight, trying to see what or who she had just missed.

"A mother skunk and her babies. They were walking across the highway liked they owned it and I turned to keep from hitting them."

I thought of Driver's Ed training as I got out of the car to see if anything was damaged: "NEVER swerve to avoid an animal on the road; more single-car accidents are caused by stray animals than any other known cause."

There was steam hissing – something escaping the radiator? It had been a hot, dry drive so far, but nothing was broken that I could see through the settling dust and dimness.

Except for one of my fingernails, which hurt like hell and had been almost ripped completely off when I was thrown against the side window and I reached out to keep my balance. And except for my lips that were bruised and split from the flashlight. Good thing I'm not a horn player.

"Everything okay?" she asked as I got back in.

"Yep. We were lucky. You okay?" She nodded, her tears had dried but she was still a little shaky. "We need to add water to the radiator again, so let's just sit here awhile and let her cool down, okay…?" I said.

Allie nodded again as I searched through the glove box for our home-made first aid kit and a band aid.

"Alex, I'm really sorry." She turned to me in the darkness, her eyes big and earnest. She looked like she was going to cry again; I didn't want that.

"Sorry…? Whoa, it wasn't your fault. You did what you thought you should - you reacted – your reflexes took over. I'd have probably done the same thing," I assured her, patting her arm.

"That's not what I meant. I'm sorry for dragging you into all this" She sort of waved her hands around helplessly.

"Hey," I said cheerily, "I've never had more fun in my life" And I really meant it.

* * * * *

We stopped in Stockton – another McDonald's that had a pay phone outside – where I called in and dictated my last column to the teletypist. I made it up on the fly, throwing in a few of my own flights of fancy, like: "Mr. Kennedy bounced to the microphone…" I changed that to, "He seemed to glide to the waiting microphone with all the grace of a boxer…"

And: "He looked tanned and rested, relaxed, in his finely-tailored dark suit, white shirt, and signature striped necktie…"

And: "The famous Coliseum, home to the mighty University of Southern California Trojans' football team…" Stuff like that.

Actually, Kennedy had sounded to me very tired, his voice hoarse. But what the heck? I figured the people who put the paper together could pull the text of the actual speech off the wire services and print whatever they wanted, if anybody was interested in reading the whole thing, short as it was.

* * * * *

Saturday morning. The Kennedy clan – John, Bobby, Teddy, wives, kids, sisters, uncles, aunts, cousins – all loaded on private planes and flew east for a badly needed and much-deserved two-week vacation.

The Republicans made final preparations for their own upcoming nominating convention in Chicago.

CHAPTER TWENTY-TWO

Grandfather – a badly shrunken version of him – was sitting up in his hospital bed, raving, wildly flailing his arms. Two male nurses had to exert everything they had to restrain him. He clawed at them, got a hand free and pointed a bony stick of a finger at Julia, yelling, "It's that French whore with you again, isn't it? It is! It's that goddamn French slut of yours, Bud! Get her out of here…she makes me want to puke, just the sight of her!"

The orderly got him to calm down. He lay under the sheets, pulling them clear up around his throat, and said, "I used to be married to a nice Jap woman. But she doesn't come around to see me any more. I wonder what happened to her. Boy, she was a nice piece. She could really turn me on!"

Then he sat upright again, pointing his finger at Julia again, screaming, "Get her out of here!" The orderlies struggled to restrain him, frantically searching for the alarm button or whatever it was they pushed in emergencies. It was awful.

About then another nurse arrived with a doctor, white smocks everywhere, Grandfather struggling with alarming strength. Omigosh! They're going to kill him. He's going to die of heart failure. The doctor produced a syringe and shot him up with some kind of sedative. He relaxed, they gently laid him back down, and he was soon deeply nestled in the arms of Morpheus, snoring between bouts of hacking, raspy breathing. His skin looked as transparent and yellowed as old parchment; his hair was thin and ragged across his forehead and a nurse smoothed it for him. His eyes bulged under their lids; his veins stuck out.

I was sickened at the sight of this old man ravaged with cancer, dying. He wouldn't live to see another sunrise. There now lay before us a small, mummified version of the hearty grandfather I had grown up with. Sure, he had been a womanizer, feisty, hard-drinking, hard-swearing. He was a hopelessly addicted gambler; he never could hold a steady job for all his boozing. He had married and unmarried several times - no decent woman could put up with his bull crap. But he was my grandfather – the only one I had ever known – and I loved him in spite of it all.

I took Allie's hand and led her out; we were both too stunned to speak, so we just held each other quietly out in the hall until Julia and Bud joined us. I felt a sudden anger at Bud for dragging us home just to witness this. Why? To hell with the family-at-all-costs thing!

It had been awful to witness; worse than awful. It was a total disaster. With a minimum of protesting back at the Beverly Hills Hilton, Allie had agreed to give up her last night of the convention to please Bud. Then we had nearly gotten ourselves killed avoiding a stupid mother skunk and her babies. But what the hell was that all about - what we just witnessed in there?

They had come out quietly. Julia, seeming smaller than I remembered, her head down, slowly shaking her gorgeous brown curls, while Bud just looked straight ahead, his shoulders back, jaw set, head high, like the good soldier he had always been.

Grandfather, heavily doped up, quietly passed to the other side late that evening, joining Hugo and hosts of others. Would Mrs. Karnekis be next?

We had a simple memorial service attended only by our immediate family – Bud, Julia, Allie and me – and Mr. Ulrich, the mortician, and his assistant, after which grandfather was cremated. His request.

After the short service we had a private family dinner at Mama's Place - no wake, no guests invited for ham, no potato casseroles, no green Jello with shredded carrots or pineapple back at the church or someone's house. Julia was quiet; Bud tried to be lively and engage us in conversation. Allie fidgeted with her meal, poking at her lo mein until it got cold. I finally tried to break the ice; the five-ton elephant in the room was Grandfather's tirade about Julia in his last hours of pain-induced hysteria.

"So, what was that all about the other day, when Grandfather was screaming all that crap at Mom?" I asked, leaving out the French whore part. Bud looked at Julia, who could only look down at her food getting cold and greasy, pushing it around aimlessly with her bamboo chopsticks. The bamboo reminded me of Jackie.

"Not now, Alex," Bud started. "Right this moment we're feeling pain, a lot of sorrow. Someday, when the situation is more conducive, we'll tell both of you. But for now, let's just drop it - pretend it was the drug-induced ravings of a sick old man dying of cancer, okay?"

I looked at Allie, who was staring back and forth between Julia and Bud, sensing something needed to be said, but not knowing how to find the words. I shook my head, and she excused herself, said she needed to go to the bathroom. I took that as my cue to exit also, and excused myself.

"I really need to get to a job interview… I've applied to work at the Lucky Store. Can I be excused?" I felt like a crud leaving them sitting there like that, but what else was there to talk about? Bud said "We'll tell you later."

* * * * *

Whenever I'm angry or frustrated or depressed, there are three things that can pull me out of it. I play the piano, something really fast or loud, or a hard piece. Or I play tennis, aggressively. Or maybe I'll sit down and write something. I'll write and write until whatever's bothering me is all worked out of my system.

It was past midnight and I sat at my little desk trying to work out my anger and depression on my portable typewriter when I heard a soft tapping on my door. It had to be Mom. Bud knocks loudly and Allie never knocks. We just walk into each other's room any time we want. "Come," I said.

Mom walked in and stood behind me. I was still close to tears, so didn't dare turn around because I knew if I saw the hurt in her eyes I would lose it completely. I hunched over my typewriter and she gently placed a hand on each of my shoulders.

"Let me tell you a story," she began. I straightened up. "Once upon a time, there was a little French girl. She was born in a little village in France, in the Pyrenees, a place called Ville du Sapin, close to Spain. It was a lovely little town. A pretty little river ran down from the mountains over white granite boulders and through our village. There were trout in the river, and lovely watercress grew in the shady banks of the river that the little girl liked to pick and eat. She was raised in a close, loving family. Her name was Juliette LaForte. Her father was a *maquis*, a mountain man, a forester. He worked and lived in the forests nearby and knew all the trails over the mountains into Spain. When the war with the Germans became a reality, he went to work for the Resistance and helped many people escape to freedom over the mountains. He was a very brave man, her Papa.

"When the war finally came to France, she was nineteen and went to live with her older sister in Paris, where she met a handsome young man, an American. He was working under cover in espionage for the OSS and had false identity papers. He worked in a café in the Rue de la Huchette with the girl. Before the war it was a jazz club at night, but the Germans had very strict rules about the music that could be played there. They would not allow any music to be played that they called *American swartzer* music. The girl was a waitress.

"The young American's name was Bud, and she fell in love with him, which was more dangerous for him than for her. For her, it was a good thing because the German soldiers would force many young girls like her to become their *putins*, their prostitutes. So she wore no makeup and cut her hair short and shaggy. She wore outlandish eyeglasses and frumpy clothes, anything to make her look ugly. She refused to bathe for days at a time and wore no fragrance. That, mixed with the garlic and other kitchen smells, made her even more unattractive, she hoped. But if a soldier gets drunk enough, any girl becomes a target of his lust. So she began to wear padding under her dress to look like she was pregnant.

"The little French girl and the American boy were secretly married and then she really did become pregnant with you and your sister. We were so happy. But your father was worried and got permission from his military bosses to move us out of the country.

"We were smuggled out of Paris on a river boat up the Seine. Then the Resistance helped us back to my village where my Papa took over and guided us through the mountains into Spain. It took us many hard days sleeping in safe caves or huts by day and moving only at night, and

I was so heavy and close to your time to be born, and it was so dangerous because of the many German mountain patrols. We finally made it to Spain where you two were born in a monastery."

I turned and looked at her in surprise. "Then…? Then what happened? How did you…we… get to America?"

"From Spain we made our way into Portugal, found passage on a freighter to Liverpool, and then flew to America on a military transport."

"Hooray for the red, white and blue!" I said, afraid that she took it as sarcasm.

"It's a wonderful country and we are lucky to live here. You don't know what it's like to live under the rule of gangsters like the Nazis, and I hope you never do."

Chastened, I apologized. Then I asked the question everyone had been avoiding: "What was all that stuff Bud's father, Grandpa, said about you in the hospital?" I feared to know the real truth; I feared that the stuff she had just told me how she avoided being forced into prostitution and all that was just a story she made up. There seemed to be so much mystery, so much intrigue, what was the truth? I also desperately hoped that what my grandfather had said was just the deranged ravings of a sick, dying man.

"Your grandfather was a rough type, a most uncouth man." I shifted uncomfortably to hear the anger in her voice. "I think you know that much is true," she insisted, her chin sticking out defiantly. Much as I wanted to honor the dead man, I nodded my agreement.

"I believe he had the notion that all French girls were loose and easy. When we first arrived back here, we all lived with him for a short while until we could find our own place. One day, when your father was gone looking for work, your grandfather tried to force himself on me and I fought back. I told Bud about it when he got back that afternoon, and he had a loud, angry talk with his father – lots of shouting, threats, and cursing. Bud said if he ever laid a finger on me or you children, he would be the fifth man in his life Bud would kill. A day later, we moved out." A long silence settled on us, while I absorbed all this.

"So let me get this straight," I finally deadpanned. "Your name really is not Peters and you don't come from Louisiana?"

We both alternately laughed and cried as we hugged.

"Do we still call you Julia, or do you prefer Juliette?" I whispered in her ear.

" *Mom* would be nice," she whispered back.

CHAPTER TWENTY-THREE

Chicago, July 27, 1960: *Vice President Richard M. Nixon is nominated by the Republican convention for the office of President. In his acceptance speech, Nixon made a prediction: "Just as in 1952 and 1956, millions of Democrats will join us, not because they are deserting their party but because their party deserted them at Los Angeles two weeks ago..."*

Mr. Nixon pledged to visit all 50 states during his campaign for the presidency.

Carla patiently worked with me as I struggled to learn the guitar. "It hurts my fingers," I complained.

"You have to build up calluses on the pads of your fingertips," she said.

"But I don't want calluses," I said back. "I want to keep my fingers soft and sensitive for my piano playing," I argued. "Why don't you and Gary play guitar, Freddie can play bass, and I'll do something on rhythm," I suggested. Then she told me to wait while she left to fetch something. She came back with a smaller guitar, a four-string version she said was a "baritone uke or a tenor guitar, whichever." The strings were gut instead of wire and were a lot easier on my fingertips. I could now concentrate on the music and ignore my tender fingers.

We had our first gig on a Saturday night at a Mormon youth party. Gary insisted we wear our red blazers. "What about Freddie and Carla?" I argued. "What will they wear?" We gave up on the blazers; it was simply too hot anyway.

I think the Mormon kids enjoyed listening to us. Carla insisted on singing her tune about the seducing man-fish. Afterwards, when we were packing up our stuff, some young guy came up to her and started speaking Portuguese. Carla started to blush bright pink and got all flustered. I was no help to her; I only know a few phrases in that language. Freddie, seeing something was wrong, came over and asked in Portuguese what was going on?

It turns out the guy had just come back from a Mormon mission to Brazil and was now fluent in Portuguese. He understood the words in her song and was letting her know that he knew. He had heard the story about the seducing man-fish while he was on his mission in Bahia. He promised Carla that he was the only one who knew what she had been singing and said he wouldn't tell anyone else. She blushed again and whispered, "Obrigada, obrigada."

"De nada," he smugly replied, as he swaggered off to join his friends.

* * * * *

"Hello, Alex. This is Donna Hostetter, secretary at the high school. I have a letter here for you. Do you think you could drop by sometime soon to pick it up?"

A letter? "Who's it from?" I asked.

"Doesn't say, but the return address is in Florida. I'll have some cookies waiting for you if you come by tomorrow morning," she tempted me sweetly.

I didn't need the offer of cookies; the mysterious letter was enough to motivate me to stop by. But the fresh-baked chocolate chip cookies with walnuts didn't hurt either. I sort of missed my little early-morning chats with Mrs. Hostetter in the bookstore before classes started.

As it was, I could swing by the high school office on my way over to Yuba College. I had an appointment with the Registrar to review what I needed to complete for acceptance. I had decided that, no matter what else – Allie's political work, dating, part-time job, playing with my combo – I needed to get back in school.

"Did I ever tell you about how I was born and raised in a tiny little town in the west desert of Utah?" she asked, as I nibbled on my second cookie.

"No, Mrs. Hostetter, you never did. I really don't know much about your personal life."

"Oh, there's not a lot to tell. My father owned a hotel, a sort of guest house right next to the railroad station in this little town named Deseret. That means 'honey bee.' When my sister and I were barely in our teens he bought us a player piano and about a hundred and fifty rolls of tunes with it. My favorite song was *La Golondrina.* That's Spanish for 'the swallow', you know, the little birds that return every year to Capistrano," I acknowledged that I did know, as she hummed part of the tune, her eyes closed in sweet memories. She had a pretty voice.

"When the War broke out, my sister left to live in Alameda, where she got a job in an aircraft factory. I joined her the next year and that's where I met my future husband, Frank, Mr. Hostetter. He was a test pilot for the factory – Lockheed. My sister got me a job as a junior bookkeeper at the plant. I learned how to operate a huge mechanical bookkeeping machine; it had about a hundred keys, but I learned fast. She also introduced me to Frank through one of his friends she was dating at the time."

I took another cookie. "After our first date Frank took me up for a ride over the Bay Area in one of the test planes, my first airplane ride, and I knew then I wanted to marry him. He was so handsome, with his wavy hair and his rakish moustache. All the pilots wore a moustache in those days, you see." I nodded; she wasn't finished with her story yet, so I settled in and reached for my third cookie.

"Well, we were soon married, and guess where we went for our honeymoon? You'll never guess, so I'll just tell you: Frank had to go back to Buffalo, New York, to bring back a new airplane made by the Fairchild Company, so he took me with him to be his navigator. We rode the train to Buffalo and flew that darn plane cross country, all the way back to Alameda.

"We'd fly all day, following major highways, stopping only when we needed fuel or for the night. It was an open-cockpit thing with two seats, one behind the other, Frank in the front and me in the rear. He got me a leather flight suit, the smallest he could find, and I'm glad he did, because it's darn cold flying in an open cockpit airplane. It had a sheepskin lining.

We slept under the wing on the ground.

"A couple of times Frank took some of the locals in those little towns for rides when we'd stop for fuel."

She paused and stared off in the distant past; I broke in. "Mrs. Hostetter, I don't mean to be rude, but I sort of have to go." She kept on staring, a faraway look in her eyes, lost in the glorious past.

She came back to her narrative: "I'll never forget how Frank decided we should take a little detour over the Grand Canyon and we dropped down so low you could see the wild burros and it was so beautiful and that darn song *La Golondrina* kept running through my head, and then I understood that I was probably seeing the Grand Canyon the same way the swallows did when they flew over it."

"Thanks for the cookies." I started to leave.

"Here, take a few for the road." She wrapped several in a paper napkin, thrust them towards me. "Frank knew Amelia Earhart, you know…"

I stopped. "I didn't know." She now had my interest. This was a story; the registrar could wait.

"She wasn't a very good pilot, Frank would say. One time, when she was practicing take offs and landings at Alameda, she landed way short of the runway in marshy ground and it took two tractors and quite a few men, including Frank, to pull her plane out. Caused a lot of damage to the landing gear and whatnot. So we weren't too surprised when she got lost on her famous last trip. She was mostly in the flying business as a publicity stunt for her company, you know… Well, I've chattered too long. You get on your way. Thanks for visiting with me again - always nice to see you, Alex."

As almost an afterthought, I inquired about her daughter Sally, what she was doing for the summer, where was she planning on going to school in the fall.

"Sally's fine. She teaches piano lessons…"

"I didn't even know she played piano," I interrupted.

"Oh, yes, she's very good, too. But she never gets asked to play in church because Janeen Brown's mother always leans on our bishop to let *her* play and Sally never gets to share in the glory, not that we should seek after glory. Still, it sort of brings out the mother bear in me."

Utah. Church. Bishop. Janeen Brown was a Mormon. Was Sally, too? "I didn't know you were a Mormon."

"Oh, yes, we are. You see, there are a lot of things you'd learn if you only asked… Sally's going to Yuba this fall. Have a nice day, Alex."

Well, that explained a lot: Sally had given a prayer at our baccalaureate services a couple of days before graduation. You don't learn to pray from reading books; you either learn prayers at church or in your home.

* * * * *

I sat in the now nearly-deserted high school parking lot and tore open the envelope. The letter was from Miss Jensdatter. Or should I now say: Mrs. Taylor Randolph!

"Dear Alex,

I'm sorry I left so abruptly, but as you have probably learned by now, we had a true elopement, and the fewer people involved, the better for us to carry out our plans.

I am truly happy, married to a wonderful man who literally (in true Jane Austen fashion) swept me off my feet. He's a major in the Air Force (so handsome in his uniform), a Lutheran chaplain, and soon to be promoted to Lt. Colonel. We met through a church group when I first arrived in YC; I was very lonely with no friends, but we met and soon became fast friends. We had been secretly seeing each other throughout most of the past year and finally admitted to each other we were in love and asked what were we going to do about it?

Taylor, my husband, was due for a transfer in June anyway, so we got married in South Lake Tahoe by an old friend of mine and honeymooned our way across the country; we stopped in just about every National Park on the map: Bryce and Zion in Utah; Rocky Mountain National Park in Colorado; The Ozarks in Missouri; the Great Smoky Mountains one in Tennessee (I think that's the name -, can't remember for sure); the Everglades, and so on, until we settled here at Homestead AFB in Florida. Florida reminds me a lot of the years I spent working for Standard Oil in Venezuela.

160

Please write and keep me posted on your doings; I do hope you're still writing.

All the best,

L. Randolph, nee' Jensdatter

P.S. Before I had a chance to post this, my morning mail came, and with it a bundle of recent issues of the Appeal-Democrat. As poor an excuse for a daily paper as it is, I subscribed for six months just to keep up on the old hometown and was pleasantly surprised to read your columns about the recent convention. Congratulations, good work, keep it up! L.R.

* * * * *

The Registrar at Yuba said yes, I would have to take the college placement exam in August to confirm my qualification for English, math, science, and history. Otherwise, my transcript looked good and I was ready to sign up for classes. The fall schedule had a new instructor, a certain H. Hill, teaching English 105-American Lit., the AP class. I wondered if this could be the same H. Hill, Jensdatter's friend from Berkeley, I met at the Robinson Jeffers seminar at UC-Davis? Was it possible? We'd see.

I stopped by the Appeal-Democrat offices to fill out paperwork for expenses and pick up my compensation for the convention work last week. I signed and turned in the voucher, and the payroll clerk handed me a brown envelope with cash in it; I counted it out and signed a receipt for five hundred plus expenses. "Could I talk with Mr. Tate?" I asked

"You'll have to see his secretary."

The secretary said Roscoe was busy but she'd take my number and perhaps he'd call me later. I was hoping to nail down a permanent job writing part-time for the paper; I felt I had earned a shot at it and Roscoe had sort of promised, but obviously it would have to wait until the great man called me back.

* * * * *

Jim Arnoldy puffed on a stump of a cigar as he scanned my job application, alternately scowling and smiling at what he saw. He set the paper aside and looked at me with gray eyes set in deep sockets under heavy dark brows. "Have you ever had any retail sales experience?" he asked, a strange question, I thought.

"I'm not sure what you mean, sir," I honestly replied.

"Have you ever sold anything to customers who walk in off the street and buy things? At Lucky Stores we sell groceries, and the public comes in and buys them. The clerks and bag boys are the main contact our customers have with our store. The way you interact with the customer, the way you treat her, that's very important, and it leaves an impression with them, either favorable, or unfavorable, depending on how you treated them here in the store. Follow…?"

I nodded – it wasn't rocket science; I could do this stuff. I mean, how hard is it to bag groceries, anyway?

"We have a short training program that I personally teach. We hire you on a 30-day trial basis and during that period you get trained and we evaluate your progress weekly. What hours can you work? Can you work late nights and Sundays? I especially need Sunday part-timers. The Mormon kids who work for me won't work Sundays, which I try my best to honor and respect. I'm religious, but, by darn, sometimes I have no choice but to work Sundays. I'm the manager, and everything that goes on here falls on my shoulders, even if things go wrong on a Sunday!" He chuckled, snuffed out the stub and fired up a fresh cigar.

Jim took me into the back of the store to show where I would have to spend some time on every shift, sorting empty returned soda bottles; there was a place to hang my jacket and put on the Kelly green apron and bow tie that, along with a clean, white shirt, was part of the uniform. He expected clean nails, fresh breath, shined shoes, trim hair cuts. No eating in front of customers; no talking about our personal lives in front of customers; and NO TIPS!

I put on the green apron and bow tie, feeling kind of dorky, but relieved that I now had a real job. After my 30-day trial I would be required to join the retail clerks' union, pay dues, and vote on union stuff. But belonging to the union also meant we got a much higher pay than the other part-time jobs around town that only paid minimum wage. I had to admit I had a good deal going here.

Mr. Arnoldy had a table set up in back with a bunch of stuff off the shelves and stacks of various sizes of brown paper bags with the store logo printed in green on them. He showed me a chart, which explained what each bag was and what it was used for, how much stuff it would hold, then proceeded to show me the proper way (meaning the Jim Arnoldy way) of bagging groceries. He did it a couple of times, slowly at first, making it look so very easy, then let me try. I fumbled around, tearing the big bag on my first try.

"Alex, Alex, relax. Take your time. There's no hurry back here while you're learning. When you finally get up front on the line, things will speed up but you'll get the hang of it. I have confidence you'll be a fine worker. I went to high school with your dad, by the way."

"Were you part of the infamous basketball team?" I asked.

He puffed on the omnipresent cigar, coughed, laughed, and said, "No, I was a year behind, so I was part of the scrub team that had to step in and try to salvage the season after he and the others got the boot, But he's a great guy and I have a lot of respect for him. Funny that you're not working for him, but I think I understand why you're not. I've noticed that fathers and sons don't always make for good working partners."

* * * * *

July just sort of melted away in the Valley heat, and August slowly oozed in like warm salt water taffy. The aroma of ripening tomatoes, melons, peaches, and prunes filled the air. The heat was oppressive, but I didn't mind: I was working in air conditioning while most of my buddies were out in the fields or orchards, or working at the Wilbur Ranch in the prune dehydrators, sweating their butts off.

A lot of the girls were sweating and slaving too, at the Del Monte cannery, steam and water everywhere, slopping around in big rubber aprons, boots, and gloves and up to their waists in tomatoes or peaches – minimum wage jobs. Sure, the guys had great tans and bulky muscles, but I was making almost twice the money in the same comfort as an air-conditioned office.

Jack Kennedy also had his summer doldrums: he was stuck in Washington while Congress fiddled around with a lot of meaningless legislation, hearings, making a show of earning their paychecks while appearing to tend to the nation's business. He chafed, itching to hit the

163

campaign trail. But everyone in politics knows that no real campaigning gets done until after Labor Day, anyway. So Allie says.

All during the last of July and into August, Allie also stewed and brooded, waiting for something to start happening so she could spring into action. Personally I was glad for the break from politics for a couple of months – I had plans to spend time with Jackie, take guitar lessons from Carla Gomes. I planned to mess around with Gary and his new folk singing gig. I also needed to take the college entrance exams at Yuba.

At the end of my 30-day trial as a grocery bagger, Jim Arnoldy came to me and asked if I'd mind being promoted to the position of apprentice cashier. Two of his other apprentice cashiers had decided to go back to school, one going to Sac State and the other transferring up to Chico State; they could only work weekends… maybe.

Mind? Why would I mind? I was ecstatic – my paycheck almost doubled from a buck twenty-five an hour! "What do I have to do?" I asked. He turned me over to his head cashier, a woman named Mavis, who would be in charge of my training. Again, I would be on another 30-day trial, but I didn't mind.

Mavis had been a grocery checker going on twenty years and seemed to know everything about the grocery business; she also seemed to know all the customers by name and always took a little time to be friendly with them. She was our union shop steward and was supposed to represent all the rest of us in discussions with management, comprised solely of Mr. Arnoldy and his assistant manager, Archie.

Mavis was very punctual about taking breaks and returning from them on time. She was a heavy smoker but only on her breaks, which I took with her while I was in training. She showed me a coin box she kept in her locker.

"This is my sin box," she said. I must have looked perplexed, so she explained, "I have a daughter, and she tried to get me to quit smoking. She knew it was bad for me. I couldn't quit, so we made a deal: every time I buy a pack of Salems, I put the equal amount of money the smokes cost into this coin box for her college education someday. You can't believe how expensive this habit is! Don't ever take up the weed, Alex." I made a promise to myself I wouldn't; I didn't need her preaching to make up my mind on that.

Mavis trained me well. She ended by reminding me that we were never to ring up any purchases for ourselves; we had to get someone else to ring it for us. Company policy. She told me that especially included Archie and his secret purchases of whiskey when he closed up the store and I might happen to be on the same late-night shift. "You'll have to ring up Archie's secret booze that he buys. His wife is not supposed to know he's a closet drinker! If I was married to that woman, I'd probably drink, too," she laughed.

CHAPTER TWENTY-FOUR

One of my first customers to come through the check out line was Jackie with a girl friend of hers that I didn't know. I also didn't know how she'd heard I was now a checkout clerk. They were buying stuff for some church youth social planned that night at Parks Bar up on the Yuba River. She invited me to go with her. "I don't know..." I said.

I'm not much on religion and wasn't sure how I would fit in with a bunch of fanatical church kids sitting around a campfire praying and singing churchy songs. If all they sang were the usual camp songs like "Kumbaya" and "Michael Row the Boat Ashore" I would probably be okay. The main thing would be I'd get to spend some time with Jackie; I had been so wrapped up in my Lucky Store training that I had ignored her. I think she could tell I felt bad that we hadn't spent any time together since that day at Lake Ellis.

"Aw, come on," she teased, "it will be lots of fun; you'll like it. I promise we won't try to baptize you or anything like that." I agreed to pick her up about seven o'clock after I got off work and showered.

When I got to Jackie, I said hello to Pete and Mrs. Presser. Jackie was wearing blue jeans and a pink long-sleeved button down shirt, with rope sandals; she threw a sweater over her shoulders in case it got cold on the river. She scooted over and cuddled close to me as soon as we were out of sight of her folks, and planted a sweet little peck on my cheek. "What was that for?" I asked, giddy at her closeness. She smelled like Coppertone instead of Chanel No. 5, and I liked the change. It made me think of tanned curves – hers – in a skinny, lime green, two-piece bathing suit by a private pool, perspiration beading up on her soft golden skin. My throat closed up and I had a hard time swallowing. I switched to another image of Jackie, dressed in a heavy winter coat.

"That's because I like you a lot and I've missed you." She put an arm through my right one, giving me another pleasant tingle, but it became a little harder to drive, so I switched the wheel to my left hand and slipped my right hand into hers, small and soft. She squeezed an affirmation of her attraction to me. "What were you thinking just then?" she asked.

"You'd blush if I told you honestly," I said.

"You're bad!" she chirped.

"Seriously? I was thinking how great it would be if we could just wave to your friends at Parks Bar as we crossed the river, and we'd just kept driving all the way to South Lake Tahoe where we could find a justice of the peace and…" She glowed in the burgeoning twilight.

Then a wave of guilt washed over me; I need badly to unload it. Now. I knew this romance was not going to go anywhere and I knew why. I felt like Huck Finn when he had tried to pray: I was living a lie with Jackie and we both needed to face the truth. I pulled off the road into the elementary school parking lot in Hallwood, killed the engine and faced her. "Why are we stopping?" she asked.

"We need to talk," I said. She frowned; I sensed she's afraid of serious talk at our young age. It scares me a little, too. I was thinking of the panic thoughts I had when I was alone with her in that hotel room in San Francisco.

"So, talk." She waited. I took a deep breath, took both her hands in mine and faced her full on.

"Jackie, I like you a lot, more than I've ever liked any girl. I haven't dated a lot of girls, so I don't have that much experience. But in a few weeks I'll be starting college and I don't really know yet what I want to do, what I want to become." She nodded, her dark eyes serious, fitting my present mood. "I think I should date some of the girls I meet in college, you know, just date a lot of different people and have a lot of fun before I ever start to settle down." She faced me, her chin firm, eyes clear and steady, looking into mine, waiting.

"You still have another year of high school and if we were going steady, I'd be cheating you out of the fun you should be having before you graduate and your crowd scatters to the wind."

I paused to let this sink in and continued: "Then there's the religion thing. You're religious and I'm not. You'd naturally want me to get serious about your church, and I'm not interested. I don't think I could honestly ever offer you the hope of my being interested. Maybe some day in the future I'll believe… You understand what I'm saying, how I feel?"

She nodded, leaned up and kissed my forehead. "I'm okay with everything you just said," she said gaily, much to my relief. I slowly let out the breath I'd been holding back. "Let's just go to this party and try to have a good time. If anybody tries to corner you into a discussion on religion I'll whack them with a piece of firewood or something."

We roasted hot dogs on willow sticks, ate macaroni salad and potato chips and olives and pickles and watermelon dripping wet from the cold river; we drank gallons of A&W root beer. We hand-cranked ice cream and made S'mores with our willow sticks over the campfire. Someone brought out a ukulele and began plunking chords while we sang some church songs like "Amazing Grace" and "Just a Closer Walk With Thee."

Then somebody else got up and suggested they should all share their feelings about each other, their friendship, and their love for Jesus. It's funny, but I didn't feel the least bit creeped out when they all got up one-by-one and "gave testimony," as Jackie whispered to me what they were doing. Jackie refrained from standing herself, though I knew if I weren't there she probably would've given testimony with the rest of them.

We finally closed the evening by singing "Kumbaya" and "Michael Row the Boat Ashore" and someone stood up and thanked God for the nice time we'd all had under "this big, brightly-lit, starry sky you made for us to enjoy together in our love for thy son, Jesus." And then everyone had to hug each other several times and tell each other how much they were loved and appreciated. Including me. I jumped right in and hugged with the best of them. Jackie and I didn't talk much driving home; I felt good and clean inside and wished this night and what I was feeling could last.

As I said good night to Jackie on her door step, I held her close and we kissed for what we both knew would be the last time as a giant Luna moth batted around the porch light.

I hoped Jackie and I and our families would always be good friends.

CHAPTER TWENTY- FIVE

"Down the way where the nights are gay,
And the sun shines daily on the mountaintops.
I made a trip on a sailing ship and when I reached
Jamaica, I made a stop.
But, I'm sad to say, I'm on my way,
Won't be back for many a day..."
— Harry Belafonte, "Jamaica Farewell"

Jack Armstrong called to see if I was interested in playing in a pickup band he was putting together for a Portuguese picnic gig over in Sutter the next Sunday. I told him I'd have to check my schedule at the store and get back to him. "Can Freddie and Carla Gomes play with us?" I asked hopefully. He said sure, that would be all right. I didn't tell Jack I was planning to drag Gary Kinnersly along to let him maybe sing a couple folk tunes in his ridiculous red blazer.

Allison found out and saw it as a keen opportunity to tag along and pass out Kennedy campaign brochures, so I said, "Sure, what's one more warm body in the back seat?" I figured we'd have to strap Freddie's bass into the trunk somehow so we could make room for Allie. Gary and Carla could hold their guitar cases on their laps.

Because there are a lot of Portuguese farmers in our area, we musicians get frequently to play for their picnics in the summer. The day starts out with a local parade some time before noon, usually on the one main street of these little farming towns around the valley. The parade starts at the local Catholic church, with the priest in his robes leading the procession, chanting and waving incense. He's followed by a gaggle of choir boys in their red robes with white lace, and after them comes a float with a statue of Our Lady of Fatima, their patron saint.

We – the band – follow somewhere in the middle of the parade on a flatbed truck that Jack always borrows from some farmer friend; we play Sousa marches while the parade moves to some local park. Then there's always the local high school band – what's left of them during the summer – with their majorettes in spangles tossing their batons; and local politicians riding in spanking new convertibles carrying signs that say they were loaned by the local car dealer. There are lots of American and Portuguese flags. Fortunately, for obvious reasons, they always put the sheriff's mounted posse at the very end of the parade.

We finally got to the park where we backed the truck under some big trees and set up to play a concert, while Allie lost no time circulating through the crowd, handing out Kennedy pamphlets. The hometown folks shuffled into long lines to be fed by the cooks who have been at it for days, roasting big slabs of beef in huge pans with lots of black pepper, garlic and mint. You could smell the delicious odors for two blocks before we got to the park. They sliced off big chunks of the tender meat, spooned the juices –called *sopa* – over meat and big chunks of bread torn French loaves, added a big serving of fresh potato salad, and there you have your picnic. You could also have a helping of chick peas, too, if you want. I usually skip those. We are invited to eat with the locals after we've played for an hour or so.

Our so-called concert always has to start out with a rendition of the Portuguese national anthem, a really catchy tune; I don't know where Jack managed to find the music, but the Portuguese love it: everyone stops eating or serving; the little kids are shushed by their mothers to stop playing on the monkey bars, and, out of respect for the mother country, they all stand, the old men take off their hats and hold them over their hearts. I sneak peeks while I play and sure enough, many of them are openly weeping, tears running off the ends of their big droopy moustaches. When it's finished, everyone claps and cheers, then they go back to what they were doing before.

We got into our concert, doing a repeat of some Sousa marches, mixed in with some other school band arrangements Jack brought along. In between, I persuaded him to let Carla sing a couple numbers in Portuguese, and introduced him to Gary and asked if he could perform a couple of numbers, too, just to let the band rest for a bit. Jack gave me the fish-eye, shook his head, then broke out laughing, all three hundred-fifty pounds of him.

We also mixed in and played a few dance numbers for the teenagers in the crowd, who got out on the open-air concrete slab of the basketball court and danced to Glen Miller's "In the Mood," or slow danced to one of the pop tune arrangements I supplied. The Portuguese girls were pretty in their pedal pushers, swaying their hips, kicking off their sandals; their dark hair swishes down around their shoulders, green eyes flashing with excitement, flirting with the guys. Sometimes jealous fights broke out.

Carla was a hit, as I knew she would be. Freddie and I accompanied her; even Gary in his red blazer, which was way too hot for the weather, picked up the key and softly strummed guitar chords under hers in a kind of counter-melody. How does he know to do that? Our drummer picked up the rhythm and kept a halfway decent bossa nova beat on the tom-tom with us. We hadn't practiced any of this stuff, but it came off okay.

When she finished the first tune, which was of course all in Portuguese, Carla said something else to the crowd into the mike. They must have approved of what she said, because there was applause. Freddie leaned over and translated for me: "She wants to sing that number about the half-man, half fish seducer. I think it's in the key of F." I must have made some kind of reactionary face, because Freddie just shrugged his shoulders, and started out a bossa vamp on his bass. The drum picked it up, as did Gary. I started in with some chords on the ancient piano, and then Carla, in this clear, pure voice, began making love to the mike. It was enchanting and the crowd loved it. Carla bowed and said "Obrigada, obrigada…" several times.

Jack paid us each twenty-five bucks in cash, including Gary, who had wowed them with his imitation of Harry Belafonte singing "Jamaica Farewell," and "Scarlet Ribbons."

* * * * *

It was dark when I pulled *The Elliott Ness* (the name I had decided to give my Olds) into the Gomes' farm yard. We had our windows open to take advantage of the cooling night air; the aroma of ripening peaches hanging heavily from the laden branches was everywhere. With an overriding odor of eau de skunk. "Smells like Frio's been chasing skunks again," Carla said, as both she and Freddie laughed.

As we drove slowly down the dirt road to their farm house between neat rows of peach trees, I asked Freddie if they weren't just about ready to harvest. He said their picking crew of migrants should have arrived today; they'd start picking tomorrow. "See all the ladders stacked and the pallets of peach lugs?" he proudly pointed through the dust cloud. "All ready to go at dawn."

We pulled up in front of the big house; in the headlights we could see Mr. Gomes with a hose, spraying their family dog, a big, friendly Chow named Frio (they say it *FREE*-oo, the Portuguese way). A can of tomato juice, now empty, lay on the ground where Mr. Gomes was kneeling. He'd tried to wash away the skunk smell with the tomato juice.

I should explain here. Mr. Gomes had found Frio as a puppy in an irrigation canal, desperately trying to keep his head above water as he paddled around looking for a place to climb out. He was cold, miserable, and very happy to be rescued. Mr. Gomes brought him home wrapped in his own coat, and although he was now safe and warm, the little guy shivered for an hour. That's why they named him Free-oo.

Besides being huge, Frio had a black tongue and mane like a lion's, the two identifying marks of a Chow. Mr. Gomes gave up trying to restrain the lunging dog, and Frio immediately headed for my car. He walked around, sniffing the tires, lifting his leg to mark each one.

Then, through the settling dust cloud, the headlight beams captured the migrant camp, set slightly back against an irrigation canal bank under a grove of English walnuts and twenty yards beyond the two corrugated tin tractor sheds that sat opposite each other. Unlike most farmers who provided merely a two-holer and a cold-water hydrant for the workers' convenience, Mr. Gomes had built a comfortable bath house of concrete and cinder blocks, complete with flush toilets and hot showers for his workers.

The migrant pickers had already settled in, cooked their dinners over campfires, and were going about final chores before getting to bed early for the next day's work. We unloaded from the car, stretched and scratched Frio's ears – the aroma of skunk still clinging to him – and greeted Mr. and Mrs. Gomes, answering their many questions about the Portuguese picnic: to Carla and Freddie in Portuguese, and to Allie, Gary, and me, in English.

We were suddenly interrupted by a young migrant couple approaching us hesitantly out of the darkness, the young man carrying what looked to be a baby or young child in his arms. Pedro Gabriel said, "Can we help you?"

The young man looked distressed, his shoulders stooped from years of hard work in the fields and too many worldly cares. His dark eyes, hooded under heavy lids, were downcast. His Big Ben coveralls were worn threadbare; he wore no shirt. His bare feet in old shoes scuffled nervously, involuntarily, in the soft earth. He was thin and rawhide tough; his one free bony hand hung limply at his side. His skin, permanently tanned, the Romanesque nose, high cheekbones and coarse black hair which spilled out from under his sweat-stained John Deere cap all had the trademarks which stamped him as a genuine Oklahoma Indian. Maybe just half-blood. What was he, Pawnee, Cherokee, Chickasaw? Maybe Chocktaw…? We'd never know because that question would never be asked.

He stood patiently, stoically, waiting, shifting the small human load to his other arm, causing the baby to stir; it cried out in pain, hacking and rasping with a bad croup.

The young woman at his side, dressed in a faded flower-print dress, barefooted, blond – her hair pulled back and held with a scarf – spoke first: "Sir, we don't aim to be no trouble, but our daughter here, Martha Dawn, well she's sick, and in a really bad way and we don't know what to do. We took her to that big hospital in town and they made us wait outside all day in the heat and wouldn't even see her, and now she's gettin' worst by the minute. I'm afraid if'n we don't get no doctor real soon, well, she jes' might…" her lips quivered, she choked on a sob; she couldn't finish that awful thought, couldn't face the finality of what might happen.

Allie was the first to step forward. "Let me see," she said, as she pulled back the thin, dirty blanket. The child's skin was ghostly white; her eyes glazed, almost lifeless, bulging from their sockets. Her curly brown hair was soaked with perspiration, plastered against her forehead where little blue veins stuck out starkly against that pasty skin. Allie put her hand on the child's forehead and gasped. "She's bad; she's burning up with fever!" The parents nodded.

"What we gonna do…?" the man said.

Allie headed for the front door, asking Mrs. Gomes for a phone book. "You wait here," she ordered. "I'm gonna go call Doc Hamilton. He's a friend; he'll know what to do." She disappeared inside with Mrs. Gomes trailing in her wake.

"But, Leroy Leon, you know we ain't got no money for doctors," the woman cried pathetically to her husband.

"Now you shush, Lola Pearl," the man comforted her. "We'll jes' have to try'n work sumpin'out with him."

"Marianna…? Hi, this is Allison Rodgers, you know – Alex's sister? I'm fine. Actually, we're not too good right now. We have a kind of medical emergency, you might say. Is your father, is Doctor Hamilton at home and can I talk to him, please…?"

From what Allie described over the phone to Dr. Hamilton, he guessed the child had a really bad case of something akin to strep-throat, possibly something worse. He didn't want to guess any further – it could possibly be diptheria – but cautioned Allie not to say anything to the young parents yet. He said we should get the child to the hospital as fast as we could; he'd meet us there and admit little Martha Dawn into emergency.

I asked Allie to ride with me in front; the parents rode in the big back seat with the baby. We drove as fast as I could make The Elliott Ness roll east on Butte House Road. All the way in to town the baby gasped and struggled for each breath, and as she did, the hollow rattling sound in her little chest – almost a death sound – was awful. Lola Pearl sobbed quietly while Leroy Leon stared straight up the road into the searching headlights, his stoic, dark Indian eyes defying doom.

We left the parents and little Martha Dawn in the care of the hospital emergency personnel and drove back to pick up Gary, whom we'd left at the Gomes' farm.

By the time we got back, Doc Hamilton had done his work up and his diagnosis was in fact diptheria. We were all shocked. Who ever heard of a case diptheria in our time? Weren't all little kids vaccinated against that kind of disease now? It didn't seem possible. We didn't have a clue what the disease was like or how contagious it might be. Like the Good Samaritans Bud and Julia had taught us to be, Allie and I were at risk by being so close to the infected baby. Dr. Hamilton said that under the circumstances, he had no choice but to order the entire migrant camp out at the Gomes place quarantined. He'd be sending out the public health nurse within the hour to take care of all the details. He suggested that Allie and I have the nurse give us Diptheria booster shots, just to be safe.

Freddie took me aside and said what a bad place this put his family in: how would they be able to start the harvest in the morning? The peaches had to be picked or the crop would be ruined, and his family would be in big trouble with the bank. I called Allie over and told her the problem. Again, she had the answer: "Leave it to me!"

She got on the phone again and started calling around for help: Jackie and her church group, and they said yes, no problem - what time do we start? Allie called her Mormon and Catholic youth friends, who all gave the same response. She called several of her Young Democrats and they too were counted in the yes column.

Right at midnight, two gray Chevvies - county cars - pulled in and stopped directly in front of the migrant camp. Mrs. Heaton, our school nurse, in a starched gray uniform and hat, got out with her big black medical bag. I went straight to her and asked if she was there with the public health nurse. "I *am* the public health nurse. And who might you be?"

I'm Alex Rodgers, a friend of the Gomes family. My sister and I, well, we've been trying to help out…"

She cut me off, holding up her hand as four other women in nurses' uniforms, tired and nervous, joined her, waiting for orders. "Thanks, but I'm in charge now, and everyone here will follow my orders. Now the first thing we need to do is get this area cordoned off." She waved an unsympathetic hand toward the camp. Her minions advanced on the camp with rolls of plastic ribbon with QUARANTINE! printed on it every two feet. In a few minutes they had the migrant camp sealed off, and Mrs. Heaton and her small army advanced toward the first ratty-looking tent.

A few hours later, Mr. Gomes – all of us – stared open-mouthed when Allie's young army of volunteers, about fifty strong, drove in before dawn and, without saying much, started for the tin shed where the picking buckets were kept. I was happy to see Jackie, gamey-smelling as I was from being up all night. Frio, still reeking of skunk, circled all the newly-arrived cars, greeting the kids with wet muzzle and uplifted paw for a friendly shake. Then he made his rounds of the cars, lifting his leg to mark their tires.

When all of Allie's rescue army had their picking buckets, they gathered in front of the house, waiting, I guess, for instructions. Patsy Ethington's younger brother Harold, spoke up and said that maybe, under the circumstances, they should have a prayer and ask for the Lord's help. Hats came off and heads bowed, while he humbly asked God to help them as they helped their friends and neighbors, the Gomes family in their hour of need. He also asked a special blessing on little Martha Dawn, that she would be healed, and that the entire migrant camp would be blessed through all this adversity. They put their hats back on and fanned out through the orchard to start this season's picking.

As much as I wanted to stay and help, I really had to run home for a shower and clean clothes; I was due at the store at 9 o'clock to start my shift. I dragged in right at nine, and Mavis said I looked like I had "been rode hard and put away wet." That's how I felt, too; I had trouble staying awake, I was asleep on my feet.

I told Mavis about what happened the night before; she listened with more than her usual rapt attention. "Oh, my gosh! How will those people get food to eat if they're quarantined?" I hadn't thought about that problem. "Wait right here," she said. "I'm going to go have a union meeting with Jim. We'll fix this right now!"

I watched her register for several minutes while she talked with Mr. Arnoldy; I could see them through the window of his corner office that sits up high so he has a view of the entire floor. He puffed on his cigar, nodding his head in apparent agreement as Mavis gestured constantly with her hands.

She came back with a big grin. "Pull your car around back; we're going to do the Christian thing for once: we're going to do some grocery shopping for those poor people."

I did as I was told. We loaded boxes into my car clear to the top, including the trunk, with stuff that Mavis took off the shelves, the dairy and meat cases, the produce section: forty loaves of bread, dozens of fresh eggs; ten-pound bags of #1 Russet potatoes from Idaho; bags of yellow onions from Vacaville; bags of carrots and celery from the Salinas Valley. There were gallons and gallons of fresh milk for the kids, butter and cheese, bottled tomato and orange juices. And meat - my gosh, such a lot of meat! Fresh meat: hams, sausage, bacon, and two-pound packages of hamburger.

"Who's paying for all this?" I asked her.

"Don't worry about that. Jim has a discretionary fund for community purposes, and this falls under that category. I think that's all; now get going. I'll bet those people haven't had a decent meal in weeks."

Jim Arnoldy sent me back out to the Gomes Farm with my load of food. "But what about my shift… don't you need me? Who's going to do my work?" I wondered. Jim told me not to worry, and that as far as he was concerned, I was still on the payroll.

Nurse Heaton and crew had settled into the bath house "…just so we'll have hot running water to wash our hands frequently!" She had two big folding tables set up to do her work from. There were two lines of migrants: in the first line a nurse helped them fill out forms while the pickers answered questions about their health, naming the last three locations they had worked in and what were sanitary conditions like there (deplorable, I'd bet), etc. Did any of the other children have similar symptoms to little Martha Dawn? Had any adults been sick? What with?

From there the pickers and their families moved to the second table where Mrs. Heaton and an assistant were administering diphtheria vaccine. Mrs. Heaton and the assistant would first wash their hands using hot water and a generous dollop of shaving cream from a big green Palmolive tube, drying their hands vigorously on a fresh white towel, before they injected the patients. The line moved slowly; babies and children cried loudly while Frio kept vigil outside the bath house, his barking adding to the organized chaos.

I asked her how it was going. She was grim, her jaw set; she shook her head. "These people don't know the meaning of personal hygiene," she whispered. "The kids have Pellagra or scurvy, every one of them. They don't get enough nutrients in their diets. All they eat is starches and fatty foods. Bad, really bad… And lice! My goodness, they're all infested. And then there's that case over there…" She nodded towards a young girl in line who I guessed was only thirteen, and obviously very pregnant. "She's not married; claims she doesn't have a clue about who the father is. She thinks maybe some farmer's son back down south in Lodi, grape country. She says she can't remember for sure. Or maybe she's just protecting someone – family maybe? I don't know and I don't really dare to ask…" Her voice trailed off. She sounded tired. We all were.

I could understand a poor migrant girl easily being seduced by some rich farmer's playboy son; but pregnant by a family member? I had heard rumors of teenage girls in these migrant caravans supposedly getting pregnant by their own brothers, maybe even some by their own fathers. But I couldn't imagine that ever happening in my own community. It sounded so uncivilized, but I guess it happens. I had been lost in my own thoughts, when Mrs. Heaton brought me back to the subject.

"I do know that girl hasn't had any good prenatal care. She hasn't had any milk to drink for weeks or months since she got pregnant. I was depressed about the pregnant girl; I'd heard enough and excused myself to get back to the groceries.

Mrs. Gomes volunteered to help me put the perishables – meat, milk, eggs, veggies – in a huge reefer they kept in one of the big tin-covered shops to keep fresh until needed.

Word of the food delivery traveled fast throughout the camp; migrant workers and their gaggle of kids craned their necks from the lines or strained against the plastic ribbon barrier Mrs. Heaton had set up, just to get a look at all that fresh food. Because the migrants, mostly out of economic necessity, lived on diets of cheap, starchy foods, like Mrs. Heaton was so worried about , fried potatoes, rice, pinto beans, white bread and bologna sandwiches, supplemented by occasional over-ripe fruit they could steal from the farms who employed them – they rarely, if ever, got to eat the foods we casually take for granted in our daily diets. Who would think that eggs or hamburger - Velveeta cheese, even - would make someone else's mouth water in anticipation?

In all the confusion of the past day and a half, I had lost track of Gary. He was with us when we arrived at the Gomes' last night, but what had become of him? Wasn't he needed back at his own farm to help milk cows? I asked Mrs. Gomes and she said he was somewhere out in the orchards helping with the peach harvest. What a guy!

As I got into my car to leave, Mrs. Gomes put her hand on my arm and sincerely thanked me, us for all we were doing. "I have never seen such kindness. Those are total strangers over there." She pointed to the camp. "Why do you want to help them? Why Mr. Jim give them so much free food? And Dr. Hamilton, to help that poor little baby like that on a Sunday when he's supposed to be at home with his wife? Why your sister get her friends to pick the fruit for us. Why…?"

"What if it had been one of *us* who needed help…?" She smiled and nodded.

I slowly drove down the dirt lane to the highway so as not to stir up more dust, taking in all the community activity of fruit picking on both sides of the lane. There were over a hundred acres of fast-ripening peaches that needed picking in less than four days. Allie and her crew of volunteers were doing a great job and seemed to be happy to be there.

I dragged back into the store, unaware of how grungy I must have looked – and smelled. I hadn't bothered to take off my green apron before I loaded the food and stuff into my car, and I certainly hadn't taken it off when I was unloading all the stuff at the Gomes' place. "You look pooped," Jim said to me. "Look, you've done enough; go home and get some sleep." He checked the schedule on the wall of his office, running his finger down the columns until he came to my name. "You're off tomorrow. I'll see you Wednesday at one o'clock." He grinned, puffed on his cigar, blew out a cloud and squinted through it at me. "You're a remarkable kid, Alex. I hope my son grows up to have half the backbone you've got. Now get out of here and get some sleep." He turned back to his paperwork and I left.

As I drove home I felt guilty that I wasn't out there in the orchards picking with Allie and her crew. I felt guilty that I wasn't doing more, that I was actually allowing myself to go home and rest. I heard a police siren and saw the flashing red lights in my rearview mirror, so I pulled over.

"License and registration." The young officer had graduated from high school only two years ahead of me; I knew him but couldn't remember his name now.

"What's the problem, officer…?"

"Step out of the car, sir, slowly, please." I complied. What was this all about? "I need to smell your breath, sir." I exhaled and from the distasteful expression, must have given him a good whiff of moose-breath, as Allie calls morning breath, the kind that, before you freshen up with Crest, comes with its own little green cloud.

"You suspected me of drinking?" I asked.

"Well, you were driving about ten miles an hour, and you were sort of weaving," he said.

"I can explain, officer. I've been up for two days now without any sleep, I'm pooped, and I'm headed home to get some rest. He nodded his understanding.

"What's your address? I'm going to follow you home just to make sure we don't have any accidents. Is that all right?" I nodded. As he got into his cruiser, he said, "Nice apron. I like that green color. It suits you, goes with your eyes!" and laughed at his own lame joke.

CHAPTER TWENTY-SIX

Penicillin: another of the miracles of modern medical science to rise up from the ashes of death and devastation of the recent War; relatively cheap and plentiful, now benefiting millions of mankind.

The migrant workers' quarantine was lifted on Thursday afternoon when Martha Dawn was released from hospital. Everyone was relieved and happy to see her running around at nearly full speed with the other little children; you would never believe she had been knocking on Death's door just a few days earlier. But thanks to the skill of Dr. Hamilton, and the miraculous healing powers of penicillin, there she was. Lola Pearl hovered close by, her eyes ever watchful for any little sign of a relapse. Without penicillin, Martha Dawn would probably have been just another pathetic tiny corpse hastily buried in an unmarked grave next to some farmer's remote ditch bank.

Word spreads quickly in our little town of Yuba City. Softened hearts went out to the plight of the migrants. Many mothers of small children – some of whom had perhaps been daughters of a previous generation of migrants, now lucky to be settled in a home and a community – generously came forward with used clothing and toys that they would otherwise have donated to Goodwill. Father Bevan delivered these offerings to the mothers in the camp, who took them with eyes averted, mumbling whispered words of thanks.

By Thursday night, the work of picking was done. Allie and Gary had stayed the entire time, sleeping with some of the others on couches or the living room floor of the Gomes' home. They all looked whacked but happy. I looked for Freddie, who had been acting as foreman of the field crew as well as liaison to the public health nurses. Freddie was also go-between with the elderly leader of the migrants.

He was an old, stooped patriarch who, because of his age, had sort of been appointed by voice vote as their spokesman. Certainly nobody would campaign for such an office; you didn't seek for it, you were "called." This bent man with shoulders sloped by decades of hunching over field crops, hands gnarled by arthritis, missing most of his teeth, had lived through decades of picking seasons; had seen nothing but hardship and with it, much want. He'd lived with his wife and brood of children - those who survived childhood now all grown and gone with families of their own – through near-starvation, crop pestilence, a few total crop failures. He had witnessed brutal police camp cleansings, had had his own skull cracked a few times while protecting his wife and children and their few worldly possessions. He had seen more than one little child taken by disease (his own, maybe?), hastily, stealthily buried in an unmarked grave in the soft earth in a long-forgotten place somewhere yonder down the long road. Yes, he had seen it all.

Until now: by his own admission, he had never seen such an outpouring of "downright Christian kindness. No sir, I ain't never seed nothin' close to this generous hand out to undeservin' strangers. We just don't know what to say, 'cept thank yew. 'Specially them young boys 'n gals what stepped in to help with the pickin'. Tell them all thank yew and God bless."

Twenty-five years later, the Joads are still among us.

* * * * *

I had almost forgotten the college entrance exams scheduled for Saturday morning at Yuba College. I didn't study for them because I really didn't know what or how to prepare. I looked through my old notes from Jensdatter's class and found a couple pages of notes I had scribbled when she did a unit on how to take exams. Luckily, she had given us some advice on taking the college entrance exams and how to do some

182

preparing.

Of course, her slant was on the English section, and included such tidbits as: Directions. Read the direction on each question <u>carefully</u>, more than once, until you understand what the question is really asking. Stick to the directions; DO NOT answer more or less than what the question is asking.

Outlining. Take time to think about the question and outline your answer, organize your thoughts before you start to write. Think of all you know about the question, jot down your thoughts as they randomly come into your head. Rule of thumb: if the question is a twenty-minute answer and it's maybe 40% of the total grade, then use half your time (10 minutes) planning the answer and half the time (10 minutes) actually writing down the answer. Practical stuff like that.

Her suggestions really paid off when it came time to take the exam Saturday morning. There were about a hundred of us that registered and showed our drivers' licenses as proof that we were who we said we were. They herded us into the Little Theater of the college and passed out the exams, along with a blank Blue Book, at exactly fifteen minutes after nine.

About fifteen minutes into the exams, one girl, obviously under some kind of stress, jumped up, flung her papers at the stage, and ran out shrieking, "I can't stand any more of this f***ing pressure!" But who had time to worry about her?

I sort of breezed through the civics and current events section, first in the test, thanks to my recent first-hand whirl in the world of *realpolitik*. The math and science portion took a little more hard thinking; I was amazed at how fast my brain had let slip the familiar, memorized formulae for radius, circumference, basic physics, square roots, longitude-latitude (which was up and which was across? Oh, crap…).

We took a short lunch break then came back for the literacy part, which would be the afternoon session. I aced the objective part, the true-false, multiple-choice stuff. I was well warmed up for the essay when it came, and which would count for 20% of the entire grade.

We had a list of ten topics we could write about in the Blue Books, or we could choose a subject of our own. I already knew what I was going to write about, and it wasn't on the list of ten.

My title was: "TWENTY-FIVE YEARS LATER – ARE THE JOADS

STILL AMONG US?"

I was relieved and pleased when the proctor gave us the two-minute warning - two minutes left to complete our papers. I gathered my things and handed in my paper. She flipped open the Blue Book, read the title, smiled at me and nodded. She must have taught either English or civics. I'd bet on English; she just had that tweedy-fusty look about her.

I reached the Gomes' Farm just as the gypsy caravan of migrants was loading up, ready to move on up the road to pick pears and apples in Paradise. Then it would be on to Idaho for potatoes, Walla Walla for onions, then who knew what they'd do for the winter.

I searched for Leroy Leon and Lola Pearl. They had just finished loading their meager belongings into their rusty '36 Ford pickup with the ubiquitous (expired) Oklahoma plates. Matha Dawn was nowhere to be found and Lola Pearl was frenzied, fast heading for the cliff of hysteria. After what they'd just been through with their little precious, you'd be too. While she went searching, Leroy Leon approached me shyly.

"I ain't much for words, but you'n yer sister, all the other kids, and that Catholic priest, hell, even them public nurses, why ever body's been so kind. Ain't never see'd nothin' like it. Cain't thank ye enough." He reached out a thorny hand and we shook.

"Well, you're welcome, and good luck. Stop by again next year…" I offered.

"I found her!" Lola Pearl announced, as she came up to us breathlessly, dragging a very sleepy little Martha Dawn by the hand. "She fell asleep in one o' them flush toilet stalls in the bath house."

"She's all right now…?" I asked.

"Yep, she's fine, thank yew. That Doc Hamilton, he sure taken good keer o' her. Cain't thank him enough. He wouldn't take no pay. Wouldn't even talk 'bout it. Said he had some kinda oath to live up to. Cain't unnerstand whut he was talkin' 'bout, kin yew all…?"

I started to tell them it was called the Hippocratic oath, the one all doctors take the day they graduate from medical school, but figured it would only confuse them. "Must have made a promise to himself to help other people like you without charging, is all I can guess. Maybe it's just a Christian thing he wanted to do."

"And then there's yer little sis an' her friends…!" Leroy Leon cut in, his dark eyes on the verge of tears.

"What about her?" I asked, curious.

"They donated all they's wages from pickin' peaches for Mr. Gomes (he pronounced it GO-mez) to us!"

I nodded and smiled. That, plus the five hundred from my convention reporting I had secretly handed to Freddie to add to the pile of cash. I didn't need it; I was the lucky one: I had a home to go to every night, a comfortable bed to lay my head down in, plenty of nice clothes, good food to fill my belly, a fridge I could go to any hour and pour myself a drink of fresh, cold milk.

Toothache? Teeth turning mottled, black, or simply falling out because of our famous rotten-egg-smelling-foul-tasting Yuba City water? No problem, just ring up good old Doc Jenkins; he'll fix it. Belly ache? No problem, just make an appointment with Dr. Hamilton. Good as new.

"That's not all," Lola Pearl interrupted my thoughts. "Some guy, cain't 'member his name, he come and fixed one o' our friend's old Chevvie, fer free!" That must have been one of Bud's shady friends, an ex-con who owed Bud a favor or two, who'd most likely borrowed the parts at night from some junk yard.

Leroy Leon pulled a folded Kennedy brochure from the hip pocket of his Big Bens. "And this...? Tell yer sis we don't vote, don't know any of our kind whut ever has done so. But yew tell her, all we heered 'bout this here young Kennedy feller, If'n I was a votin' man, he'd sure's hell have my vote!"

"I'll tell her and she can pass the word on to Mr. Kennedy. That's a promise," I said.

* * * * *

Jim Arnoldy stepped out of his office and called to me, waving a pink phone message. "Alex, when you have a minute..." It was from Roscoe Tate; I held my breath as I dialed the phone in Jim's office, crossing my fingers behind my back for extra luck.

"Mr. Rodgers...?" Butter wouldn't melt, as they say. Why did I not trust this guy? "Hey, long time no talkie! Listen, I'll cut to the chase. How'd you like to do a weekly column under your own byline? Lots of folks have called and written in saying how much they enjoyed the

reporting you did from the convention last month. It pays fifty a week.
No benefits, we're non-union and I aim to keep it that way. Even if that
Socialist Kennedy does manage to buy the election with his daddy's
money." I decided not to tell him I already belonged to a union, but I
didn't want him calling me *comrade* in that condescending way he has
when dealing with his reporters. I also wondered what he'd say about my
new JFK hair cut; I'd been letting it grow out since the convention. No
more Kingston Trio crew cut for me.

"For now, I want you to focus on your sister, how she's doing locally,
that kind of human interest crap. Those parts you wrote about her at the
convention really lit up our readers, especially the ladies. What's your
answer?"

"How come it's only fifty? You paid me a hundred a day for covering
the convention," I reminded him.

"That was a special situation; I was in a jam and had no choice but to
pay you more. Now things are back to normal. It's fifty, and that's final."

"When do I start?"

* * * * *

Sunday I had the day off from the store. I was invited by the Sargenti
family to a special event, the unveiling and blessing of Sarge's headstone
to mark his grave. Even though the weather was still August sticky and
hot, I wore a navy blazer and tie for the occasion. We gathered at the
gravesite and waited for Father Bevan. When he was a half hour late,
Sarge's mother asked, Becky, his older sister, if she had remembered to
actually invite Father Bevan. "Mom, I did! You think I'm some kind
of idiot what doesn't remember the important things? I mean, this is an
important thing!"

"I was only asking," Mrs. Sargenti said, trying to smooth things.

"Well, I did," Becky snapped. "I called him, and I told him the date
and time. And the place, too." Things were getting more tense by the
minute and nobody seemed to be wanting to do anything except stand
around and bitch at each other. If this is what money does to a family...

"Look," I finally spoke up, breaking the impasse in negotiations, "it's
only a few blocks from here to the church. Do you want me to go find
him? I don't mind; I'll go." I wanted to get away from the tenseness, out

of the heat and the thought of some air blowing in the car window sounded good. I waited, sweating, while they formed a scrum and huddled.

Mr. Sargenti looked at me and nodded. "Go," he said, "there's a good boy." I went. As fast as decorum allowed. "He's such a good boy," Mr. Sargenti said again.

I looked through the opened church everywhere, but no Father Bevan. I heard what sounded like a basketball being dribbled on a court out back; then the sound of a ball bouncing off a rim, voices, laughter. I followed the sounds and found the good friar out back behind the church, his shirt off, playing a game of pickup basketball with a couple of kids from the parish. I waited until it was sides out, and called to him.

"Father?"

He looked at me, wiping sweat from his eyes with the hem of his sweat-soaked tee shirt, grinning, his face scarlet from the heat and exertion. "Yes?"

"The Sargenti's… The blessing of Hugo's head stone…"

He looked at his watch. "Good Lord! I must have forgotten. I'll be right there. Sorry boys, game's over, and I was winning, wouldn't you know it? Luck of the Irish!" He ran through the church grabbing his vestments, dressing on the fly.

I drove him back to the cemetery as fast as I dared push The Elliott Ness. "You have a fine car here, my boy," he praised. I nodded my thanks, concentrating on the road.

"I named it *The Elliott Ness*," I said.

"And I can see why," he responded, smiling, patting the dash again. "Almost reminds me of the car I had when I was your age." He fondly rubbed the walnut glove box lid. "Nope, they don't make them like this any more, do they?" I shook my head..

We pulled to a screeching stop behind the line of fine Sargenti vehicles; Father Bevan straightened his vestments – burgundy for the dead – as he casually strolled over to the grave site, all smiles, rubbing his hands with relish at the chance to serve his fellow beings. "Parce mihi, Domine," he said to nobody in particular.

"What's that?" I asked.

"It's Latin. It means *Lord, give me strength.*"

I nodded as I marveled again at this remarkable man. Only a few years ago he'd been a highly successful investment banker in San Francisco: rich, educated, cultured, married, with a family, a nice home in Sausalito on the water front, with a nice sail boat and all the time in the world to take rich clients out on it. The world was his oyster.

Then he blew it: too much drinking, affairs with secretaries, gambling trips to Reno. "I lost it all and finally hit bottom so that I could find Christ," he explained. He became a priest and asked to be sent to a small community where he could make a difference. He tackled the toughest, nastiest jobs with relish. I could still see him the morning he arrived with the CYO kids at the Gomes' to pick peaches. Dressed in old khakis and combat boots, he jumped out of his old Volkswagen bus, literally rolled up the sleeves of his faded chambray work shirt, scratched at his furry arms, pointed to the peach orchard and shouted, "Give me this mountain!" Some Biblical reference I figured.

A woman's scream shook me out of my reverie. It came from the Sargenti cluster. Mrs. Sargenti had fainted or was making a good imitation of a swoon and had slumped back into her husband's unready arms. He was struggling manfully with the load of flesh, trying to support her. Hugo's older brother Sal helped his dad get the substantial Mrs. Sargenti laid out on the grass. Mr. Sargenti was furiously fanning his wife with her broad-brimmed hat while shouting at her, "Don't die, Stella! Please don't die on me, Stella. Forgive me for my sins against you, Stella!. I've only loved you; all the others didn't mean a thing to me. Honest!"

Everyone had been shouting their opinions on what was needed in the emergency when Papa Sargenti had been spilling his guts out, confessing his sins over the fallen hulk of Stella: Water! Shade! Doctor! Ambulance! Fetch a priest! We have a priest, he's right here! An eery silence began to settle, as they all stared at their father, then each other, eyes wide, straining to hear what would next come out of his – or one of the siblings' – mouths.

What would Holden Caulfield do in this situation? I casually strolled over and peered over Becky's shoulder. Mrs. Sargenti looked okay to me; a little overweight maybe, but far be it from me to criticize. What shee was to have some of her tight clothes loosened up, then have everyone back away to give her air so she could breathe. They were all locked in such a tight cluster around her I doubted if any of them could even breathe either.

Then, out of curiosity, I looked around to see what might have caused this family crisis. Becky had pulled off the purple velvet covering from the head stone; the cloth lay to the side. I looked at the head stone; then looked again. Nothing seemed out of the ordinary; it was just a simple, gray granite stone with the usual: name, dates, sentiments, and so on.

Then I spotted the culprit: a badly misspelled grave stone that said HUGE SARGENT.

Suddenly, Becky turned her grief (surprise at her father's recent confessions? fury?) on her brother Sal, hitting him over the head repeatedly with her purse, screaming, "You stupid bastard! I give you one simple job and you f*** it up! Bastard…! F***ing village idiot, that's you…!" Stuff like that, which no lady should ever say in mixed company.

Sal replied with his own mixture of Italian insults, which I guessed meant something like slut, etc., but with a lot of his own "F*** you, too!" thrown in for good measure. Stuff like that, which no gentleman should ever say in mixed company.

Apparently Becky and Sal had decided to surprise Stella with the headstone. Nice plan from loving kids. Becky had assigned poor feckless Sal the job of ordering the head stone to be cut. One problem: Sal wasn't the brightest kid in his graduating class; anyone could have told her that. She should have known the limits of her own brother's ability to execute such a mission, shouldn't she?

I looked at Father Bevan; he shrugged and went back to doing his priestly work, calming troubled waters as he rolled his scarf into a tight ball and stuffed it into his khaki pants pocket under his surplice. He took Becky by the shoulders, hugging her, patting, whispering soothing words until she nodded, relaxed her tense body and just stood there, limp, overheated, crying.

Mr. Sargenti did something Stella would never have approved of: he lit a big cigar, sat down on the ground next to his still-prone wife, loosened his tie, tears from his recent cleansing confession still freely flowing down his ruddy cheeks, puffing away on his big Corona, while patting Stella's still-unconscious butt. To comfort her, I guess.

I learned from Father Bevan while driving him back to the church that Sal had decided to make a few bucks himself off the head stone transaction. But he made a strategic error: instead of hiring the local head stone cutters – people of honor, traditions of excellence and service, so on and so forth – Sal had contacted a cousin in Sacramento, who was in for a small cut of the *vig*, who had highly recommended a young Sicilian immigrant stone cutter he knew in Live Oak. It seemed like a traditional Italian business transaction. Everyone would be happy: Mom and Dad would be so pleasantly surprised by their kids, Becky would be happy, Sal and his cousin would each pocket a hundred bucks from the transaction, nobody the wiser. Until the innocent-looking purple velvet had been pulled away from the head stone and the misspelling was revealed.

"How long will it take the family to forgive poor dumb Sal?" I asked Father Bevan. "Or their Dad?"

He laughed and scratched at his wooly arm, stroked his chin, then laughed some more. "I'll preach a sermon on forgiveness next Sunday."

"Think it will work?"

"Nope. Won't faze that family. They're Italian; they have long memories and they never forgive sins like Sal's."

"What do you make of what Mr. Sargenti…?" He cut me off with a wave of his hand; I noticed it was small, soft looking, out of proportion with the rest of his bigness.

"I've learned never to set too much store on what people say under extreme stress, such as in battle or family gatherings, like weddings or funerals." He sighed as he heaved his bulk out of the car. "Jesus – and probably his Mother Mary and a host of other saints and angels – will have to work this one out… Some time in the hereafter, would be my guess." He chuckled to himself as he walked away.

I learned that the only thing more dangerous than a Greek wedding is perhaps an Italian family gravestone blessing.

One thing the family gravestone event did for me: At last I felt free from the ghost of Sarge; he was now buried and finally laid to rest.

CHAPTER TWENTY-SEVEN

Friday, September 8, 1960: *Senator Kennedy makes brief stop at the Southern Pacific train depot in Marysville, part of his old-fashioned whistle-stop tour through California's Sacramento and Central Valleys, as he kicks off his campaign to become president of the United States. He faces Californian Richard M. Nixon, Vice President and the Republican nominee, in the general election in November. Our reporter, Alex Rodgers, was on the scene, and files his report.*

I had my lunch hour, one hour, to race over to the train depot in Marysville, try to see John Kennedy make his historic whistle-stop in our community, and hustle back to Lucky Store before I was clocked in late by Jim Arnoldy. Mavis wished me luck as I dashed out the front door and fired up The Elliott Ness. I sped east on Bridge Street, but as I approached Sutter, I sensed trouble. Traffic going over the bridge to Marysville and the train depot was already beginning to back up considerably, so I cut a quick left on Sutter and tried for the 10th Street bridge, figuring I'd double back to the depot by a few back streets on the Marysville side of the river, find a parking spot as near to the depot as I could get, and hoof it the rest of the way. My one consolation was that JFK's train was probably running late anyway.

My plan worked, sort of. There wasn't much traffic on the 10th Street bridge, and as I glanced to the south I could see a long line of cars stalled on the 5th Street bridge; I felt I was in luck. I patted the seat beside me to make sure my pad and pencil were still handy; I wasn't going to miss the chance to write about this historic event as the first story of my new job which I intended to submit to Roscoe Tate that night.

I turned right at the first light after the bridge, and sped south on the back streets as I had planned, running every stop sign. I found a parking spot across from the park, a couple of blocks from the depot, grabbed my stuff, and ran. As I jogged along, dodging in and out of the gathering crowd of curiosity-seekers, gawkers, and secretaries on their lunch breaks hoping to catch a sighting of the handsome senator – now presidential candidate – the thought struck me: I had somehow moved beyond a detached news reporter. I had now actually become another one of his growing army of admirers.

As I remembered some of the phrases from the few Kennedy speeches I'd heard, I realized I could identify with the lofty phrases and goals he had challenged us with. I began to feel a little of the excitement Allie had for this cause – for it had become a cause, a mission – and the adrenaline charged me up, moving me forward with the crowd.

I found a spot as close to the front as I could get, staked my claim and stood my ground. I craned my neck above the crowd, wishing I were tall like Orly, so I could get a better view. I was hoping to catch sight of Allie; if she were closer, I'd cheat my way up to her and watch from that spot. But no Allie to be seen. She had vowed she wasn't going to miss this event for anything.

We heard the train – you always hear it – long before we could see it chuffing into the old Southern Pacific station. That whistle sent a ripple of excitement which began to spread like an epidemic through the crowd. I felt a sense of local pride: that track had originally been laid by my ancestors (or ancestors of my friends), pioneers, Coolies, and gold rush opportunists gone bust barely a century ago. This levee, atop which the track now ran, had originally been laid down to keep the flooding Yuba and Feather Rivers in check to save the town of Marysville. Stanford University, that great school of higher learning, where some of my classmates would be enrolling this very week for college, had been endowed and built thanks to the largess of one of those early railroad men, Leland Stanford.

It was a warm early-September day, the clear sky an autumn blue above, as the train shuddered to a squealing, steamy, smoky stop; the last car, the one he would speak from, draped with patriotic campaign bunting and JFK posters, was conveniently stopped directly in front of us. The brakes let out a hissing fart; the crowd quieted down, other train noises still underlying human and traffic sounds. A dog barked a block away; a few babies in the crowd fussed and mothers shushed as Senator Kennedy stepped out onto the rear platform on the last car and waved to the crowd, to us. He's waving to us! A roar of recognition and approval swelled up to meet him; he grinned, brushed at his rogue forelock of hair, waited a full agonizingly nervous minute while the Kennedy advance men lifted a microphone up to his train platform.

Another advance man vaulted himself over the railing onto the car platform and seized the mike, blowing into it, tapping it, which set the sound system to screeching loudly and with it, the inevitable barking dogs and crying babies. Kennedy just stood awkwardly with one hand shoved in the side pocket of his suit coat, the other brushing at his hair. "Testing-testing…" The sound system worked well enough for most of us to hear Kennedy's set stump speech, and he launched in.

"Thank you. It's a pleasure to be here in… uh, in the town of Marysville…" He was interrupted as someone – I couldn't make out who for all the heads in the crowd limiting my view - the Mayor, perhaps? - handed him a wooden bowl of locally-grown fruit wrapped in yellow cellophane. He thanked them graciously, handed the bowl to an assistant, and continued.

"Uh… Every town we stop in, someone asks why my wife, why uh Mrs. Kennedy, isn't with us. Well, my wife uh has other duties right now… My wife, she… uh, she's going to have a baby." The crowd laughed and cheered.

Someone close to the front called up to him, and asked "What's it gonna be, Jack, a boy or a girl?"

Jack Kennedy leaned down to acknowledge the questioner, pointed and grinned. "She's going to have a boy. It's going to be a boy!"

"How do you know?" the questioner asked back.

Unfazed, enjoying the human warmth of the moment, the questioner, the crowd's response (he had them eating out of his hand, now), Jack responded back, "Uh… because she told me so." The crowd cheered, whistled, stomped their feet and clapped some more. Someone whispered something in Kennedy's ear; Jack checked his wristwatch, and resumed his speech.

"Governor Brown and I have... ah... been riding this train from Portland since yesterday morning, picking up food along the way - grapes, olives, corn, canned salmon, and now it's some... some uh..." He turned to an assistant - or perhaps it was Pat Brown - asking for help, then back to the mike, "... uh, it's some locally-grown uh ..." He turned again for help. " ...uh some almonds." The audience clapped. "And some peaches and prunes. We've been gathering foodstuffs like this all the way down this rich state of California, and I think this just proves what a bountiful country this is. We thank you." [Applause]

Preliminaries over, Kennedy tossed out the meat of his stump speech for Marysville and Yuba City to pounce on: "I campaign for the office of president in a hard and dangerous time in the history of America, and I do so without promising that if elected, I can solve all the world's problems in a first term." He stabbed the air with his hand for effect, "But I can promise I will try my hardest. I'm a Kennedy, and we Kennedys always give it our best! [Applause]

"We must move this country forward again. If you believe we can provide better schools for the children of this community, more assistance for the elderly in our country; if you believe with me that we can do more to develop the resources of this great state and the West; if you believe with me, that we can do more to strengthen the image and prestige of America around the world, then come along with me, with us." Again, with every point he made, Jack stabbed at the air for maximum effect. There was more applause.

"But if you are tired, or you want the status quo and don't want to move forward, then stay with the Republican Party." A few scattered boos greeted him from the crowd. He held up his hands to shush the booing. "I'm reminded of the elephant, you know – the symbol of the Republican Party. Well, when you see elephants in a circus, you see big lumbering, slow-moving animals. Their heads are full of ivory, they have long memories about the glorious past, and they just go around and around in circles, each elephant holding blindly on to the tail of the one in front of him. That's the way they see the world, the way my opponent, Mr. Nixon, sees the world. I want to change that!" The crowd roared and laughed again.

Kennedy grinned broadly, waiting for the noise to subside. Then he moved back to a more serious tone: "But I believe we are ready to move forward toward a New Frontier in the history of this great country. Come with me; I ask for your help. Thank you!"

More applause as the train whistle blew. The crowd began to disperse and I saw a skinny red-headed kid with a flat top standing there, not moving away; he looked familiar. He was at the front of the audience, close to the rear of the car where Kennedy was standing. It was Harold Ethington, Patsy's younger brother; with him was another kid I didn't recognize, sort of pudgy, dark hair, flat top. I wedged my way to where they were standing as quickly as I could;; I felt like a salmon swimming against a strong current. Jack Kennedy was leaning down from his speaking platform, gesturing with one hand, nodding his head, speaking to Harold. The train slowly began to roll forward; I got one photo as Jack Kennedy waved, turned, and disappeared back into the last car, brushing at his hair as he went.

I made a final push against the wall of humanity, broke through and rushed up to Harold and his friend. "Hi, Harold," I panted. He smiled at me. "I saw you talking with Mr. Kennedy." Harold nodded and smiled back at me, obviously proud of his accomplishment. I nodded to his friend, a somewhat familiar face that I had probably seen around school a few times.

"This is my friend Don Fossum," Harold gestured. Then I recognized the round cheeks, the sad, Basset-hound eyes behind the horn rim glasses. They both had been a couple of years behind me in school.

"You were talking with Jack Kennedy. What did you say to him? I saw him saying something back to you. What did he say to you?"

Harold sort of laughed, a triumphant little chuckle, and said, "I said to him, 'Mr. Kennedy, are you really going to do everything you say you'll do?'" Then Harold slipped into a perfect Kennedy accent: "You can, uh, count on it. Everything I said!"

I laughed and said, "Wow, Harold! I'm doing reporting for the Appeal-Democrat now, and I'd like to put that in the paper. Is that okay with you?"

Harold grinned and said yes, it was okay. Lucky kid.

* * * * *

I retraced my circuitous route back to the store in time to meet Jim Arnoldy in the parking lot. Had he also gone to the Kennedy train stop event? "How was it?" he asked me cordially, lighting up a fresh cigar. He crushed the match under his foot.

I was nearly breathless, like I'd just run a 440-yard sprint. "It was great, just like I thought it would be," I said. "I think it's one of those events you'll end up telling your kids about some day."

He nodded his agreement. "Good. Then let's get back to work."

I couldn't wait to get home after work and write my story. Allie was already there, working on more Kennedy stuff, post-train stop. Her room, almost that entire part of our house, had been taken over by the Kennedy campaign. She was again driven to prove to the community that she could in fact live up to her brash pledge, made in the flush of a nomination victory: that she could deliver the vote for Jack Kennedy even though the majority of voters in our congressional district hadn't seen a Democratic presidential majority since FDR.

Her door was closed; she was on the phone, the new extension Bud had allowed her to have installed "for the duration of the campaign only - understand? Agreed?" I knocked on her door and she yelled for me to come in.

I poked my head in. "I looked for you at the train stop." She nodded, listening, her hand over the mouthpiece. "It was great; I'm doing a story on it for the paper," I added. She nodded again, furiously scribbling notes. "I saw Harold Ethington, you know, Patsy's little brother? He actually talked with Kennedy just before his train pulled out." She grinned and waved. I went to my room.

Julia called up as I was changing into jeans and a clean tee shirt. "Alex, do you want dinner down here, or should I bring it up to your room?" I wavered. I enjoyed Bud and Julia, our few dinner meals together. And somehow, when we sat around the table, eating and talking in our relaxed way, her gourmet French cooking always tasted better than when I ate it on the run or in my room or warmed up hours later.

But the lure of the story pulled me towards my desk and the typewriter. I was itching to write the story from the moment I'd left the train station, heading back to work. I wanted skipped my afternoon shift to write the story, but how would I explain my absence to Jim Arnoldy? "Would you mind if I ate it up here while I work? I want to get this story done."

I heard Julia throw some comment back up the stairs at me that sounded like, "Writers…!" But I knew she said it out of pride.

He Doesn't Dress Like Your Father… I began my story. *Senator John F, Kennedy, Democratic candidate for the presidency, made an historic appearance in Marysville today. Speaking from the rear platform of a Southern Pacific Railroad car, as Kennedy's campaign made another brief whistle-stop, one of many as he winds his way down California's great Central Valley, accompanied by California Governor Pat Brown…*etc. as I described the crowd, and quoted a few lines from his stump speech.

I finished up with: *Senator Kennedy, if elected president, may well end up forging an entirely new fashion trend among the men of this country. For eight years we have had before us the gray, but kindly, image of Ike – and before him Truman –both staid and balding, in their double-breasted suits and wide silk-screen printed neckties. Now comes Jack Kennedy: tanned, slim, athletically-fit, his now-trademark shock of, unruly hair, white teeth, with his own unique fashion statement.*

Mr. Kennedy appeared- as he almost always does – in a two-buttoned, single-breasted dark business suit, <u>plain-collared</u> white shirt (no button downs, please!), and a conservative, somewhat narrower striped tie, which has also become part of the Kennedy wardrobe.

Will Jack Kennedy have men tossing away their three-buttoned coats in favor of the new silhouette? Will men be growing out their hair and having it cut to the new "JFK look?" We'll just have to wait and see.

On a local note, Yuba City resident and a junior next year at Yuba City High School, Harold Ethington, was lucky enough to speak with the candidate as his train was leaving the station. He said he asked Mr. Kennedy if he would really do all the things he said he would do if elected. Ethington said the Senator promised him, "You bet I will!"

* * * * *

Classes started at Yuba College the Monday after Kennedy's whistle-stop appearance. My first class in the morning was human physiology. As I pulled the Elliott Ness into the college parking lot, I had a let-down feeling. It started when I saw the high school across the street in a whole new light.

I had never paid much attention to Marysville High School - I mean the physical aspect of it: the location, the layout of the buildings; the actual design and construction of the buildings themselves. Here you had a group of classic-looking red-brick buildings, most two-storey in height, ivy crawling up their outside walls; surrounded by a spacious campus, playing fields, and ample parking in back. Tall oaks, elms, eucalyptus trees adorned the old lady, with beds of flowers in the spring and fall.

Across the street, by stark contrast, was Yuba College. Old, run-down, pasty-yellow war surplus, single-level huts (except for the Little Theatre, which stood somewhat above the rest of the huddle). It was a gaggle of shacks that seemed to expand as enrollment grew and needs arose. Pathetic. I was almost ashamed to be seen on the other side of the street from where Jackie and her friends gathered to learn, play, and socialize. I should have been enrolling in a classic-looking school like Chico Stateor Berkeley.

I took comfort by telling myself that at least I was getting an education virtually free, thanks to the California system of higher education, that offered college to almost anyone who wanted to enroll. From junior college (or community college, as many were starting to call it), moving on up the food chain to the state colleges, and on to the university system, almost all of the grades we earned could be transferred, should we wish to matriculate up the ladder.

I also took comfort that first day realizing that right after lunch my only afternoon class would be English. Not just *English*, but advanced English, made possible by the grade I'd earned on the Blue Book I had written in the entrance exams. Apparently someone recognized good writing. And the professor was none other than Jensdatter's young friend, Harold P. Hill, M.A. Hons. English & Phil., freshly bestowed from the august UC Berkeley.

I breezed through the morning schedule: human physiology, American government, and my PE class – golf – which I had never even tried. There were a couple of cute co-eds in the golf class. Things were starting to look up. I ate my lunch, a hamburger, fries and a coke, in the student union cafeteria. It wasn't too bad; I listened to a new folk group on the PA system singing "Green Fields" while I ate and watched a bunch of freshmen gathered on the quad, sitting in the grass outside, holding nominations for elections for the freshman class officers. I wasn't interested; that would be Allie's thing if she ever came to Yuba; she'd end up as one of them. I checked out the school library: about the same size as ours at YC High. Not too impressive; I'd have to do my research at either the Yuba County or Yuba City libraries.

Time for Hill's English class. As I passed the quad where the nominating meeting was just breaking up, I saw my sister handing out Kennedy literature. "What are you doing here? Aren't you supposed to be in school?"

"I *am* at school," she laughed. "Vote for Kennedy. Thank you," as she passed out brochures.

"I meant at your own school!" She just laughed and kept handing out brochures. I loved her.

Hill's English class. Open seating, so I headed for a seat in the front. On his table, which served as his desk from where he would lecture, sat a portable record player spinning an LP, a piece of classical music, but I didn't recognize it or the composer. I sat next to a cool-looking brunette in a green sheath dress. She nervously smiled at me; I nodded and smiled to her as I sat down.

Mr. Hill had his back to us as we entered, writing stuff on the chalk board. Even though it was still fairly warm weather, he was wearing a camel-toned three-button Harris Tweed jacket with suede arm patches and bulging pockets; a light blue button-down shirt (Gant or Brooks Brothers? I needed to know) with a fine woolen dark green paisley tie; gray flannel slacks; badly scuffed desert boots completed his ensemble. When we were all pretty much seated, he sat himself casually behind the small table, stretched out his legs and opened his textbook, the same one we had all recently bought in the student bookstore. He pushed a stray lock of reddish-blond hair out of his blue eyes, reached deep in a jacket pocket and brought out a briar pipe, stick matches and worn leather pouch of tobacco, and sat back to fill it and smoke at his leisure.

He began the roll call, alphabetically, filling in a seating chart as each person responded to the call. We were all seated, about 35 of us, in several semi-circle rows of desks. The desks were well-worn clones of the ones I had occupied at YC High only recently.

Mr. Hill studied his chart, ran his finger down a column, stopped and picked out a person to call on and said, "Miss Pettigrew? Sandra Pettigrew? Did I pronounce it correctly?" A pert blond girl in the back row had raised her hand, had acknowledged his polite call for her to perform. She squirmed slightly; I think we all squirmed while he was running that finger down the chart.

"Miss Pettigrew, on page 36 of your textbook is printed a poem by Robert Frost. Do you see where I'm citing?" Sandra Pettigrew nodded she was with him. So far. "Good. Now I wonder if you'd be so kind as to tell us – in a general overview sort of manner – what Mr. Frost was possibly thinking when he penned the words in his poem *The Lone Striker*." He waited for Sandra Pettigrew to think for a minute, marshal her thoughts before she sent them marching forth as words. We had been given an advance syllabus of the course and what reading we should come to class prepared to discuss; we had all bought the text and the other books: *The Dialogues of Plato, The Lottery, To Kill a Mockingbird, Alas Babylon, the Poetry of Robert Frost, The Grapes of Wrath, A Farewell to Arms, Crime and Punishment.* It was going to be a class with loads of reading; I figured out we'd be reading at least 100 pages a night, including weekends. But I relished the challenge.

I liked his teaching method; it wasn't at all what I had been used to in high school. There it was lecture. Here it was a question and answer approach. He did the questioning; we were supposed to supply the answers. If ever I had the good fortune to become a college English professor, that's the way I was going to teach. While Sandra Pettigrew was struggling with her answer, the rest of us were furiously scribbling notes.

————————————

CHAPTER TWENTY-EIGHT

September 12, 1960: *Senator John F. Kennedy makes an appearance at the Greater Houston Ministerial Association in Texas, to make his case why religion should not matter in a presidential race. In a short, nationally-televised speech, Mr. Kennedy said, "I am not the Catholic candidate for president; I am the Democratic candidate for president who also happens to be a Catholic."*

I have a light class load on Tuesdays, and I wasn't at the store; I was home sitting in our living room eating a snack when Allie said, "Hey, let's watch Kennedy's speech on TV." I didn't know he was speaking on TV. Allie switched it on and we watched as Kennedy made a brief prepared statement to the assembled ministers:

"I believe in an America where the separation of Church and State is absolute. Where no Catholic prelate would tell the President (should he be a Catholic) how to act, and no Protestant minister would tell his parishioners for whom to vote.

"I believe in a President whose views on religion are his own private affairs, neither imposed on him by the nation nor imposed upon him as a condition to holding that office.

"I do not speak for my church on public matters – and the church does not speak for me."

Allie thought he looked great, had done a great job. I thought he looked tired, taut, slightly nervous, but I didn't share my opinions with her. Bud and Julia agreed with Allie.

"I'm going to be at *your* school again tomorrow," Allie announced. "Gary's going to be helping me, too."

"What for?" I asked.

"The usual: handing out brochures, trying to get people to vote for my man."

"Most of us at Yuba aren't old enough to vote," I reminded her.

"Some are, and most of them have opinions and may try to influence others to vote, like their parents, maybe," she pointed at Bud and Julia.

"You already have their vote," I argued. "Doesn't she?" I asked Bud and Julia.

"What happens in that voting booth is strictly between us and our consciences, isn't it sweetie?" Bud asked mom.

"But maybe I like Nixon," Julia countered, a mischievous twinkle in her eyes. "Maybe I'll just vote for him, then what?" she asked Bud.

"Then our votes will just cancel each other out," he said. "Pfft, like that…!" He snapped his fingers.

"But you two promised me your votes for Kennedy!" Allie shouted, jumping up to face them.

"Easy, Missie," Bud calmed her. "We're just kidding, having some fun with you. I have not only one, but *two* Kennedy posters in my shop window, as you know. What more can we do? I can't tell a guy to vote Kennedy while I'm waving a straight razor around his throat, now, can I?"

"If it works," Allie replied.

"What's this about Gary helping you?" I asked.

"Oh, yeah, his mom gave him her old Buick, so now he can drive me around since you seem to be too busy in school."

I let that one drop. "That's great," I said, raising my eyebrow at Bud, who nodded back at me knowingly.

"I saw that!" Allie said.

"Saw what?" I asked, innocently.

"That look. You gave each other *The Look*. There! You just did it again! What's that for - what's that supposed to mean, anyway?"

"It means, dear," Julia intervened, "that Alex thinks maybe you and Gary have something going now, if you know what I mean."

"That's ridiculous!" Allie responded. "Sure, he's a nice guy, and I like him a lot, and he's helping me, but that doesn't mean anything." She was blushing, the first time ever I saw my sister blush because of a guy.

She needed rescuing, so I jumped back in with, "So back to the main subject, why is Gary helping you at my school tomorrow?"

"I already told you, there's a Young Democrats Club rally and I've been invited to represent Kennedy. I can also pass out literature afterwards, and Gary was nice enough to offer his car. I have boxes of brochures to carry, and I don't have my own car, unlike a lot of other girls my age." She gave Bud a pointed look, who glanced at her through his half-moon reading glasses over the top of his paper.

"When I was your age, young lady, I was lucky to even get to use the family mule occasionally."

"Look at us," Julia cooed. "This is the first time we've been all together in the same room as a family since when? It's so nice to be here in the company of loved ones, sharing scintillating conversation, don't you think?"

True to her word, Allie was there in the Student Union at noon setting up her table, laying out her Kennedy literature. Gary was there to help her, too. Feeling a bit ashamed for not having done more recently, I pitched in and helped them hang a banner on the wall across the corner where they had set up. Several members of the Young Democrats Club – mostly girls - dropped in to help Allie.

Gary took out his guitar, pulled on his goofy red blazer with a straw boater, an oversized Kennedy button stuck on the front, and began playing and singing folk tunes: *Michael Row the Boat, If I Had a Hammer, Blowin' In the Wind,* and, yes, even *Kumbaya.* I stuck around for awhile to hand out literature until I had to leave for Hill's class, my guilt somewhat assuaged.

* * * * *

Sunday, September 26, 1960, Chicago, 8:30PM, Central Time.

"Good evening, this is Howard K. Smith speaking to you from Chicago, where the first of four nationally televised debates is about to get under way.

"The television and radio stations of the United States are proud to provide a discussion of the issues in the current political campaign by the two major candidates for the presidency.

"Tonight's subject will be questions on domestic policy. Each contestant will have approximately eight minutes to make his opening remarks.

"Seated on either side of me are the two men representing their respective parties for the office of the presidency of the United States."

So began the debates that would, revolutionize American presidential politics into the future. This was another historic moment in politics, just one of many in this campaign, for it marked the advent of television as a campaign tool. Political scientists and pundits, commentators and analysts, would debate just how much the first televised debate influenced the outcome of the 1960 election. And we were witnesses to the unfolding of this live drama; we were there to watch it on television and afterwards to debate, to discuss, and to form our own opinions as to who won and why.

But the question would be not so much who won the first debate, but who won the hearts and minds of American voters as they watched, some 65-plus million of them, by the networks' own estimates.

Looking at it from a writer's point of view, I had my own thoughts about the several themes playing out in this campaign. I started out as a distant observer until I caught Allie's enthusiasm for the game of politics and the personal charisma of Jack Kennedy, who had a way of drawing you into his personal quest, making it your own. So that's one theme: candidate vs. candidate in a noble quest to win the hearts and minds of the American voters.

But the theme I saw playing out was the Old vs. the New. Nixon, closely identified with the stultified Eisenhower administration, was stuck with that label whether he liked it or not. That image stood for the past, the old way of doing things. Kennedy represented a new generation, change, a forward look. He constantly hammered on the theme of his campaign: Let's Get America Moving Again.

Nixon had arrived only that afternoon, with little time to rest or prepare. Earlier in his campaign he had banged his knee on a car door, causing a bad case of phlebitis. Apparently he had banged the same knee again getting out of his car in Chicago, and was in pain, though he tried to mask it. He looked tired, frazzled, nervous, jowly, and uncomfortable.

One close-up shot of him showed beads of perspiration on his brow and his upper lip seeping through his heavy pancake makeup. He wore a light gray suit, which only served to highlight his pasty complexion. He also looked like he badly needed a shave.

Nixon had secluded himself in his hotel room to undergo his own preparations, confident of his own abilities "to take this guy." Nixon had a reputation as a successful, aggressive debater and had no doubts he would "win" this first debate.

Kennedy, on the other hand, arriving at the studio in a freshly-pressed dark gray suit, white shirt, and conservative necktie, appeared calm, sun-tanned, relaxed, and refreshed by a leisurely lunch with Bobby, Ted Sorenson, and Lou Harris, friend and pollster. Jack had also insisted he take his usual afternoon nap.

Jack had arrived in Chicago the previous day, where Bobby and his staffers had set up a mock TV set in their hotel suite. They had brought in a large foot locker – a traveling research library - which contained stacks and stacks of papers and file cards with possible questions and answers based on exhaustive research by staffers. Kennedy also had his personal Brain Trust, captained by Ted Sorenson, who would help the candidate prepare for the debate. They had a full day, plus part of Sunday, for their preparations, preparations the Kennedys lived by as an article of faith. Details would make or break the campaign, and no detail leading up to this first crucial debate was overlooked by them.

One man was assigned to be Nixon and would badger Jack and adopt Nixon's attack-style of debating . They went about the preparation as if Jack were cramming for his Harvard final exams. They wasted no time in getting to work, practicing, grilling their candidate, who lay on his hotel bed in slacks and a tee shirt, relaxing.

They spent several hours drafting and discussing and proposing ideas for Jack's opening remarks, which he finally rejected. He drafted his own opening speech, dictating it over the phone to his personal secretary. By Sunday afternoon, the Kennedys were ready to take on the Vice President.

* * * * *

We gathered in the living room to watch the debates: our family plus over a dozen of Allie's friends from the Young Democrats, a couple of

205

new staff workers whom I didn't know, and Gary; Jackie came with her new boy friend, a Marysville High School jock, a football player, who looked like he could dismantle a truck with his bare hands. Mom had made a load of snacks - hors d'ouvres, she called them - and lots of drinks. I was perfectly okay with Jackie being there, even if I disapproved of the way her boy friend's hand kept wandering down to proprietarily stroke her lower back. I kept mentally willing him – his name was Josh something – to keep his attention on the snacks. Jocks were always supposed to be hungry, weren't they?

With the introductions over, Mr. Smith turned the time over to Kennedy, who opened with his view that the world could not endure half slave – half free. The Democrats have a history of being more aggressive about domestic policy, offering more government involvement in the daily aspects of our lives. Kennedy's point was that America and the world would be more secure if we had a stronger domestic policy. He argued that what we do to move domestic policies forward at home not only affects us, but it also affects what we are able to do abroad.

He wrapped up his opening with, "Can freedom be maintained under the most severe attack it has ever known? I think it can be. And I think in the final analysis it depends upon what we do here. I think it's time America started moving again."

Of course, Nixon politely disagreed with most of what Kennedy had said in his opening. He praised the accomplishments of more than seven years of the Eisenhower administration, noting advancements in building hospitals, schools, highways, dams, etc.

It appeared from the start that Nixon was debating as if he were trying to score points with a panel of judges: he wanted to *win* the debate.

But Jack Kennedy ignored Nixon's non-existent judges. He knew who his audience was; he delivered his message in a way designed to appeal to the hearts and minds of the greater audience, the vast number of Americans who had tuned in their TVs and radios that night.

At the end of the night, it was clear to me who had won: Jack Kennedy.

Bud and Julia excused themselves and went off to bed; Allie and her guests rolled their eyes. Like, they're going to be doing anything upstairs while there's a gang of teens downstairs? Allie asked Gary to get out his guitar, and we all sang folk songs for another hour until the snacks and drinks were all gone and Allie's guests had to get home; it was a school night and classes came early.

* * * * *

Mr. Hill pulled a sheaf of papers out of his beat-up leather briefcase, stuffed his pipe – a sure signal that the lecture was about to begin – cleared his throat, and began to read:

"I have here in my hands a student essay. I want to use it as an example of clear, concise writing, and I hope you take note and aspire to some day write on the same level as this student.

"Twenty-Five Years Later: Are The Joads Still With Us?" he began. My jaw must have dropped. My mouth got suddenly as dry as the Mojave; my pulse began to race, and my heart pumped. He was reading my entrance exam Blue Book as an example of good writing! He didn't look up at me, but continued reading.

Being an aspiring writer is one thing; you hope many people will read your work. You hope, if you get lucky enough to be published, that a lot of people will buy your book. That's what you live for.

But to have your work held up as an example? I wasn't ready for this experience. I didn't think of him as I would a literary critic, the kind that reviews books or feature articles for a magazine or major newspaper. I could see he was trying to make a point with the students in his class. All the same, I was a bit unnerved.

CHAPTER TWENTY-NINE

Thursday, October 13, 1960, *Pittsburgh Pirates win World Series: Bill Mazeroski hits the game-winning home run to lift the Pittsburgh Pirates 4-3 over the New York Yankees in game seven of the World Series.*

Wednesday, October 19, 1960: *Dr. Martin Luther King, Jr., with 52 other Negroes, was arrested during a sit-in at the famous "whites-only" Magnolia Room Restaurant in Rich's Department Store in Atlanta. King was the only one jailed, then he was quickly sentenced to four months hard labor and secreted away to the State Penitentiary in Reidsville. John Kennedy intervenes, calls Mrs. King, and puts pressure on Georgia state authorities; he secures Dr. King's immediate release.*

I'd secretly hoped the Yankees would win Game Seven of the World Series, even though I was a Giants fan and should have been cheering for the National League team. With that final run in the bottom of the ninth inning, Pittsburgh put an end to the last major distraction of this political season. The country could now get down to the task of choosing its new president.

Allie was falling behind in school with her campaign work, and I could tell her health was barely holding up, too. Normally she's strong, full of energy, charging out of bed early in the morning to take on the world. But lately we almost had to kick her out of the sack and then listen to her groaning and complaining. I suspected it may have something to do with Gary. They had been spending a lot of time together since his mother gave him her old Buick and Allie leaned on him more and more to get around.

I had a brotherly talk with her about it being okay to have fun, but just be sure to be careful and all that kind of stuff. Jeez, I was starting to sound like I was *her* father. Whish pop!

She just gave me a disgusted look and said to mind my own business. Add to that the fact the Kennedy campaign had pulled their financial support for our congressional district, choosing instead to put their chips behind several other California districts where the historical poll results favored a win by the Democrats. Allie was bummed that she had to close the campaign headquarters – formerly an empty store on Sutter Street.

She cheerfully put the arm on Bud, who let her use a small unused back room in his shop. As I've said, we're family, and we stick together. Bud chalked it up to advertising: more teenagers traipsing through his shop just might translate into more customers needing JFK cuts, at least for the guys.

So with about three weeks left to go before the general election, we all pitched in: Bud, Julia, I; Gary, plus Jackie and some of her Marysville friends. Then there were all of Allie's friends from the Young Democrats. Father Bevan showed up in his army fatigues, black shirt and collar with his rolled up sleeves. I took his act of rolling up sleeves as symbolic – he had a willingness to attack any job, no matter how dirty. He brought with him several kids from the church's CYO. Allie wasted no time in handing out job lists.

We all got to work stuffing envelopes, licking stamps, making phone calls and canvassing door-to-door to encourage people to turn out for the vote on Election Day. "I didn't know people could be so nasty on the phone," one volunteer with a very red face said. "You should've heard what that old coot told me I could do with Jack Kennedy...!"

Except for a few hours a day when those of us who were students had to be in class, we worked almost around the clock helping out. We survived on pizza and cokes, donuts and coffee, and hamburgers and potato chips. Allie seemed to grow stronger as the days to election wound down. I was amazed to see her rising to the challenge of little or no support from Kennedy's national campaign people; her senses got sharper, and even her voice seemed to take on a cold, calm certainty. She seemed to sense that somehow, in spite of the rebuffs from voters on doorsteps or over the phone, with hard work and determination we could pull this thing off.

With John Kennedy intervening in the Martin Luther King jailing, our campaign got a bit of a bump locally. Yuba City isn't exactly known for its ghettoes teeming with Negroes; the minority population around here consists more of a mixture of Mexicans, Sikhs and Japanese farmers. We all got along pretty decently in this polyglot community. White kids worked in the summers for Japanese and Sikh farmers. Sikhs, Mexicans, and Japanese shopped in the stores alongside white folks.

Without a large Negro population in our town, we really had no way of identifying with the folks who lived in the Deep South, with the problems they faced daily. We didn't have their long history of racial discrimination, of separate facilities, for blacks and whites. We can't imagine what it was like - the racial tensions that seemed to be growing and seemed to become more prominent in the news with this particular election.

But I doubt Kennedy's intervention on behalf of Dr. King made as much impact locally as it did in other communities like Newark, Detroit, Chicago, Atlanta, or East L.A.

Nixon made the tactical error of waffling, trying to buy time on the King issue, while Kennedy took decisive action. I wondered if that would cost Nixon Negro votes. It surely wouldn't hurt Kennedy.

In between helping out Allie and her growing staff of volunteers at campaign headquarters, college classes, and trying to keep up my schedule at the grocery store, I was constantly running behind with my column for the paper. Allie's campaign experience was supplying me with a lot of first-hand material, but I sensed Roscoe was getting fed up with the constant stream of Kennedy touting I was submitting. I tried to squeeze in some Nixon reporting: local voters who favored the Republican and why they intended to vote for him. That claque consisted mostly of older voters, the over-forty crowd. Kennedy had the young vote in our community truly locked up.

I had also pretty much given up on dating and playing piano (except for my church commitments on Sunday mornings) for the time being. Gary had turned down several requests for us to sing, thank goodness. I already had my post-election party planned: I was going to take a solitaryy ride over the hill to South Lake Tahoe and enjoy some live music for a couple of days.

‎ * * * * *

There's a tiny village in New Hampshire – Hart's Location it's called– that tries to be the first community to report the vote on Election Day. Their polls open just after midnight. Based on some advance polling, the Nixon people knew they had five of the twelve voters; Kennedy knew he had five, too. That left two undecided. Who would get their vote?

So Election Day 1960 dawned, and the nation quietly trooped to the polls to cast their votes for the next president of the United States.

In his civics class Tommy O'Farrell welcomed his juniors. When they were settled down and relatively quiet, he dramatically pointed to the big Regulator clock on the wall and announced, "By now, it's noon in South Boston, and both sets of my dead Irish-Catholic grandparents have already gone to the polls and voted for Jack Kennedy… Three times each!" Except for a few of the brighter ones who laughed at his irony, they just didn't get it.

Bud had rigged up a borrowed TV set for Allie in the temporary Kennedy headquarters. By early afternoon business had dropped off, so he took off his apron and donned a blue blazer covered with Kennedy buttons and a straw boater with a big button in front just like Gary's. Gary showed up in his red blazer, also covered with buttons. Julia had arranged for lots of pizza and soft drink, and had spent the better part of Election Day decorating the shop with red-white-and blue bunting, American flags, and the last of the Kennedy posters. She had brought in a portable record player and a stack of LPs – mostly Ray Conniff, Sousa marches, stuff like that – and was keeping the music (and morale, she hoped) up to a high level. The kids, Allie's Rangers, as they came to call themselves, were too excited to notice the lame music. They began to pour into the shop a few minutes after seventh period ended; even Jackie and some of her friends from Marysville dropped in and settled down for the duration.

"Have you and Bud voted yet?" Allie cornered Julia.

"We haven't, dear. There's been so much to do to help you get ready."

"Mom…" It was the first time either of us had called her that since we were kids. "I'm okay - everything's just fine. Now get your butts out the door and vote!" She handed them each a clip board with polling sheets they were to use after they voted. Bud and Julia had agreed to split up and each cover a voting place to ask voters their preference after they left the

211

booth. Allie handed one each to Gary and me and scooted us out the door. We wouldn't be back to the party until the polls closed at eight o'clock.

Allie's election-night party went well into the night as the returns trickled in. Sometime after midnight it was projected that California would go to Nixon by a very slim margin. The few kids that were left at the party booed and hissed; the rest, under strict parental orders, had gone home. Tomorrow was just another school day. We watched anxiously for any returns from our congressional district.

About two in the morning, Mayor Daley of Chicago pulled a hat trick, and released the upstate votes: Illinois went for Kennedy, thus electing him as our thirty-fifth president. We were all exhausted, drained of energy, but Allie hugged me, hanging on to me, crying, "We did it! We did it! We did it," she blubbered again into my collar, soaking me with her tears.

"Yes," I said, "*you* really did it."

Out of 6,507,000 votes cast in California, Nixon won by the narrowest of margins: 35,500 votes, or one-tenth of one percent.

Kennedy carried our congressional district by an even slimmer margin: seven votes (the same number that voted for him in Hart's Location, New Hampshire, over twenty-four hours earlier), or a mere one-twentieth of one percent. The Democratic congressional candidate rode into office on Kennedy's coattails; the Republican incumbent would not concede, bitterly vowing a recount.

I rode home alone through the foggy, silent streets, musing at how brilliant the Founding Fathers had been in drafting our Constitution. We had all just witnessed a quiet revolution; not a change of power at the end of a rifle because not one shot had been fired. It was a revolution of the supremacy of the rule of law.

I went in the house as quietly as possible; Bud and Julia had gone to bed around midnight. I was dog tired but not the least bit sleepy. I sat down at my typewriter and began to write out the next to last article I would do for Roscoe. He had become so curmudgeonly toward me in the last couple of weeks of the campaign that I'd be very glad to be rid of him, and I'm sure he felt the same way about me.

My last article would be a report on Allie attending Kennedy's inauguration in January if I was still employed then by Roscoe Tate.

I lay in bed listening to the lonely cry of geese circling above the valley fog, looking for fields of recently harvested grain stubble.

* * * * *

Two weeks after Kennedy's razor-thin victory, a hand-engraved, ivory vellum envelope addressed to Allie came in the mail. *Miss Allison Rodgers, the pleasure of your company is cordially requested by President-elect and Mrs. John F. Kennedy...*

The invitation arrived along with two dozen red roses, and a personal note from Ted Kennedy which read, *"Allison Rodgers of Sutter County: Well you did it. You said you would be elected as a national delegate, and you did it. You said you would deliver the vote for Kennedy, and you did it! I look forward to seeing you again at the Inaugural; please drop by and say hello. Kindest regards, Ted Kennedy"*

* * * * *

Mid-January, 1961: While Allie, Bud, and Julia were getting airline and hotel reservations preparing to attend Kennedy's Inaugural, I was studying for final exams at Yuba. After our last English class of the semester, Mr. Hill asked me to stay after class for a minute.

"I have a letter for you. Well, actually, it's addressed to me, but it concerns you. Here, go ahead, read it." He handed me the letter. It was addressed to him from a former colleague, a distinguished English professor at Cal Berkeley, and I was the subject.

He stated that he had read my college entrance essay and was duly impressed with my writing ability. He had circulated my paper to several others of his colleagues on the English faculty, who were also impressed. So much so that he was inviting me to become a student in their English department, along with "an academic scholarship to assist, should your financial needs so require."

For once, I was nearly speechless. "What can I say?" I asked Mr. Hill. "How, when, why did you do this?"

He smiled, tamped his pipe and struck a match, sucked thoughtfully and blew a cloud in the air. "I think we both know that you're just marking time here, Mr. Rodgers. It was only a matter of time before you'd be off and gone anyway, answering the siren call of some English faculty at a more – shall we say - *prestigious* school than Yuba. So I thought I'd help the process along. I think if you were to act with some degree of

213

haste, they would matriculate you into Cal Berkeley in time for the spring semester..."

* * * * *

January 20, 1961: *Inauguration Day. Washington, D.C.*

I was studying for finals in the Student Union, having a donut and coffee, when the Inauguration came on the two TV sets hung high on opposite walls. The room became hushed as the President-Elect took off his top hat, approached the podium in formal morning coat with tails and striped pants, and began his speech. By now I had become comfortable, familiar even, with his style of oratory: the flat, New England vowels; the stabbing gesture with his hand; the jutting of his jaw in defiance of any tyrant, any despot who dared challenge America's greatness.

He acknowledged the distinguished guests, and began the meat of his speech by saying, "Let the word go forth from this time and place, to friend and foe alike, that the torch has been passed to a new generation of Americans – born in this century..." Would that be me, my generation?

"...tempered by war..." That would be Bud and his army buddies who fought in Europe, Africa, and the Pacific, wouldn't it?

"...disciplined by a hard and bitter peace..." In one of the debates with Nixon, the subject had been foreign policy. The two candidates had laid out for the American people the harsh realities: America had a duty to protect the freedoms of peace and freedom-loving peoples around the globe. They had ticked off the many places where there was war, or serious danger of war breaking out: Quemoy and Matsu Islands off the coast of Taiwan; Berlin; East Africa; French Indo-China; North Korea; Israel and Palestine; Russia and its oppressive influence behind the Iron Curtain. They debated the Gary Powers U-2 fiasco. On and on the list of problems grew. Yes we had peace; but it was tenuous. War could break out at any moment anywhere in the world. What if we had to go to war again in my lifetime? Would I be called up, would I have to fight and take the lives of other humans?

"...proud of our ancient heritage..."

Then he made a call to every citizen to be prepared to sacrifice as others before us had done: "We shall pay any price, bear any burden, meet any hardship, support any friend, oppose any foe to assure the survival and

214

success of liberty…"

I felt then that our generation was entering into a new period of history when we would likely see some pretty dramatic things happen: would it be another war? Would it be racial unrest? Would it be another Great Depression like our parents had gone through? I felt a small chill of danger creep up my neck.

Kennedy finished by a call to all of us; the chord he struck resonated through the Student Union of Yuba College: "Ask not what your country can do for you – ask what you can do for your country!"

Another chill went up my spine and left my scalp tingling. I think the others in that room felt something, too. I'll never forget that moment when he made us feel like we had important work to do for our country, great things perhaps, that could benefit generations yet to come.

A couple of days later, before I left for Berkeley, I was scheduled to work at the store, my last day there. In the back room, as I was putting on my green apron and bowtie, Mavis told me to read a new company-wide memo to all clerks. It was pinned to the cork board and said that due to an ever-increasing number of bad personal checks being accepted by our stores, we now had to require the person writing the check to provide identification which we had to write down on the face of the check and add our initials before cashing. Okay, no problem.

I had only two customers before my lunch break who wanted to write personal checks for their groceries. They were very nice about the new policy; no objections, just some head-wagging and tsk-tsk-ing about what a sorry state this country was in…

Then a young mother with her four-year old son came through. I rang up her groceries and was waiting while she counted out the cash when I noticed her little boy was acting really funny. He was jumping around in a tight little circle, waving his arms. His face was red, turning blue; he seemed to be choking on something. I grabbed him, turned him over my knee and pounded on his back. His mother must have been surprised when I did this; she screamed and told me to stop beating her child. What the hell was I doing to him? That sort of stuff. I ignored her and kept pounding. On about the fourth or fifth whack, a coin shot out of his mouth and rolled across the floor: he'd swallowed and was choking on a quarter!

The kid immediately sucked in a huge gulp of air and his color began to return to normal as he wailed for his mommy. When the mom saw what had happened and how I had saved her kid she apologized and thanked me. Then, normal motherly reaction: she yelled at the kid for being so stupid. "I've told you a thousand times never put things in your mouth you could choke on, now haven't I…!?"

Well, that was exciting.

Shortly after that, at a quarter to twelve, Mrs. Arnoldy, Jim's wife, came in the store, all dolled up to go out to lunch or somewhere swanky. Mavis usually waited on Mrs. Arnoldy, but this time she was busy with another customer. Since I didn't have any customers at the moment, Mrs. Arnoldy headed straight for my register.

She pulled a checkbook out of her purse and began writing. "I want fifty dollars cash."

Not "*I need fifty dollars, please…*" I opened the till and she handed me her check.

Before I counted out the money, I informed her of the new policy and said I would require some identification like her driver's license. I thought I asked in a nice way, but she went ape on me. "You little snot!" she shrieked. "I don't have to give you any ID! Where's Jim? I'm reporting this outrage to my husband!" She stalked off to his office, charged up the stairs, nearly stumbling in her blind anger. I could see that Jim was on the phone; he made her wait a full minute before he finished and hung up. That only made things worse.

Mavis finished with her customer and asked me what had happened. I told her I asked Mrs. Arnoldy for ID so I could cash her personal check. Mavis clucked her tongue, laughed, shook her head, like boy-are-you-in-big-trouble. We stared while Jim opened the safe in his office, took his wife's check and counted out two $20s and a $10 for her. She stomped back down the stairs and flounced past us without acknowledging our presence when Mavis wished her a nice day.

When she was safely gone, Jim stuck his head out of the office and motioned for me to come see him. "The walk of shame," Mavis stage whispered as I marched to my doom. What was he going to do, fire me? On my last day? I decided that if things started looking bad I'd just chuck it all and quit before he could fire me. I'd never been fired from a job in my life. – yet.

"Alex, take a seat." I sat. "Alex, you've been one of my best employees ever. But gosh dang it, you need to learn a few things about human nature. She wanted me to fire you on the spot. I'm not going to do that, but I did promise I'd give you a good chewing out." (Here it comes, I thought.)

"What's Arnoldy's Rule Number One of customer relations…?" he asked. Huh?

"The customer always comes first," I mumbled.

"Yes. And what's Rule Number Two…?"

"When in doubt, refer to Rule Number One."

"Good. At least you've learned something. Now I want to take a minute and add to your store of knowledge." He sounded just like Bud whenever I screwed up around home. "Alex, you just need to add a dose of good old-fashioned common sense to the way you deal with customers and you'll be on the right track. Just now, for instance…" Oh, boy, I thought, here it finally comes. "…if my Boss's wife had come to me with a check, and I *knew* she was the Boss's wife, no question, you think I'd ask for her ID?"

"I guess not. I'm sorry, sir…"

"Of course I wouldn't! Look, it's okay this time, but next time take a minute, inhale a deep breath, and count to ten before you act. Okay, are we clear?"

"But I was only trying to do my job. It was a new policy…"

He cut me short. "I know, but…"

"All clear, sir."

He put his arm around my shoulder and said, "Alex, if you ever need a job, the door is always open for you as long as I'm here. Got that…?"

"Yes, sir."

"Good luck at Berkeley."

"Thanks, sir."

CHAPTER THIRTY

Fifty years later...

Mostly out of curiosity, I opened the email from an unfamiliar sender's address; something I rarely do – there's always the possibility of a virus. It was an announcement from a committee of my high school classmates inviting me to our fifty-year class reunion. Fifty years! I know *where* the time went; but what did I do with it? Fifty years!

I wondered about my old friends and classmates and what had become of them, what they had done with their lives. I began to look forward to seeing them all again. I wondered if they had been happy, had married, had children, now had grandchildren, had retired, had joined AARP? Had they gone on cruises, shopped weekly at Costco or Sam's Club? Fifty years!

Then I thought back over the last fifty years; what I would tell them I had done if they asked. I had a few regrets, but not many. I had a lot of things to be pleased about: my career, my marriage to the same woman for over forty years – Carla - our three wonderful children, and now three grandchildren that we spoiled. I didn't really have any burdens or regrets or guilt.

As I thought back on those youthful experiences, those few months back in 1960, I felt suddenly free: free now to tell my story, to tell what happened then and after, in the fifty intervening years, free to talk about some of things I had kept to myself all these years. Some things I had seen and heard and carried around like a burden, things I had promised to keep confidential until I could talk about them now, long after the subjects were gone.

Such as why and how Jensdatter had disappeared.

Such as my accidental meeting with Steinbeck that night in the Persian Room of the Sir Francis Drake Hotel in San Francisco; how that little thing influenced the path I chose for life.

Such as the day my grandfather lay dying and ripped into my mother, and Bud had promised that some day he'd tell me a secret. I needed to know so I could get that monkey off my back. I wasn't sure what I'd learn, but I had to know, maybe to write about it some day.

* * * * *

Bud lay in a hospital bed, shrouded in white, hooked up to many high-tech medical devices that alternately kept him alive and breathing or checked his vital signs every few seconds and reported his bodily functions to some computer somewhere that I hoped somebody qualified was watching. The machines hissed, gulped, farted, drained off the bad stuff, and pumped measured injections of good stuff into him through IVs.

He didn't look good; his normal robust self was gone. The father and friend I had known all those years was missing. In his place, a stranger lay: gaunt, bony-thin, hair mostly gone, struggling for every breath.

Allie had called me two days before; she had already seen him, paid her last respects a few months ago. She urged me to see him before it was too late. She would stand by and fly out to Yuba City if needed. I hopped the next plane out of Sao Paulo, and flew eighteen hours to Sacramento through JFK and Salt Lake City, then by rental car, to get back home.

Bud's doctor was a young specialist, very young. Dr. Hamilton had long ago quit his earthly practice. Mom had left us ten years ago. I don't know why Bud hung on for so long after she was gone. Her leaving seemed to take the life out of him, one little chunk every day, one day at a time.

He was sleeping peacefully when I entered the room; I hunkered down for what was sure to be the death watch. I brought a pile of newspapers and magazines – some in Portuguese, some in English – and a new Le Carre novel I had purchased at the airport gift shop before I boarded my Delta overnight flight. I can barely make it through a day or a long flight without a stack of reading material.

I opened up the latest issue of *The Economist* and started reading an article by some British political wonk on why the American president Barack Obama is so naïve and why "he needs to look to the British model to learn the art of *compromise*." The writer suggested Obama and the country – meaning America - would "benefit greatly by his having a weekly Q&A session with Congress, much like the British PM does with Parliament." He has a good point, but I doubt it will happen in four or even eight years of an Obama administration.

At the top of the hour a nurse came in, woke Bud to check his vitals and give him a painkiller suppository. "Do you want to do it or shall I?" she asked him. Bud managed a mischievous grin and turned with some help to expose his butt for her ministrations. "I guess that's my answer," she said, as she inserted the drug. "He can be really naughty sometimes," she said to me. She tidied up the room, fluffed his pillows, entered something into his electronic chart with a mobile scanner, and left us.

Bud was now awake and I asked him if he needed anything. He said no. I pulled my chair close to him; his time was short and I wanted to talk. Allie had told me the doctor said Bud had started the process of dying, shutting down; he had all the classic indications. I'd been thinking a lot about what I needed to resolve during my long flight. I took a deep breath and went for it.

"Bud…? Dad…?" He opened his eyes. "We need to talk. Are you up to it…?" He nodded and closed his eyes. "Do you remember when we visited Grandpa when he was dying?" I asked. Bud nodded, his eyes closed. "He said something to Julia, to Mom…" Bud nodded again, his eyelids now half raised. His expression encouraged me to go ahead with what I needed to ask. "Grandpa said something that really upset her, upset Allie, upset me, too. You remember what it was he said?" He mumbled a yes. "Mom talked to me later and explained everything. Well, almost everything. She also said you had killed four men. Was that part of what you had to do in the war?"

Bud leaned painfully up on one elbow, his eyes fully open, searching the ceiling for the words. He reached out with his other boney hand and pulled me close, my ear next to his lips. His breath smelled of impending death. His lips brushed my ear as he rasped out a few words in between struggling for gulps of air.

"She was no whore! She was as pure as the Madonna; she meant the world to me..." His strength was sapped for the moment; he lay back and rested, his eyes closed, but his lips still moved; he was whispering something only he knew.

"I know," I said, and waited.

A half hour, an hour, the digital clock ticking off the minutes; he roused himself awake again. His strength was ebbing fast. Was I killing him? He lay on his back and spoke again audibly. "Hey, Pal, you really bought into that Kennedy speech, didn't you? You know the one where he said 'ask not what your country can do for you'? I nodded yes. He continued, now a little more alert, seemingly stronger, "I was always proud of you and your sister, how you made a contribution. You both did something that counted, and that's really important. I wonder what would have happened if Jack Kennedy had lived, how our lives would have been different. So what's on your mind? What's bothering you, the killing other men that I had to do? It was just part of my job, the bad part. The Nazis were evil. We had to stop them any way we could. That's about the only contribution I ever made. That and having you two kids. You're the greatest thing that ever happened to your mother and me."

He rested again for several minutes then revived briefly. "Maybe you could tell me something that I've been wondering about. I nodded. "I been wondering for a long time now - what's your code name? I know you're a spook. Look, I'm dying, so your secret goes with me to the grave."

I was somewhat embarrassed to tell him it was *Honker*. He smiled, lay back down and closed his eyes. "That's a good one. The old school mascot thing..." He dozed for a few minutes, roused again, and said, "I hope there really is a hereafter, you know, a life after this one. If there is, I plan on going up to Jack Kennedy and telling him I'm the proud father of Allie and Alex Rodgers who worked hard for his election back in 1960 in a little town called..." He broke off with a coughing fit.

He looked gray, terribly weak. I could actually see the life ebbing out of him fast. A nurse came in and gave him another shot of morphine – no suppository this time. He was too weak, too far gone to make any more crude jokes.

His eyes closed and he managed a few last words to me. "I kept a journal that I smuggled out of France when we escaped from the Nazis, Juliette and me. With a lot of help from the Resistance. You'll find it in my footlocker buried somewhere in my bedroom closet, under some stuff… It'll tell you all you need to know, the killings and all that stuff. I'm sorry we never talked about it before…"

Before I could tell him it was okay, the morphine pulled him under again. I kissed his damp forehead and whispered that I loved him. I needed fresh air. When I came back a half hour later, the room was crowded with white coats, doctors, nurses, bending over his limp body.

His last words to me had been, "I'm sorry…" I turned away, found a broom closet and wept alone.

* * * * *

We had a simple memorial ceremony; Mr. Ulrich's son now runs the family's mortuary business. Some of Bud's old friends and poker night buddies, the few who hadn't already passed away, were there. Ivy, bent and frail, was there, helped by Orly, now quite gray himself. Bud was cremated, his wish.

Allison flew in from Boston for the memorial service. "You look great," I told her.

"So do you. And how's my sister-in-law - how are Carla and your kids and grandkids?" she asked. I assured her they were all just fine.

"Believe me, Sis, Carla would've liked to come to visit Freddie and her family. But she had commitments that she couldn't get out of on short notice," I apologized. Allie said she understood.

Allison and I climbed the Buttes early next morning to scatter Bud's ashes, another wish of his. The late October air was cold, clear and calm; the rattlesnakes were in their holes for the winter. Abandoning caution, we made good time to the top of the highest peak. Allie runs the streets of Boston and along the Charles River every day and stays in good condition. I frequently hike from the mountainside villa where Carla and I have retired down to the little fishing village to pick up our mail and buy my newspapers, a distance of twelve kilos round trip. I usually swim in the ocean below our house most every day, so I could keep up with Allie. Barely. As I said before, she was the jock Bud wished I had been.

I was happy for our little reunion. I hadn't seen Allie for maybe five years, since the last time I was summoned to Langley for meetings. She flew the shuttle down to Washington and we had dinner together. She had just received word that Gary had finally died of AIDS, alone in Florida - Ft. Lauderdale, I think. He'd gotten it from a dirty needle when he was a DJ in Chicago. She hadn't seen him since she divorced him in 1998. Drugs. She seemed relieved, unburdened with this news.

Gary got hooked on smack in Vietnam after he'd been drafted in 1966; he managed to keep it hidden from Allie for several years after he got back. Then it all just seemed to fall apart. Pity – he had such a great singing voice. He would sign off his radio show every day by taking a listener request for some hit tune, some popular artist, and would sing along with the tune, doing a perfect voice-over imitation.

Back at the Hampton Inn, I took Bud's journal to Allie's room where we sat down on the bed and began to read it together.

ACKNOWLEDGEMENTS

My children and grandchildren have asked me what it was like when I was growing up. How do I tell them? I find it easiest to write it down and hope I get it right. For several years I have been trying to write this story. I kept putting it off in favor of other projects but never felt the motivation I needed until a few months ago when I got that email announcing our 50-year reunion - Yuba City High School - Class of 1960.

It was a seminal year, 1960: a lot of our history was set in motion that year, starting with the election of John F. Kennedy, his short administration, his tragic death. Who could ever forget where you were and what you were doing the precise moment when you heard the news of his shooting in Dallas? I was in Vancouver, Canada, and I remember many Canadians, perfect strangers, like one gas station attendant who came up to me with tears in his eyes, expressing genuine sorrow and condolences to me, an American!

We lived through the turmoil of the campus protests, civil unrest and urban riots, the murders of Dr. Martin Luther King, Jr., and Bobby Kennedy, the Vietnam War that pulled down LBJ, John Kennedy's vice president. A man on the moon! We saw the advent of The Pill, and the second pill, Viagra. Are we the Pill Generation? There was the Second British Invasion by the Beatles, as Gary had predicted; Cassius Clay aka Muhammad Ali; the first NFL Super Bowl. Then there was the Watergate scandal that toppled the Nixon administration followed by Richard Nixon's resignation and dramatic farewell. It was an intense time to be alive. I hope I captured some of the feeling, the mood and spirit of the times we lived through leading up to the mid-60s and beyond.

Writing a mostly historical novel requires a fair amount of research. If for no other reason, I needed to verify that my memory wasn't playing tricks on me. When it's written down in history books or newspapers, it's much more reliable than my memory.

Thank goodness for the invention of the Internet to help with research. I guess I should first of all thank whoever invented it: Al Gore, Ross

Perot, Steve Jobs, Bill Gates? I don't live in a major metropolitan area like Washington or New York, with an abundance of research facilities and those marvelous libraries. So the next best thing was the Internet, where I was able to access data from public sources online - such as the University of Southern California, the University of Washington, the John F. Kennedy Library, to name just a few – for much of the campaign material and details of that 1960 presidential election used or referred to herein. It was very helpful.

I also wish to thank the archivists at the Appeal-Democrat newspaper in Marysville, California (I hope I didn't make the paper come off as bush league, because it's really not); the librarians of Yuba County's Library in Marysville, Yuba City's Library, and Salt Lake County's Library System in Utah. One of Yuba County Library's archivists, Diane Barbaccia, was especially helpful to me in correctly identifying the exact date John Kennedy made his historic whistle stop in Marysville. I lived in Yuba City at the time. Like some of you might have done, I drove over to Marysville during my lunch break on that warm September day to try and catch a glimpse of Senator Kennedy. I saw him from behind at a distance just as his train was pulling out of the station. Thanks also to Hal Ethington for his first-hand account of that day.

I want to thank my editor (and wife), Janet Landerman, for her suggestions and assistance (as well as her long-suffering and patience). I appreciate the work of Danny Taber, for his assistant editing and layout; he's a summer intern from Arizona State University, working with my publisher. Thanks to my friend, artist John Fackrell, whose ideas for the cover art merged with my concept of the man this story is about. Mr. Fackrell's favorite medium is water color and his touch is true and certain. And thanks to Bob Pearson for the author's photo on the back cover.

Thanks, again, to my publisher, Mike Webb, for his enthusiasm for this project, and for agreeing to let me set aside a prior publishing commitment so I could finish this story in time for the reunion. Thanks also to his graphic designer, Leslie Thompson for text layout and cover design.

Thanks to our many inspiring teachers and counselors at Yuba City High School, and for the tireless, friendly staff. I remember those early-morning visits and freshly-baked cookies in the bookstore with Donna Hostetter, where she shared stories of her early years. It was my privilege to visit her again recently at the Emerald Oaks care facility in Yuba City just before she passed away at the age of ninety-four.

Thanks also to the administration at our high school – fond appreciation goes out to all of you. I'm especially grateful to Matt Spears for helping guide many of us students through those critical, formative years of our youth. My wife taught high school English and French for over two decades, so I know first-hand that you never really know whether what you teach kids will stick until years later – maybe even fifty? If you're lucky, you may get to see some of the seeds you planted grow and ripen into good fruit.

Thanks to my classmates for inspiring this story. Friends are an important part of our lives, more important than we sometimes realize. You were my friends back then, one of my main reasons for wanting to trudge off to high school every day. I watched you, listened to you, and some of what you were, collectively – mostly the good things - rubbed off and stuck on me. Looking back, I am impressed by how many of you went on to higher education, meaningful careers, families, community service and leadership, and became just good people, when you could just have easily been burn-outs like many of the next generation. You are a unique group of Americans. You were, and always will be, an inspiration to me. Thank you. Thanks to the good people of our community: Yuba City, Marysville, and yes, even good old Olivehurst. Yuba City was a good place to grow up.

Finally, thanks to John F. Kennedy, to the memory of the man. I will ever appreciate him for the way he inspired and challenged a generation of young people – our generation – worldwide. He raised the bar when he asked us to make a lasting contribution to our society. In early January, 1971, I visited the hut of a Peace Corps volunteer, a teacher on the Island of Yap in the South Pacific, who had joined up because of John Kennedy's call to service for our country and the peoples of the world. On his wall was a picture of President Kennedy. He said that most of the islanders had pictures of Kennedy in their huts, too. I've seen the same thing in Brazil; other friends of mine have related similar experiences they had in as diverse places as Africa and Puerto Rico. Thanks, Mr. Kennedy. We miss you.